I0614616

Calueria

Book 1 of Legend of the Dea Regia

by

Jessica Munn

W & B Publishers
USA

Calueria, Book One of Legend of the Dea Regia © 2015. All rights reserved by Jessica Munn.

No part of this book may be reproduced or transmitted in any form or by any means, graphic, electronic, or mechanical, including photocopying, recording, taping, or by any informational storage retrieval system without prior permission in writing from the publisher.

W & B Publishers

For information:
W & B Publishers
9001 Ridge Hill Drive
Kernersville, NC 27284
www.a-argusbooks.com

ISBN: 978-1-942981206

Cover Art by: Jer-Miah Angell

Book Cover designed by Dubya
Printed in the United States of America

Prologue

Calueria: When It All Began

LONG AGO, BEFORE OUR world existed, before our galaxy came into being, there was Calueria. The Omnideum, the most powerful being in the universe, decided it was time to create a new realm with new life. On this world, he decided on magical beings that would have the power to conjure and create on their own. He began by creating the Majori, demideums who had much of the power of the Omnideum, but not one of them possessed it all. There were twelve of them to be exact, six male and six female. The Omnideum commanded the Majori to rule over the world of Calueria and to create all manner of species and races that they deemed worthy.

Together the Majori agreed upon their domains in the world. They split, male and female into six groups. One pair was to rule over the land; they called themselves the Dea Terra. Another was over the water; calling themselves the Dea Aqua. Another was over the air; taking the name of Dea Aer. Another still was over the fire; being called the Dea Ignis. Another was over plants and simple animals; known as the Dea Vita. The last pair, the Dea Genesi, was to rule over the Essent Medei, the magical creatures who would inherit this realm. Together the Majori lived in the Temple positioned on the tallest mountain in all of Calueria, Magmons, where they could oversee their stewardship.

Almost a thousand years had passed while the Majori busily worked to populate Calueria with life of all sorts. Plants of all kinds spread throughout the world, covering the barren soil and filling the ocean floors. Life swam in the seas, flew in the skies, burrowed in the ground, and even danced in the flames of the deepest volcanoes. Lastly, the Dea Genesi, working with their peers, created creatures with powers of transformation, powers over the water, powers over the air, powers over fire, and powers over plants and simple animals.

They shaped the creatures using the elements over which they would have power. A Saga Lymph, or water witch, was shaped using the water. The Lipus were created using the skins of the animals they would transform into. Strigae, or witches, were created who could manipulate one's mind, foresee events yet to occur, and even alter reality. The Essent Medei did not take long to begin creating their own spells and discovering new ways of using their magical abilities.

After a couple thousand years had passed, the Majori were quite pleased with themselves as they sat back and observed their creations. That is until the Essent Medei, who were immortal, began getting sick and dying. The Majori rushed to find the cause; they searched the realm over for a reason and a cure. Years passed while they searched; and as they searched, the Essent Medei were increasingly contracting the illness and dying. One day, an Essent Medei approached the Majori with a possible solution. What if they could have the power of procreation? What if they could have power, not just over the elements and animals, but over their own procreation as well?

The Majori found this idea fascinating and set to work immediately to figure this out. Working together, the twelve discovered that it was harder than it sounded. The power of procreation was not something that could just be given to magical creatures. Magic and the power of procreation continuously would cancel each other out when they attempted to combine them. They could manage one without the other, and vice versa, but they could not give an Essent Medei the ability to procreate. As they struggled to find the answer, one of the Majori stumbled upon a creation that could be the answer they'd all been searching for. They called them Mortals. Thus the Majori created a male and a female mortal, whom they called Abram and Eva.

Without the ability to use magic of any kind, the mortals also had no control over their own life spans as the Essent Medei did. They would be born, grow up, grow old and die; whereas the Essent Medei were simply created as they were and were supposed to have eternal life. Hoping to have found the answer, the Majori mated a mortal with an Essent Medei. The outcome was just what they had hoped for: a child that could procreate and that could wield magic. The child would not have eternal life, but would live longer than a mortal. Depending on the amount of magic the child could wield, he or she would be that much less or more likely to have offspring. It was a give and take situation. The more magic the child could wield, the least likely he or she could procreate and vice versa.

Many full mortals were born to Abram and Eva as well, in order to be used for procreative purposes among the Essent Medei. Three hundred years went by and the mortals multiplied and multiplied and multiplied. It seemed that as long as they were in Calueria, the magic of the realm granted them unnaturally long life. The mortals were also very covetous of the Essent Medei's magic and were desirous that they too should wield magic of their own. They became so numerous that they began to make plans of overthrowing the Majori and demanding their own magical powers.

Meanwhile, a Saga Spectare, named Selene, approached the Majori one day with a vision she'd had concerning the destruction of all magical creatures and all Essent Medei in Calueria. She prophesied that a child would be born to a Majorus who would fall in love with Eva, the first mortal woman. That child would bring about new death of all Essent Medei and all magic as they knew it. In order to prevent this, the Majori forbade any of their own to procreate with a mortal and least of all to fall in love with one.

As the Majori were convened during this discussion, Selene had another vision. She foresaw the mortals coming against them in mighty force. There were so many of them that sheer numbers would be enough to capture the Majori and take control of the temple. Selene told them that on the marrow, the mortals would attack the Temple, led by Abram. In haste, the Majori worked through the night to create a world in which the mortals could live and have the power and control that they desired. They created a world in which the mortals would not know magic; any memories they had of Calueria would be nothing but a fairy tale, a legend, a nursery rhyme to tell their children.

With the rising sun, came the first mortal invaders, but the Majori were ready for them. Once at the top of the great Magmons, the mortals would not find the Temple, but rather would be sucked into a portal leading them to this new world. As soon as the mortals came near enough to the portal, there was no escaping its pull, and they were drawn into it. One of the effects of the portal was that it would alter or erase the mortal's memories; leaving them to draw whatever conclusions they would about their history on their own.

What the Majori Didn't Know

Eva and her Majorus

    During all of the Majori's hasty planning, the very thing they had hoped to prevent happened. One of their own did fall in love with Eva, and she did give birth to his child. In an effort to escape the Majori, it was Eva who had stirred Abram's anger enough to organize the mortals against the Majori. And, it was Eva's Majori lover who had brought up the idea of creating a new world for the mortals to go to. They had a plan which involved leaving Calueria with their baby in order to be free from the Majori's ridicule and their ridiculous prophecy.

    After the exile of most of the mortals, a few staying behind to continue aiding with reproduction, the Majori realized that one of their own was also gone. Then, the search for him began. The Majori spread themselves out around the globe of Calueria. A few even began searching nearby planets to see if he was possibly there. Being stretched thin as they were, the Majori began to neglect the people of Calueria and they continued to die without a cure or knowing the reason for their ailment. As the years passed, the Majori lost hope in ever finding their companion.

The Caligro Striga

    All the while, Anngora, the Caligro Striga or the Dark Mist Witch, basked in her triumph. She believed that the Majori were far above the Essent Medei; that the Essent Medei didn't deserve magic. More than that, she believed that the Majori should be worshiped like Deus, or Gods. Filled with anger, jealousy and hatred, Anngora set out to destroy the Essent Medei. It was her secret plan and spell that was draining them of their magic and their lives; and it was succeeding! She was becoming more powerful than she could have dreamt she would.

With the Majori busily searching for their lost companion, she had free reign over the Essent Medei. Years passed and the Essent Medei became accustomed to dying. It was all but forgotten that they had ever been immortal. Immortal life had become a legend, as had the story about the Majorus who fell in love with Eva, the first mortal woman.

Chapter One

IT'S DARK AND COLD AND the middle of the night. Crashing and thrashing, banging and clanging echoes up the stairs. I shiver beneath my blankets, pulling them tightly around my face. I can't bear to cover my eyes in case they come up to my room. I don't know where Dad is. He said he had some business late tonight like he often does, so I just went to bed. Now, as I lay here listening to the upheaval downstairs, I can't help but wonder, 'Where is he?'

I force my eyes shut so I can focus all my efforts on my ears. Imploringly, I strain to hear every crash and tumble, every creak in the floor boards and every sigh of the walls from the blustery winds blowing outside. As if the storm wasn't bad enough, they had to choose tonight to invade my house. Lightning flashes outside my window and I shudder ever so slightly. I don't scare easily, especially not by lightning; but with the combination of Dad being out of the house, the storm raging on outside and whoever is trashing the house beneath me, I am terrified.

My eyelids are still winced shut when I hear them. Sirens ail out on the street; blaring so loudly that the entire world could have just woken up despite the howling wind, roaring thunder and crackling lightning. I hear the screen door slap shut and bounce off like it does when you slam it too hard. Maybe they ran off? Maybe I'm safe?

Just when I start considering getting out of bed, I hear a creak on the floor boards just outside my bedroom. Frozen, I am suddenly glued to my bed. I can't move. I can't blink. I can barely breathe. I watch the door as the handle begins to turn.

Lightning crackles through the sky right outside my bedroom window, hitting the tree next to our house. A branch is struck and crashes through my window. But, all the while, I am frozen, petrified, staring at the bedroom door; mesmerized by some low hum coming from the other side of the door. The wind is now furiously whirling around my room. Rain blows in so hard and fast that it stings when it hits my face. I cling to my blankets as if they can protect me from the elements and whatever, or whoever, is at the door.

Steadily, slowly the door begins to push open. Although the wind beats against it, the hand on the knob compels the door forward; still moving at such an unnatural, crawling pace compared with the fierceness and speed of the wind and rain that now floods my room. Still the door opens steadily, not even rocking when the gusts of wind rush at it. The door opens so slowly that it is sickening to wait.

The hum grows stronger as the door opens, inch by inch. Wind rushes around the room wildly, throwing the stinging rain in every direction. Another crackle of lightning outside the window, followed by the roar and rumble of thunder, all too close by. Still, I am mesmerized by the hum and the ever increasing gap in the open door. All I can see is the darkness that waits beyond the door; there's no figure there, just empty darkness.

All of a sudden, the low hum now sounds a roaring, rumbling racket like the steady, furious beating of a base drum. The door is thrown open. Just when I don't think I can bear anymore, lightning strikes. It crashes through the roof, through my ceiling and down through the center of my bedroom! Now, I am screaming! Now, I am moving, standing on my bed, clawing at the wall, wailing in sync with the blowing wind, and praying that I will survive.

Blackness. Stillness. Peace. Aside from the light bird songs that drift on the breeze flowing through the open window, there is no sound.

It is too quiet, Calley thinks and opens her eyes. She lifts her head off the pillow. Calley stares out the window. *Where are the cars? Where are the horns? Where are the sirens?* Calley wonders.

Grumbling, Calley begins to remember, *Oh, right, I'm in Texas now.*

Calley lets her head fall back onto the pillow. Calley's mom lives about 15 miles north of Round Rock to be exact. Gradually, the memories all come back to her. The night of the storm. The night of the break-in. The night he disappeared. The night Calley's world fell apart.

"Calley, you're going to be late for school!" Mom shouts from the bottom of the stairs.

I could care less if I'm late for school. I don't want to be here in the first place. I should be back in New York, going to my school, meeting with my friends, Calley mourns as she rolls over in her bed. *With the time change,* she thinks and glances over at the clock on the side table, *Beth*

and Gable should be about getting to Algebra I with Ms. Haney. I hated Algebra anyway, but at least I'd be with my friends if I were there. And, if I were there now, I wouldn't be here. If I weren't here, then maybe that night might not have happened at all, Calley thinks longingly.

That wasn't the worst part though and Calley began to think, *What's worse than not being at my school, in my neighborhood in Brooklyn, with my friends? Not being with him. I still don't believe what they told me about it all. And, they didn't believe me when I told them about the intruder at my bedroom door either. Could I have dreamt about the lightning that struck through my bedroom? Because when the cop opened my bedroom door, the only damage was from the branch that was struck outside my window and crashed through it.*

I know what I saw. I know what I heard. Still, could I have been dreaming it? Shaking her head and sitting up, Calley brings her knees up under her chin. Resting her head on her knees, she wraps her arms around them. Calley sighs and closes her eyes.

Thinking about all of that makes my head hurt too much. I only just got out of the hospital a couple of weeks ago. They only let me go because I stopped telling them about the man at my door who didn't exist and the lightning that didn't split my bedroom through the center. I wasted too much time there anyway. It was stupid of me to think that if I just kept telling the truth, eventually someone would believe me. I should have known that people only believe what they want to regardless of factuality or reality, Calley rationalizes.

"Calley! Get a move on young lady!" Mom's voice comes closer now, probably from half-way up the stairs.

She's coming. I guess I better get out of bed before she gets in here. Last time she made it all the way to my room, she dumped a cup of ice water on me. She's so annoying. Calley rolls her eyes and plops her feet on the floor.

"Okay, I'm getting up!" Calley yells towards the bedroom door. It has a dead bolt on it, but her mom has the key. Mom had let Calley have the lock to make her feel safer, but she insisted on keeping a key to it since Melanie shares the room. *Why'd she even bother with the lock if I can't keep anyone out anyway?* Calley thinks as she gets dressed.

By the time Calley gets downstairs, there isn't any time for breakfast; not that she would eat anything anyway. Calley hasn't had much of an appetite since that night.

"Bye, I'm leaving for school," Calley yells as she pushes through the front door. The spring air hits her face bringing with it the smells of daisies, tulips and daffodils from Mom's flower garden. Spring is in full bloom for sure! It was a long, cold winter, but now everything seems to have woken from its winter long slumber.

It is the last day of school, but Calley doesn't even bother going to school. Instead, she spends the entire day at the nickel arcade; spending all of her nickels on arcade games.

There isn't any point in going to school here anyway. I don't know anyone and I've only gone there for a couple of weeks. It's not like anyone was really going to miss me, Calley reasoned to herself.

It was an entire month ago that Dad disappeared. The cops said that chances were he was killed by the intruders that night and that his body had been hidden somewhere off the freeway that runs so close to their house. The other theory as to what happened that night was so absurd that Calley refused to entertain it at all.

To suggest that Dad could have been part of the break-in, that the whole thing had been staged, was just absurd! Calley thinks as she walks home from the arcade.

There was no way in a million years that Dad would just up and leave me during some kind of elaborate ruse! Besides, he never went anywhere without his brown leather jacket. It was so old and smelly, but he wore it even in the summer! Dad would never have gone anywhere without it by choice! Thinking of that night, Calley argues in her head with the imaginary officers.

***

At dinner, Richard talks all about his last day at school and the traditional 'Field Day' that they had.

"I got to dunk Principal Reeves! And, there was so much food at the snack bar! I couldn't even make up my mind what to get and I ran out of money before I could get everything I wanted! They had a snow cone machine, a cotton candy machine, popcorn, laffy taffy's, fruit snacks, box drinks, bottled waters with kool-aid mixers, candy bars, chips! There was so much food!" The little kid is practically bouncing off of his seat while kicking his legs hard under the table.

"I got Tommy to run in the three-legged race with me! And we all played against Mrs. Kenneth's class in the tug-of-war! And, we won! Then, Tommy and I played horseshoes and water balloon volleyball and oh, oh, oh!" Richard puts his food-covered fork straight onto the table abruptly and blurts out, "Tommy got hit right in the face with a huge water balloon! He was soa… soaking…wet-" Richard starts laughing so hard that he can't go on with his description.

"That sounds like so much fun. I think it's so wonderful that the PTA puts that together every year to help earn money for the next year at your school," Mom says. "What about you, Calley? How was your last day of school today?"

"Oh, you know, pretty much the same as Richie's. Food, fun, games," Calley lies. She stares at her plate, pushing the mixed vegetables and pot roast around with the fork, hoping that Mom won't see through it; although by the tone in her voice, she already has.

"My name's not Richie, it's Richard! How many times do I have to tell you to stop calling me that?!" Richard protests and Calley rolls her eyes at him.

"I thought they said they'd hired a local band this year to play right after lunch at the high school? What were they like? Were they any good?" Mom pushes.

Yup, she knows, Calley thinks but she decides to continue the façade anyway; for Richard's and Arthur's sakes of course.

"They were okay I guess. I liked them all right," Calley tells another bold-faced lie straight to her mother's face.

"Well, that's funny because the PTA president sent out an email, this morning, to all the parents apologizing that the band couldn't perform because there just weren't enough funds to hire that band. So they were cancelled last minute," Mom says convincingly.

Why can't she just drop it? She already knows I'm lying about being at school. Why does she have to draw it out at dinner in front of Arthur and Richard and Melanie; not that I really care what they think anyway, Calley thinks as she glares at Mom.

"So? There wasn't a band… Okay…" Calley says rolling her eyes and then looking at the ceiling in the corner of the room. "I spent the day in the library, so I guess I missed that part." *Couldn't hurt to try again, right?*

"What book were you reading? You wouldn't be doing any studying on the last day of school," Mom persists.

Really? Why not just let it go? Had she really expected me to go to that school where I don't know anyone and where I didn't even learn anything I didn't already know? What was the point anyway? Calley thinks.

After staring at Mom again to no avail, Calley says, "I'm going to my room." Calley gets up from the table with her plate and turns toward the kitchen.

Just as she turns, Mom says, "Calley, are you forgetting something?"

Calley stops, glares some more at Mom, and says, "May I please be excused?"

"Yes, you may. I'll be up to talk to you in a little bit," Mom says and then goes back to eating. Everyone at the table is silent now as they watch Calley leave the dining room.

Why does she insist on always being so proper? What's the point? She knew I was leaving, I just said so, what's the point of specifically asking to be 'excused'? Calley thinks as she rinses her dishes, puts them in the dishwasher and heads up the stairs.

Melanie's little toddler bed near the door reminds Calley of how little privacy she has here. *I'm almost 16! You'd think I would get my own room. But, of course, Mom has to do the proper thing.*

"A girl and a boy cannot share a bedroom. It would be improper." Mom's voice rattles around Calley's head.

"But they're so young! They wouldn't even know anything was wrong!" Calley had argued back.

"That's my point, Calley. They don't know any better; unless we teach them. They need to learn what's right and wrong; what's proper and what's improper," Mom had said. Her voice is now ringing in Calley's ears.

Looking at Melanie's bed again, Calley's eyes linger on the various stuffed animals on her bed. There's a plain, old fashioned teddy bear dressed in a newer pink dress, but that's the only animal. The rest of Melanie's bed is covered with princess dolls. There's a princess doll which Calley assumed was Princess Aurora from Sleeping Beauty, one that looks like Belle from Beauty and the Beast, another that looks like Snow White, another that resembles Princess Jasmine and even one of Ariel, the Little Mermaid! Calley rolls her eyes and plops onto her bed, still staring at the dolls.

Princesses! Hmph! There's no such thing as a 'Princess'. I don't get why Mom lets her play with those things! 'Oooh, I want to be a 'Princess' when I grow up!' What's so great about that? They get pampered and waited on their entire lives and then grow up to be stuck-up, conceited, snobs; not like they portray in those fairy tales. They're not real. That's not reality. It's not real life. Real life is ugly... and mean... and dirty... and hard...Real life sucks! Calley thinks as she rolls over onto her side and grabs her MP3 player off her night stand.

Calley puts the ear buds from her MP3 player into her ears and switches it on. Imagine Dragons blasts into her ear drums; the beat pounds them as if they are Native American war drums. She doesn't even hear the knock when Mom comes to the door.

Chapter Two

"CALLEY, I'VE SAID YOUR NAME about five times now!" Mom says after taking an ear bud out of Calley's ear while standing right beside her bed. Calley rolls her eyes, sits up and takes the other one out. "You know how important school is, Calley."

"But the seniors don't even show up on the last day of school! It's another of your town's weird traditions; they call it Senior Skip Day," Calley counters.

"And that is a sanctioned and acceptable tradition for seniors who are graduating high school to participate in. However, you are not a senior...," Mom stops, shaking her head and then starts again. "But, that's not why I came in here to talk to you-" Mom pauses, looking at her hands as she sits down on the corner of Calley's bed.

She's nervous, Calley realizes.

"Have you been sleeping well, Calley?"

"All right I guess," Calley sighs, not really wanting to get into it with Mom right now.

"You've been having nightmares. You wake up screaming. We share a wall, remember? You wake up practically the entire neighborhood with your screams, Calley."

She is right too; Calley's been having terrible dreams about that night.

"Do you want to talk about them?" Mom offers.

"Not really," Calley answers. *After the way they treated me at the psych ward of the hospital when I tried to tell them what I'd seen in my room that night, I'm definitely not going there again,* Calley thinks, recalling the horrible experience of not being believed when telling the truth.

"They're about your dad, aren't they? About the night of the break-in? The night he disappeared...." Mom continues. She looks up at Calley for a moment, but then looks back down at her hands again. She's popping her knuckles repeatedly.

"Mom, I don't want to talk about it," Calley says in a hope to end this line of questioning.

Mom looks up at Calley, frowning and silent. Together they sit in silence for a few moments when Melanie comes bursting through the door.

"Mommy!! Mommy!! Tickle monsta comin!" She runs to hide behind the bed and then Arthur walks in the room crouched like a hunch-backed ogre. He has his fingers curved and ready to grab at any second.

"Fee-Fie-Fo-Fum, I spell the ticklish little one!" Arthur says rounding Calley's bed.

"Honey, will you take her downstairs for a little while? Calley and I are trying to have a private conversation," Mom says calmly.

"Sure thing, dear. Come on, Melanie! I think I hear the ice cream truck outside!" Arthur entices Melanie with hopes of ice cream.

"Ice-keem! Ice-keem!" Melanie rushes out the door and down the stairs followed by the lumbering hunch-backed ogre once more.

"Calley, I love you very much. You know that, right?" Mom asks worriedly and attempts to look Calley in the face.

Calley just turns her head further away in response.

"You do know that I am here for you no matter what, right?" Mom says, looking back at her hands again.

Calley pretends to read a book she'd found on her night stand. Mom takes the book and looks Calley in the eyes.

"Sure, Mom. Of course you do; you're my mom," Calley says matter-of-factly, staring blankly at Mom.

"Calley, I have something for you," Mom says reaching into her shawl which she'd had wadded up in her lap. Calley hadn't realized she was hiding something in it.

Mom reveals a small, rectangular gift box elegantly wrapped with gold and red ribbons. She hands Calley the box. Calley looks at her, waiting for her to say something else. When Mom nods her head, Calley unwraps the box. It's a jewelry case, and inside it is a necklace with the biggest green gem on it that Calley has ever seen.

"Is this from you and Arthur? It's not my birthday until the end of August," Calley says, looking up at Mom. She couldn't help but wonder what the occasion is that entitles her to be given a present.

"It's from your grandparents; your father's parents to be specific. The truth is, I wasn't supposed to give this to you until your 16th birthday, but I thought you could use it now. You see this is a Peridot gem; and it's a rare kind too! Look at the color, such a deep olive green! Just like your eyes! Not only is this your birthstone, but the Peridot is said to have healing powers to protect against nightmares! I made sure it had a very strong, heavy duty pure silver chain so you could wear it continually. I'm sure your nightmares will be a thing of the past in no time!" Mom says enthusiastically. She takes the box from Calley and pulls out the necklace, holding it out to put on Calley.

Calley pulls her pony tail aside and turns to let Mom lock the necklace around her neck. The peridot is probably the biggest gem of any kind that Calley has ever seen! It is about the size of a quarter; maybe a little bit bigger. Set inside a silver casing, the peridot makes a fairly heavy pendant. Calley turns the pendant over and sees that there is an inscription on the back. Squinting, Calley reads the inscription, "To our beloved Regina Alleynia," Calley reads aloud. "What does that mean? Did I read that right?"

"Yes, you did. Do you remember why we call you Calley? Your full name is Catherine Alleynia. Actually, your grandparents were very upset with me when I gave you the name of Catherine. They said it was inappropriate for their little Regina," Mom says, shaking her head and remembering.

"Yeah, but no one ever told them that you call me Calley?" Calley asks while admiring the pendant.

"I've only ever met your father's parents twice; once on our wedding day and then again the day they came to bless you as a baby, and they left this with us to give to you when you were older. It was your father who came up with the compromise of calling you Calley; he said it was a good meeting point between "Catherine" and "Alleynia"," Mom explains. "'The best of both worlds', he said."

"Whatever happened to them? My grandparents I mean. I don't ever remember meeting them; I guess when I was a baby was the only time," Calley says, trying to remember them.

"They're from some tiny country in Eastern Europe. I never could remember its name. Your father told me that there was some kind of civil war that broke out in their country which prevented them from leaving and kept anyone from going in. All communications ceased actually. I've just assumed that the war has gotten pretty bad and they just haven't been able to contact us," Mom says, shrugging her shoulders and sighing.

"But, are they okay? Haven't they sent any kind of message to say they're all right?" Calley asks, now genuinely worried.

"The last time we saw them was when you were 3 months old. It was the same day that they blessed you and gave me the pendant to give to you. Marina, your grandmother, told me they weren't sure when they would be able to see us again, if ever. But, they wanted to make sure you had this. They said it would be very important to you. She always had a way of knowing things long before they happened, according to your father. So, I took her word for it and I still do. Perhaps she was referring to these nightmares of yours... I don't know, but I have faith that she was right about it being very important to you," Mom says. "Please tell me you'll wear it and give it a chance to help you?"

"Sure, Mom. Whatever. I'll try it out," Calley says, spinning the pendant between her fingers on its chain. *I have to admit, I do like it.* It seems to radiate a kind of warmth that comforts and calms Calley. Mom starts in on a different topic while Calley rereads the inscription over and over.

"Oh, Calley! I can't believe it's so close to you birthday! You'll be 16 by the end of the summer! I hope you don't mind, but I've already started planning for your Coming Out Ball! I do hope you will wear your pendant! It complements the color of your eyes so well!" Mom starts spouting off flower arrangements and color schemes and dress fashions.

Not that I care about any of those things, Calley thinks, rolling her eyes in annoyance. "Mom, I already told you, I don't want a 'Ball'! I don't even want a party! I just want to sit in my room, all alone and pass the time until it's over," Calley says, looking out the window and wishing she was somewhere else entirely. This topic always made Calley uneasy.

"Oh come on, Calley! No one wants to be alone on their birthday! You are so lucky that the community's 'Coming Out Ball' just happens to be taking place right on your birthday this year! Talk about perfect timing!"

Mom sure is excited about this stupid dance party, Calley thinks. She never was much into dances, or makeup, or jewelry, or dresses. You could call Calley a tomboy of sorts, although Mom is anything but girly girl.

Calley is staring out the window, trying to stay calm, when the fumes start to fill her ears.

"Just imagine it Calley! The music, all you girls made up like royalty, the boys just lining up for a turn to dance with you!" Mom continues without missing a beat.

Mom is having some kind of flashback, Calley thinks. *Breathe, stay calm, don't get mad...*Fumes begin to escape slowly.

"Oh, and we need to go shopping, Calley! I was thinking first thing in the morning, we could go to the mall and get some concealor and foundation to cover up those blemishes... and those dark circles..." Mom pauses and touches Calley's face, just under her eye. "We'll get some blush to bring out your rosy cheeks, some eye shadow to emphasize those gorgeous green eyes of yours; and of course you will have to wear your pendant to the ball! Maybe while we're there, we can stop in and you can try on a few dresses so we can get some ideas, and then we go to..." Mom stops and takes a big, deep breathe. A huge smile spreads across her face as she stares into space. "Wait here a minute!" Mom says and she jumps up and leaves the room and is back in a flash carrying a dress bag. Already Calley is on her feet, backing away from her mother.

"How many times can I say that I don't want a party?!? I don't want a dress, I don't want make-up, I don't want to 'come out'!" Calley raises her voice and crosses her arms. Calley taps her foot on the floor quickly in an attempt to keep from bursting out any further.

"But just wait 'til you see it! You're going to love this," Mom starts opening up the bag carefully, ignoring Calley completely. Calley's frustration has turns to anger!

I never had a choice in the matter did I? She already got me a dress! She already had everything planned! And, I don't want it anyway!

"I said I'm not going! There will be no foundation, no eye shadow, no lip stick, no dress and NO BALL!" Calley screeches at Mom, bursts out of the room and skates down the stairs on her heels.

Chapter Three

ONCE OUTSIDE, CALLEY TAKES off at a sprint for the stables. The only thing that ever calms her down anymore is riding Ginger, her mare. Dad had gotten Ginger for Calley when she was just a little girl. He said it was important that she have a friend who would always be there for her and would never let her down. Every weekend, they would go out to the countryside in upper state New York where Calley spent her time riding and training with Ginger.

As soon as she enters the stables, Calley grabs the saddle and harness and heads for Ginger's stall. There, the mare is waiting for Calley like she's been expecting her.

I swear she always smiles when I see her. Calley takes a deep breath feeling somewhat calmer. Calley doesn't waste any time in placing the saddle on Ginger and clasping the harness tightly around the horse's flanks. Once everything is tightened appropriately, Calley climbs on and guides Ginger out into the evening air. It may be late spring, but there is already a slight hint of summer on the air.

The sun will be setting in a little while, but I'll be fine with Ginger. I've roamed all over Mom and Arthur's property; all 100 or so acres of it! I know where we'll be going, Calley thinks as she heads out.

Calley had wanted to go to a little grove of trees she found that was just a little way from the house, but as the sun sets, and she can't see the way as well, Calley starts to get frustrated.

Then, the thoughts come in heavy and hard, *How could Mom have thought that I would actually WANT some stupid ball! After how Dad just disappeared!?!? After he was kidnapped..... I'm sure that's what happened. I still have his brown leather coat that he always used to* wear everywhere he went; even in the summer-time, Calley thinks, getting madder as she thinks.

The nerve of that woman! Assuming that I would like something like that!? She doesn't even know me at all does she? Dad would never have tried to push something that dainty and delicate on me! A dress!?!?!? She knows I don't wear dresses. At least, I haven't worn one since I was just a little girl. I can't stand them! They make me feel vulnerable and soft, Calley thinks as she grows more furious and frustrated.

Instead of planning some stupid ball, she should be helping me try to find out who took Dad! Why doesn't she even care? I haven't heard her say anything about that to me. She probably thinks I'm as crazy as a fruit cake like all the other people back at the hospital! Either that, or she thinks I've accepted the alternative theories about Dad's disappearance. These thoughts bring tears to Calley's eyes, and she brushes them away fiercely with the sleeve of her shirt.

I'm crying!?!? I DON'T cry! Calley tells herself and forces the tears back down.

"Hya!" Calley yells and kicks Ginger in the flanks so she'll pick up to a gallop. On and on, they gallop. Ginger jumps downed tree trunks and curves around bulky vines that have clumped together smaller trees. Calley has to keep her head low so she doesn't decapitate herself on low hanging tree branches. It feels like they've been running forever when suddenly Ginger stops in front of a tangled mass of vines and trees just in front of them. Calley can't even see where the mass ends or begins. Looking around, Calley realizes that they are surrounded by trees. They are in some kind of hallowed out spot around which the trees have grown so thick that you can't see through them. Calley turns Ginger around in time for her to start bucking and backing away from the entrance to the hollow. Something has spooked her, and Calley can't figure out what.

"Shhh, it's okay, girl. Calm down," Calley says while patting and smoothing Ginger's mane. Ginger stops bucking, but keeps backing up. "Come on, giddy-up, let's get out of here," Calley heels Ginger's flanks, but she keeps on backing up. Hopping down from the harness, Calley takes hold of the bit in order to talk to Ginger face to face.

"It's okay, there's nothing there. See," she says this while swinging her arm around to show the horse that the area is clear. Once it seems that Ginger has relaxed, Calley begins to remount her. With one foot in the stirrup and a good grasp on the harness, Calley jumps and pulls herself up. Suddenly, Ginger rears up, knocking Calley to the ground.

Calley can hear the sound of Ginger's hooves as she speeds away from her, but the pain and approaching nausea are too much to ignore and they completely consume her. Everything fades to black, to cold, to silence.

Chapter Four

THEN, IT ISN'T SILENT anymore. Snickering, whisperings, little high-pitched, squeaky voices seem to be carried on the wind. They seem so distant, so far away. And yet, they seem as though they could be whispering right in Calley's ear.

"Who is she?" "What is she?" "Where did she come from?" "My mom told me a story once about a mortal…" "Come on, you know those are just stories to scare us kids, right?" "Maybe she's a mortal?" "Maybe she's a Striga from across the Nox Pelio!" "A Striga?! No way! Look at her! It looks like she's the one under some kind of spell!" "No, she's a Nympha! Look at how soft and smooth she is!" "No, she isn't! She's a Striga!" "I think I should know what a Nympha looks like! My Grammy was one after all! She's a Nympha for sure!" The voices argue amongst themselves.

The whispers become a debate about whether or not Calley is a Striga or a Nympha; whatever those are. It still hurts too much to move or even to open her eyes, so Calley just lies there perfectly still, listening to the bickering.

Calley soon notices the trickling of a spring somewhere close by. *Wait a minute, there's no creek or river or anything like that on Mom and Arthur's land… Could I have ridden Ginger passed their lands boundaries?* Calley makes the painful effort to open her eyes just enough to realize that everything is fuzzy. The sight is enough to bring back the nausea and the weight of her eyelids seals them without another thought. Calley groans, "Ugh".

"Shhh! I think she's waking up!" "Don't push!" "Let me see!" "She's like an angel!" "I told you, she's a Nympha!" "No, she's a Striga!"

"Ugh," Calley sighs and tries to open her eyes again, this time ready for the need to refocus. Her eyelids are weighted and hard to keep open, but Calley manages to catch glimpses of the rabble of whispering voices. They're just children. Tiny, miniature sized children. "Who,.. umf..." Calley struggles to speak, "who are you?"

Calley forces her eyelids up long enough this time to get a good look at her surroundings, and lifts her head slightly from the ground. While everything still appears foggy, as if she's looking through fogged up glasses, Calley can make out the tiny shapes of the children and their child-like features. She can also make out the large, sharp edges of the rocks that line the small creek that runs alongside where she lay.

I have got to be dreaming. I know there isn't a creek anywhere near Mom's land, and I don't remember there being any people with big families living around it either. Maybe I hit my head harder than I thought? Calley wonders, rubbing her head.

Calley closes her eyes and tries to sit up, but her arm collapses beneath her weight. She tries again, slower this time, and is able to raise herself to a sitting position.

From this angle, maybe the world will make more sense, Calley hopes as she opens her eyes again after rubbing them once more. *Nope, nothing changed. They're all still there, staring at me.*

"Could one of you tell me where I am?" Calley asks the children, who look like they could be only 2 or 3 years old at the most. But, something in their faces makes them seem older than that, though their size would indicate they couldn't be much older than 3 years, if that. There are about a dozen of them, all huddled in a group not far from Calley. Almost as soon as she asks the question, a girl in the back of the group runs off in the opposite direction. *Did I scare her?*

Every one of the children has rough, auburn hair that curls messily out. The girls' hair is longer than the boys' but even the boys' hair reaches their shoulders. All of them have pudgy round faces with rosy red cheeks. They stare blankly at Calley, careful not to move a muscle or even bat an eyelash while Calley watches them. Something strange about the children catches Calley's interest. Their eyes are all a golden brown color; lighter than the auburn of their hair and more yellow.

"Please, don't be scared. I just don't know where I am." Calley looks around at all of the stone faces of the children. Now, they have all frozen in place as if pretending to be statues. Calley stifles a chuckle at the thought and tries again, "Please, someone tell me where I am so I can get home."

"Calueria," one child begins. "Shhh, she could be a Striga trying to trick you! Don't say another word," another child says. "Don't be silly, she's a Nympha, like I said before. She must be confused." "You lot listen here, she's a Mortal just like I said before!" another child speaks up; and the debate resumes once more as though they'd forgotten Calley was watching and listening to them.

Soon, Calley sees the little girl who'd left a while before heading back down the hill. Behind her is another person who looks like she could be the girl's older sister. Something in her face reminds Calley of someone older, however. *Maybe that is her mother? It's strange how small these people are. I've seen small people in movies before, but never in person and never so many at one time and in one place.*

"Children!" The newcomer yells, getting the attention of the whole group. "Scat! There is nothing to be seen here and there are chores to be done!" the newcomer yells, waving her hands as if to herd them away. The children all run back up the hill. Following them with her eyes, Calley now sees that at the top of the bank there are silhouettes of houses. She can't see above the tree tops, but if she could she would see smoke billowing up from that direction. Calley can smell the crisp scent of wood-burning stoves as the breeze picks up for a moment.

"Now, child, what is your name?" the woman asks kindly. She seems gentle with smooth, round features. She's no taller than an 8 year old. Her cheeks are rosy and dirty as if she's been hard at work. Her auburn hair falls in messy curls around her face, just like the children's did. And, her eyes are the same golden color as the children's were.

"Calley, my name is Calley," Calley says while the woman sums her up with her eyes from head to toe. "Where am I?" Calley asks, beginning to worry.

"Calueria, child. You're in Calueria. Now, if you'll come with me, Calley," the woman pauses as she notices the knot on Calley's head which is covered by dried, old blood from the night before. Calley raises a hand to feel the place where the woman is staring and realizes her injury for the first time. "We'll get you washed up and fed. And, I'll see to that bump on your head. Must have had quite the spill, didn't you, deary?" The woman turns and begins walking back up the hill.

"No, wait. Calueria, you said?" Calley is still sitting on the bank of the creek, now more confused than ever. "Where is Calueria? Is that near Round Rock?" she asks, her head beginning to hurt again.

"Yes, I believe there is a 'round rock' around here someplace. But, I don't believe it is the 'Round Rock' to which you are referring. Now, please, come with me and I'll get you fixed up. You'll need a bandage on that head." The woman has come closer to Calley now and touches

her forehead where it hit on the rock when she fell from...
Ginger!

"Wait, where's Ginger?" Calley asks and starts turning all around to look in every direction to see if she can see the horse.

"Ginger? Who is Ginger?" the woman asks patiently, crossing her hands at her waist.

"She's my horse. I was riding her, and she got spooked; I fell and that's how I got this on my head," Calley reaches up to feel the goose-egg that has formed at the top of her forehead, right on the hairline.

"She's gone now, child. I'm sorry, but you really must come with me so I can tend to that bump." The woman takes Calley's hand and leads her up the hill.

***

At the top of the hill, Calley sees that she was right about the fire, except there are many more than just one. There are dozens of little cobble-stone cabins spread out with a fire lit at each house. It's almost like a camping site except with the cobble-stone cabins instead of tents. *Cobble-stones instead of wood? These are not like any cabins I've seen before,* Calley thinks as she follows the little woman.

"Now, have a seat right here, dear, and I'll go and grab the bandages and cleanser." The woman darts into the house. Looking around, Calley can see clothing hanging on a line to dry, an iron pot hanging over the fire pit, and something smells good coming from the pot. A small dirt path connects the houses to each other and forms a kind of road in the center which continues away from them all.

"Ah, that smells delicious! I'll bet you're famished!" The woman says as she opens the pot and dishes a portion out into a tiny bowl she holds. Setting the lid back onto the pot, she motions for Calley to come to her.

Calley walks over and sits on a log bench that is set near enough to the fire for warmth, but far enough not to get burned.

"Here, you eat this while I tend to that bump." She hands Calley the bowl and begins dabbing a rag into a bowl of water and using it to clean Calley's forehead.

"What is your name?" Calley asks.

"Esther. I'm the village healer. You were lucky it was my Persephone who found you! Now, eat up, you need your strength." Esther wipes Calley's brow with the rag again before pulling out a small wooden bowl with yellow paste inside, which she then applies to Calley's forehead using the rag.

Calley scoops up the sweet smelling soup with a spoon and sips it carefully. Sweet honey fills her mouth; it's smoother than any she's ever tasted and made into a soup! It soothes her throat as it slides down. She can feel the warmth as it passes through her throat, into her stomach and then throughout each of her limbs.

Chapter Five

"WE NEED THE MONEY! WE DON'T have the luxury of owning our own slave. How else are we going to pay to fix the roof? She couldn't have fallen into our laps at a more convenient time!" A man howls from somewhere nearby.

"Just think of how much she'd make us if we just kept her and used her, Tarence! We could breed her! She is young and strong!.. Besides, she could patch up the roof for us! And, then if someone falls from the roof while attempting to repair it, at least it won't be you!" Esther's voice is harsh and cold.

"Yes, my love, but who will pay for the supplies to patch the roof in the first place?" the man asks in a sarcastic tone.

"Hmph! Fine! Take her then! She'll be waking soon; she didn't drink much of the drought before nodding off and she'll need another dose soon if you're going to take her to the market." Defeated, Esther snarled with her words. "Oh, and just get her out of here before I change my mind. There'll be no putting this off for another day like you do with everything else around here. And, I expect that roof patched up by the end of the week! No more excuses for you now!" There's a short silence and then Esther continues her tirade in a more subdued tone and from further away. "Three weeks the roof has been leaking! And I've been saying all along that we needed to get..." Esther's voice fades as she moves away from the house.

***

"Well, hello there." The man who was arguing with Esther, Tarence, says from in front of Calley, who now lies on the ground near the fire. "Yes, I know you're awake. And, you have been listening too," he says, kneeling down.

Calley opens her eyes and looks up at the man. He's not much taller than Esther, but slightly more rounded than she. His hair too is an auburn curly mess; although much shorter than his shoulders. The tangled curly auburn mess doesn't stop at his head either; it encompasses his face and neck in the form of a very thick, very heavy beard. His eyes are the same strange gold color as Esther's and the children's.

"Wha...... wha......wha......" Calley tries to speak but cannot seem to form any words.

"Oh, don't try to speak. You'll be much too doused for that any time soon. And, don't bother trying to escape, you don't have the strength for that either if my dear Esther's drought has done its job correctly. Now, she said you'd need another dose before we left..." Tarence lifts the ladle filled with the sweet honey potion up to Calley's mouth and lets it drip into her mouth and down her chin. "Your head seems to have healed up quite nicely! Yes, I think Esther's salve has worked wonderfully on you, even if you are a mortal." Tarence holds Calley's chin while he examines her forehead. He turns her head this way and that to view it from different angles. Using a long strip of twine, Tarence wraps up Calley's wrists, and holds on to the other end as he stands.

"Okay, well then, let's be going. *Badiz!*" Tarence commands and Calley feels her body begin to move without her control. She stands and begins following Tarence. "We're going to the emporium to see if we can catch a good price for you," Tarence tells Calley as they begin walking down the dirt road, away from the rest of the cobble-stone cabins.

Why is he bothering to tell me any of this? If he's just going to sell me, why bother talking to me at all?

Calley wonders as they walk and Tarence continues to talk to her. *Whatever the reason, it's beyond me!* Calley concludes.

After seeming to have walked a good two miles, they finally come upon a large open air market. Vendors have wooden barrels filled with fresh vegetables and fruits; most of them Calley has never seen before, but she does recognize some of them. Apples, oranges and pears fill one of the vendor's carts while the very next one sells exotic looking fruits. One fruit is green and spiky on the outside with a juicy, red center. Its texture looks to be similar to that of cantaloupe. A small cluster of white seeds makes up the very center of the fruit. Another vendor sells what looks like corn, but the husks vary in color from brown to green to yellow. When the husks are peeled away, the kernels inside reflect the color of the peeled husk.

The vendors' carts are lined up along the dirt road on either side. Behind the vendors are wagons filled with their produce for sale.

They turn off of the road after passing a vendor selling something like purple apples with bright red leaves still attached at the stems. They pass a few more produce vendors, and Calley hears yelling growing closer as they walk.

"Can I get 10 gold thrushes here? I said 10 gold thrushes for this beautiful specimen of canine? Breeds like this are rare these days so step up and get yours for only 10 gold thrushes! Ah! We have a bid for 10; do I hear 11 gold thrushes? Anyone in the crowd want to take home this rare breed of canine? Yes, sir in the back of the crowd! That'll be 12 gold thrushes that we're up to now!" The man continued calling out the bids as they came in. Although similar to what she'd heard of about the way that auctioneers speak, this auctioneer speaks much slower. He speaks at a normal pace and not in a mashed up, hurried mumble. Calley can actually understand what he is saying. Although, she isn't sure what a 'gold thrush' is.

Tarence leads Calley around a huge stage that has been set up behind all of the produce vendors. The auctioneer stands on top of the stage next to the item being auctioned off. Behind the stage, there are cages all over the place with all sorts of animals in them. Looking from cage the cage, Calley catches the eyes of one inmate who looks strikingly like herself. It's another mortal!

"What have you to auction today, sir?" another man comes up and asks Tarence, not even glancing at Calley.

"The name is Tarence Shay and I have a mortal to auction. I'm not late am I? I see the bidding has already begun on a few items," Tarence asks.

"No, you're not too late. We usually save the mortals for last anyway," the man looks down at a piece of parchment in his hands and starts to write something down. Calley notices that the man has nothing in his hand for writing with. Regardless, as the man's hand wisps across a line on the parchment, words do appear there trailing behind his speedy fingers.

"You'll be number 4256; here's your tag and a cage for your property. You must leave it here behind the stage and it will be brought out when it is time for your item to be auctioned." The man hands Tarence a small orange, square ticket with the number 4256 on it. Tarence hands the man the twine tied to Calley's hands and walks back off towards the front of the stage with his ticket in hand.

The auction-hand leads Calley to the empty cage he'd pointed out to Tarence. He writes on the top the number 4256, again with an invisible pen, and says to Calley, "Get in." Calley obeys and, still without looking at her, the auction-hand whispers something and the lock on the cage snaps shut all on its own.

It's not a huge cage, but at least it's not so small that she has to pull her knees up to her chin in order to fit. Calley can sit cross-legged comfortably and lean her back against the cage.

***

Time passes and animals are taken into the stage area to be auctioned off. Before long there are not many cages left and the sun has begun lowering down the western side of the sky. After a few of the little people come and take away the cage next to Calley's, which held some kind of flying snake in it, she realizes that she is in clear view of the other mortal; a little girl.

"Hey!" Calley whispers loudly in the girl's direction. "Hey!" Calley tries again slightly louder than before.

The girl is curled up in the fetal position in her cage; which is much smaller than Calley's. Although the girl is younger than Caller and therefore smaller, they have misjudged how much space she would take up in the cage because it is much too small for her. *She has no room to squirm around or sit up or roll over or anything,* Calley thinks, concerned about the little girl.

"Hey! Little girl!" Calley says a little louder, no longer whispering.

"Shh! Do you want them to hear you?" a small voice comes from somewhere beneath the heap of dirty clothe and ragged hair that makes up the girl in the other cage.

"Where are we? What's going on here?" Calley asks hurriedly! *Someone I can talk to who might give me some answers about what is going on and where I am!* Calley thinks hopefully.

"Shh! They'll be back any second!" She snaps at Calley, lifting her head just enough that Calley can see the girl's face now.

She is younger than I'd thought. She might only be about Richie's age, Calley thinks.

"How'd we get here?" Calley whispers, quieter once again.

"I don't know," the girl says.

"Where are we?" Calley asks.

"They call it Calueria," the girl answers blankly.

"How old are you? You don't look much older than my little brother's age; he's eight," Calley asks.

"I'll turn 13 next month. At least, I think so. What month was it when you left?" the girl asks.

"Then end of May. It's about to be June," Calley answers.

"Then, yeah. Next month, I'll be 13." The girl lies silently, watching the entrance to the stage from the back where another auction-hand is bound to come through any second.

"What are they going to do with us?" Calley asks.

The girl gasps in exasperation. "You haven't figured that out yet? We're being sold as slaves. They'll do what they always do. They want to breed us!" the girl gives Calley a hard look of annoyance just before the auction-hand walks back out to take in another cage to be auctioned.

"There aren't many left before us. We'll go last, but we are next in line," the girl says quietly. Then, she lifts her head again in Calley's direction and says, "You must have just gotten here. I've been here for a while. I was playing hide and seek with my friends out behind my house a few years ago. I found this cave and thought it would be fun to explore it. After I went inside, the entrance caved in. The only light I could see came from somewhere inside, at the back of the cave; so I followed it thinking that it would lead me out of the cave. It led me out all right. It led me out of the cave and into this place. I was immediately captured by some people who then took me to a different emporium just like this one somewhere else," the girl says and stops. She lifts her head and Calley can barely see the flicker of her eyes over her shoulder as she looks at Calley.

"Wait, how did you get here?" Calley asks curiously, realizing for the first time that she doesn't know how she got here.

The girl sighs as if annoyed again and says, "I guess there are these holes between our world and theirs. That's what I stumbled into that day in the cave. You must have found one too."

"Is that the only way to get here from there? Is there a way to get back? Back home, I mean?" Calley asks intently.

"Not that I know of. I mean, I guess I've heard a few of them talking about trying to open a portal. Some of the traders who have dealt with me would talk about it. They would argue about whether or not it could be done," the girl says and she lays her head back down again.

"I've been sold like this a few times, you know," the little girl offers, beginning a new line of conversation after a few minutes of silence. "I've had a few owners now. My last one sold me because his wife got jealous that he was falling in love with me. They're always so paranoid about that. I guess it's some kind of taboo for them to fall in love with a mortal, that's what they call us; mortals."

"What are they?" Calley asks.

"The people here are called Kinsfolk. They're like little people, but they have magic. Actually, all little people in our world used to have magic also. But, they over bred with mortals and the magic was bred out of them," the girl says and then is quiet for a moment. "You don't understand, do you? Okay so, pretty much everything you've ever heard about in a fairy tale or religion is probably true to some degree. This is where everything originated. They create what they want and whatever they decide they don't want anymore, they simply create a new place and send the creatures there," the girl says dryly, as if she's recanted the story a million times.

Then, the last of the other creatures is taken away onto the stage to be auctioned off. Now, the two mortals are alone for a few minutes.

"Is there any hope of escape?" Calley asks optimistically.

"I've tried. That's what ended up getting me sold off after my first master. I even tried with the second one, but he'd just drag me back and put me back to work with a heavier chain each time. I don't know why he didn't just spell it to keep me bound. He could have. He had the ability because I saw him do it to others. Maybe his wife was on to something about him having a thing for me. If he did, he never did anything about it though."

They sit silently now, staring at the stage entrance or at the ground, waiting for their turn to be taken away and auctioned. Neither of them knows who will be taken first. Finally, another question pops into Calley's mind and she asks the girl, "What's your name?"

"Sademma," she answers and then they are both silent again. It seems like forever before the auction-hand is back and takes Sademma away. Calley is left alone.

Calley can hear the cries of the audience now. Mortals must be a hot commodity by the way they sound! Loud, boisterous shouting in different languages explodes just before a loud whistle is blown and everything goes silent.

Was that a fight? Calley wonders.

Then, the auction-hand comes to take Calley away.

Chapter Six

CALLEY WOULDN'T HAVE EXPECTED one man to have the strength to lift her cage if she hadn't seen him do it to all the others before her. But when he comes to take her, Calley hears him mutter something under his breath and then he hoists her into his arms.

Is it magic he uses to lift these heavy cages? Calley wonders as he takes her onto the stage. The tide is smooth, more like she is floating than being carried.

After being carried inside, Calley is set at the front of the stage where all can see her. The crowd is instructed that they will have one minute to view her before the bidding will begin.

"This is a fine and beautiful specimen! Fresh from the mortal world and new to ours! She would make a fine breeder or even a mistress if one was so inclined! See for yourself how ripe and unmarked she is! Perfect for a first time owner also I should think! We will open the bidding at 10 gold thrushes... Do I hear 10 gold thrushes?..10 gold thrushes...Ah, good, do I hear 11 gold th-" the auctioneer is interrupted.

"15 gold thrushes!" a man yells from the crowd.

"15 gold thrushes it is! And, do I hear 20 gold thrushes?" the auctioneer poses to the crowd.

"20!" cries a woman from somewhere in the back of the crowd.

"We now have 20 gold thrushes, do I hear 25?" the auctioneer says, keeping things moving quickly and smoothly.

"Here! 25!" another man yells from somewhere in the front.

"No! 30 gold thrushes here!" the first man yells above the crowd.

"Wonderful! We have 30 gold thrushes for the bid, do I hear 35 for this fine, young mortal specimen?" the auctioneer postures towards Calley in a feminine sort of way.

"50 gold thrushes!" the second man near the front yells.

"75! Here! 75 gold thrushes! She will be mine!" yells the first man, now making his way towards the stage, pushing people out of his way as he goes. Once the second man sees this, he starts making his way to the stage as well.

"Now, now! We don't want to have to bring out the Toot-Sweet again, do we?" the auctioneer asks and the men stop where they stand and wait.

"We have a bid for 75 gold thrushes, do I hear another for 80-" the auctioneer begins.

"I'll bid one Platinum Senine!" the woman at the back of the crowd yells and a silence hushes over the crowd.

Clearing his throat nervously, the auctioneer announces, "We have a bid for one Platinum Senine; going once, going twice," the auctioneer eyes the two men at the front of the stage but neither of them seem to have this kind of money. "Sold! To the lady in the back. Again, all purchases are final, payments must be made before receipt of your purchase and may all of you have a good day! This now brings our weekly auction to a close. Winning bids may be paid for at the cashier and upon transference of your ticket, you may pick up your item behind the stage."

Calley is again lifted as before and taken back outside behind the stage. She doesn't see Sademma anywhere though.

Maybe she's already been paid for and picked up. That's too bad. I'd have liked to see her one more time, Calley thinks and sighs.

It isn't too long before there is a horde of Kinsfolk behind the stage handing over tickets and carrying off their prizes. A few of the bidders are a little taller than the rest, but for the most part, everyone here is Kinsfolk. Calley leans her head against the cage and watches as other cages are emptied or carried away with their cargo inside.

I guess you have to purchase the cage extra if you want to keep it. Calley closes her eyes and sighs. *I have got to be dreaming. If only I could get myself to wake up! This has all got to be some huge, really long nightmare that I just can't break out of!*

***

"Number 4256? This way. So you're the lucky new owner, eh? Well, she'll make you a proud one, she will!" the auction-hand is walking towards Calley followed by a hooded, taller woman walking slightly behind him. The woman's hooded cloak is a very deep maroon, almost brown color.

The woman hands the auction-hand her ticket and he asks, "Did you want to purchase the cage to keep her in or do you have your own means of transfer?"

"I have my own way to take her, thank you," the woman says with her eyes still shaded from Calley's view by the hood.

"All right then, here we go." The auction-hand whispers something next to the lock and it springs open. He reaches in and grabs Calley's arm and yanks her out.

Before she has even realized what is going on, the woman has Calley by the arm and ties something tiny and thread-like around her wrist. Then, she whispers something and she lets go of Calley's hand.

"Follow me." The woman turns and takes a few steps away from Calley. When Calley doesn't follow, the woman adds, "That is the silk of a Black Wrathian Widow Aranea, a kind of spider native to the *Nox Pelio*, that binds you to me and you will do as I say without hesitation or you will regret it." Then, turning towards Calley again, she says, "Oh, and don't even think about escape. Once connected to the Wrathian Widow's web, she can always find you. The last mortal I had that did try to run away learned that lesson the hard way. Every inch of her was bone dry of blood and water when my Wrathian Widow brought her to me." The woman crosses her arms and she shifts her weight onto one foot.

"Oh, she wasn't dead, no! That would hardly serve my purposes now would it? But, oh the agony she was in before I allowed my Wrathian Widow to give her back her blood! Ha!" The woman then comes right up to Calley with her face only inches away from Calley's. At this range, Calley can clearly see the woman's face. Red, glowing eyes burn like fire as she says, "You should heed this warning and not test the boundaries of my Wraithe!" Then, she turns again and strolls off at a good speed. Calley hurries to keep up with her this time, not wanting to meet any kind of spider, let alone a spider like the one just described to her.

"My name is Scyn. You will call me Magistre Scyn. I think you will make a wonderful pet for a wealthy client of mine in the Atsu Damscence, the Adorned City." With that, Calley's new master silently leads her back through the various vendors, weaving in and out of both vendors and customers. Once they get to the main road, Scyn turns away from the village. Calley follows on her heels as quickly as she can, occasionally tripping here and there.

***

A ways down the road, Scyn veers to the right abruptly which causes Calley to jerk and trip again. A slew of wagons, horses and donkeys are spread around a single bonfire at the center. They keep walking to a covered wagon with a door on the side. Beside it, there are several strange creatures lazily lounging in the grass, nibbling it here and there.

Scyn pounds the door with her fist and yells, "Isabol! Take this girl and place her on one of your asimuns, she is coming with us to Atsu Damscence."

An older woman opens the door and looks Calley up and down for a second. Parcels of white hair are sparse upon her head as it is mostly bald and covered with mottled spots and bumpy moles. She has an odor all her own which is almost incapacitating. Moles and more mottled spots cover the old woman's face and give her an overall look of what many in the mortal world would describe to be a witch. "What are you going to do with her?" she asks curiously in a gruff, scratchy, low voice.

"I plan to sell her for top senine to one of my wealthiest clients. Make sure that no harm comes to her and that she arrives as pretty as she is now. I don't want a single bruise, cut or hair lost on the journey."

"Yes, Magistre Duz de Comitas," the woman says, slightly bowing her head. Isabol comes out of the wagon, waddling down each step one at a time. She hops off the last of the three steps to the ground, and Calley realizes that the old woman is only as tall as her shoulders.

I wonder if she's a Kinsfolk, Calley thinks. Scyn gives Calley's wrist with the invisible spider silk tied onto it to Isabol and then leaves.

The old woman begins waddling behind the wagon and Calley follows. There is a small campfire with an iron pot settled near it. Something inside the pot is boiling because the lid keeps jumping and small juices jump out into the fire only to sizzle away into steam.

"Boy! Tend to the pot!" Isabol yells. A tall, thin boy pops up out of nowhere and hurries to the pot. He pulls it away from the fire with a slew of what Calley can only guess are curse words at the boiling liquid that has scalded his hands and arm. He looks up at Isabol and Calley while sucking on a spot on his hand. Almost as soon as their eyes meet, the boy stiffens like a block of petrified wood, just noticing the girl. Cautiously, he lowers his hand and straightens himself, without taking his eyes off of Calley.

Tall! Very tall! Calley thinks as she looks him over. *And, handsome too!* She blushes suddenly and averts her eyes, realizing that she is staring.

The boys piercing chocolate brown eyes only show against his dark amber-colored skin because of their depth and intensity. His mousy brown hair is almost as long as his shoulders as it waves and curls in a disheveled mess. He has it tucked behind his ears to keep it from falling into his face.

Calley begins to feel a little self-conscious suddenly as she realizes that she's staring and she looks at the ground, waiting for the awkward silence to pass and someone to say something.

"Boy, have you gone daft? What is wrong with you? You've seen a mortal before! Now, stop babying that hand of yours and get back to work. Tend to that burnt mess you call supper." Isabol turns to Calley and says, "Now, you'll be staying with us when we're camped. You'll do as I instruct and when we're on the road, you'll be riding in here." Isabol points to a cage similar to the ones used at the emporium. "This is where you'll sleep as well, but when we've stopped for the evenings you'll have chores to do. I'll keep you busy! Ha!" The old woman chuckles and lowers her head and shakes it, then she starts waddling back to the fire and the boy; leaving Calley to stand and decide what she will do about this predicament of hers.

For a moment, Calley thinks about running away and testing this spider of Scyn's. But, although she's not greatly afraid of spiders, she doesn't really want to test it out to see if it's real or not.

There's a lot here I've never seen before, I should probably be weary of anything they tell me. Looking at the cage, Calley realizes it's not much bigger than the last one she was in earlier. *It's going to be a cramped space for sleeping, that's for sure. I don't look forward to that.* Calley's stomach growls. *I am hungry. I wonder if they plan to feed me.*

Calley walks back towards the campfire with the cooking pot and the boy. The aroma of cooked vegetables: carrots, onions, potatoes, celery, and maybe even cabbage invade Calley's nostrils. She rounds the corner of the wagon and comes into view of the campfire. Isabol and the boy are sitting beside the fire on log seats eating out of clay bowls. They slurp it out straight from the bowl without using any kind of spoon.

"Hungry are you?" Isabol asks and points to the boy. "Boy, get her a bowl. Come. Sit and eat, girly," she says, and she pats a seat near her on the log. "Magistre Scyn did order that you remain healthy after all." Isabol slurps her bowl. Soup scales its way down through the wrinkles in Isabol's chin, at last dripping to the grey scowl around her neck. Calley walks over to the fire and waits to receive the meal.

"Here you go," the boy says almost too quietly to hear.

He truly is tall! Calley gawks in amazement. *He must be at least another foot taller than I am! And, I'm not a shrimp of a girl either, I'm 5'6"!* This time, his eyes won't meet hers as he hands Calley the bowl of soup.

"Thank you," Calley says politely, taking the bowl from the boy. She lifts the bowl to her lips and sips. The aroma of vegetables did not exaggerate the possible taste of the soup. Delicious broth fills Calley's mouth with flavors she knows well: rosemary, thyme, basil, garlic, and of course, the vegetables: carrots, onions, celery, potatoes and yes! It is cabbage!

Nothing else is said while the three eat. Calley slurps down the soup as quickly as she'd seen Isabol do. Calley is too afraid to ask for seconds, but she doesn't need to. As soon as Calley's bowl is empty, the boy fills it again. His movements are fluid, like a dancer's. He eats quickly too but spills nothing.

He has amazing control of his movements, Calley wonders in amazement as she steals a glance at the boy.

"We leave in the morning at first light. I suggest you get rested up, Luc. Girl, I'll need to lock you in at night. Come with me." Isabol gets up, sets her bowl on the log seat and walks back to the cage she'd assigned to Calley. She holds the door open while Calley gets in. Then, Isabol uses a lock like the ones at the emporium. She whispers a few words to the lock and it fastens shut. Nothing will open it now until she again speaks those words to it.

Chapter Seven

CALLEY DRIFTS BETWEEN DREAMS and night-mares. She can't really get to any good sleep. One dream, or rather nightmare, keeps coming back to her.

It's dark, lightning flashes before my eyes. Water rushes up onto my feet. My long silken, white night gown blows behind me with the wind which wraps it tightly around my body. The wind throws my hair behind me as well. Ocean spray is blasted into my eyes, causing them to sting and close automatically. I hold my hand in front of my eyes to prevent any further stinging and open my eyes. Howling wind blows furiously, whipping my hair and dress in opposite directions, but always behind me. Blinding flashes of lightning crash in the waves just before me. Veins of electricity breech through the water like the roots of a tree underground. They spread from the source of impact viciously and reach the edges of the water and sand aiming for anything in reach.

The lightning strikes get closer and closer to me. Finally, it strikes behind me in the sand causing me to jump and turn and land in the ocean. I'm breathing heavily and am a little off balance when a split second later, another bolt strikes behind me again, this time in the water. I am immediately charged with the bolts of electricity which assault my every vein and explode through my finger tips, my mouth, my nose, my eyes.

Just before her heart stops beating, Calley wakes, panting, struggling to breath. *It was just another nightmare,* Calley thinks to herself. *Just another nightmare,* she repeats in her mind. *It's not real, I'm safe... sort of...*

Morning comes all too soon. *I guess that means I slept at some point between my nightmares.* Calley is let out for bathroom needs and to eat. Then, she is put back into the cage as the caravan lines up and begins its journey. *I guess I could always attempt to nap on the road. I don't think it'll be much of a struggle seeing as I can barely keep my eyes open in the first place,* Calley thinks as she leans her head against the metal cage, her neck at a crooked angle while her head bounces off the cage with every bump in the road.

For most of the morning, Calley drifts in and out of sleep. While the nightmares don't repeat themselves, her sleep is still restless. It doesn't help that every time she wakes up and looks around, that boy is watching her. If Calley looks up at him, he turns his eyes as if trying to hide that he was staring at her. As if it wasn't obvious that he had been staring.

Calley's cage is dragged behind some kind of mule/rat creature.

I guess that's what Scyn called an asimuns. Whatever it is, it smells! If the wind were blowing in my direction, I would never have been able to get any sleep at all, Calley thinks as she wakes up again late in the morning.

***

At noon, the caravan stops for a midday rest. Calley is let out of the cage again for bathroom needs and to eat. Calley had given up on trying to get any more sleep anyway, because the wind had shifted, and that rancid smell blew right in her face as she was dragged behind those things.

"What are those things?" Calley braves a question to the boy who keeps staring at her as they sit and eat a lunch of stale bread and moldy cheese.

"They're called asimuns. They're Mother's creation. She's very proud of them." The boy shoots a look at

Calley and then it's gone in a flash and he again studies the ground.

"How did she 'create' them?" Calley asks bewildered.

"I mean, she bred them. She mixed and matched until they were born. Now, she has enough of them to reproduce whenever she wants to." He keeps shooting short glances at Calley, but will not keep her gaze for more than a second. He keeps looking around anxiously like he's watching for something.

"What's your name? I'm Calley." Calley tries, hoping for a friend. *Maybe he could at least make things more comfortable for me while I'm being held captive here. I don't know, maybe he could convince Isabol to let me walk or ride in the wagon or somewhere else other than behind that rat-thing,* Calley considers hopefully. *It's possible, it could happen, right?*

"Luc! Where are you, boy?" Isabol yells from within her wagon; where she seems to reside the majority of the trip. It, like Calley's cage, is pulled by those asimuns.

They are certainly stronger than they look. Little, wriggly, bony, hairy freaks of nature that don't look like they could pull a cage like mine let alone a big wagon like that with a person inside, Calley concludes.

With tails, whiskers, skin, and ears like that of a rat, the creatures also resemble a camel as they have two humps on their backs. The creatures are also much taller than a rat would be. They're at least as tall as a small horse, with disproportionally long legs that end with hooves like those of a camel: big, clunky and with only two toes.

The boy stands up so rapidly that his plate falls to the ground. He puts it away and rushes to the woman's aide.

So, his name is Luc. Maybe there is hope for me? He seems shy, but perhaps sweet too? Calley thinks, daring to hope.

***

That afternoon, when Isabol is back in her wagon and the caravan is on the move again, Calley sits up, facing the animal whose bane has become her torture. They smell worse in the afternoon with the hot sun beating down on their sweaty, moist, sparsely haired backs. Their heavy gray color probably doesn't do much in the way of helping alleviate the heat either as it probably soaks up as much of the sun as black might.

Calley sits up when she hears Luc singing a tune that seems familiar to her. But, when she catches the words of the song, she realizes she's never heard it before.

"There once was a prince so mighty and fine, in
his palace one night he did dine,
His mother the Queen, well they say she went
mad,
And locked him away up in the tower of Baghad,
A Striga some did call her, wicked and mean,
She delighted in pain and there never was seen,
A more cruel or foreboding old hag like the
Queen,"

Calley twists until she can see Luc, who rides on an asimuns next to her, singing.

"What is that?" Calley asks when Luc comes to a natural pause in the tune.

"It's an old nursery rhyme. You haven't heard of it?" Luc answers and asks.

"No, I haven't. It's so sinister and yet...sweet at the same time. Is there more to it? Will you sing the rest for me please?" Calley asks.

He has a wonderful singing voice...baritone, I think? It's calming and peaceful. I could listen to him sing all day. It almost makes this cage and that smell more bearable, Calley thinks and rolls her eyes.

"Afraid that they'd take him, she drugged the
    young boy, and
Carried him off to a city made of Alloy.
She turned the people into cobalts and spelled the
    city gate,
So there the young prince would have to wait.
A Striga they did call her, wicked and mean,
She delighted in pain and there never was seen,
A more cruel or foreboding old hag like the
    Queen.
So in the highest tower of the city made of Alloy,
Waits the young prince until no longer a boy.
With the aid of a maiden from a far, distant land,
The prince, at last he may take the upper hand.
For only then can he ever be free, from the
    Queen's perfidy."

Luc stops singing and looks at Calley.

"What a sad story. What is the 'Queen's perfidy'?" Calley asks because she's never heard that word before.

Looking down at his asimuns, Luc says, "Well, the story goes that the Queen wasn't in fact royalty at all but was a servant in the palace. She was the king's mistress and when she became heavy with his child, she was cast out of the kingdom. She was exiled to a small village just outside of the King's purview, where she birthed the royal child in a stable alongside the animals. She swore she'd have her revenge. Her son was royalty and would be set up where he belonged. He would have the crown. She delved into dark magic and sold her soul for the power to enslave the king, his queen and the entire kingdom." Luc pauses for a moment and looks back at Calley, who is at this point entranced by the story; her mouth is open and she is gawking at the air that she seems to see right through.

"That's horrible! What a horrible story!! And you called it a nursery rhyme?" Calley says, disgusted.

"Yes, well nursery rhymes were created to teach children lessons, were they not?" Luc asks, seeming amused.

"Sure, but what kind of lesson could that possibly teach a child?" Calley asks, completely horrified at the concept.

"That you can't do anything about where you come from, so be patient and your time will come," Luc says in a matter-of-fact kind of way and looks at Calley blankly.

"Be patient and your time will come? That's it? That's the moral of the story? What about something like, 'You can't choose who your parents are, but you can change who you are'? Or,..." Calley thinks for a minute and then finishes with, "or, whatever, but that's not something I would tell a child."

"I mean, a fairy tale should be more kid friendly. Like one I heard growing up about a princess who is trapped in a tower and a prince has to rescue her. Although, in that story, the princess is put under a sleeping spell and only true loves kiss can wake her," Calley explains. "I mean, there's a moral for you! True love conquers all!"

"Of course, true love is the ultimate power and would 'conquer all' as you say," Luc begins, "But, realistically, there isn't much of that going around these days. Here, true love is rare. We don't want our children believing in something they likely will never find. Maybe in the mortal realm, you have the luxury of 'true love'. I'm not surprised that your people changed the stories that way."

Seeing the confusion in Calley's expression, Luc elaborates, "Your stories came from ours. You see, the people of Calueria actually created Earth. Well, the Majori did anyway. To make a long story short, our Majori created mortals and then created Earth for the mortals to live in." Luc could see that this explanation only raised more questions for Calley as her face fills with confusion.

"Ok,… *Omnideum*, or God, first created the universe. Then, he created the Majori. The Majori then created the rest of the creatures and different walks of life that now exist in both our realms. When the Majori first began creating, they wanted their creations to have all the benefits of magic that they possibly could. There was just one problem with their creations; they couldn't reproduce. So, the Majori set out to fix this problem after numerous complaints and requests for something more. After many failed attempts, they finally created the first mortals, Abram and Eva. Mortals turned out to be very fertile and when interbred into other races, the gene of reproduction was passed on to the offspring," Luc pauses, looking into the sky for a moment and then continues, "However, this fertility came at a cost. They soon discovered that as they bred the mortals in with other races, although the offspring were able to reproduce, they also lacked in magical abilities. It seemed the price to pay for offspring was magic," Luc says, pausing again, this time to look directly at Calley.

"Eva bore hundreds of children; both mixed with other races and pure mortal babies. However, the Majori had not counted on just how reproductive mortals could be. The Majori had also underestimated Abram drastically," Luc says, raising his eyebrows slightly. "They didn't realize just how vile and jealous mortals could be. And, since they couldn't wield magic, the mortals grew suspicious and secretive. Eventually the mortals grew to be so many that that they got ideas of overthrowing the Majori and taking control of Calueria. Something had to be done about this so the Majori created the Earth and banished all the mortals there, except for a select few that stayed behind in order to continue to help with procreation problems." Luc finishes his story leaving silence to filter the information Calley has just gleaned.

Is that all true? So, everything I've been taught all my life is wrong? We were only created like a science experiment to serve someone else's purposes? Calley feels her head begin to throb as she tries to process this new information. *Wow, I guess I have a lot to learn if that's all true,* Calley thinks, closing her eyes and wishing that this was all just a dream.

"Okay, here's one you might like a little better," Luc starts and then begins,

"A soft breeze, a whispering wind, it plays a soft melody as it blows along the meadow,
It dances among the treetops and teases the bushes and flowers below,
Far, far, far it travels over the hills and across the rivers, its melody playing everywhere it goes,
Hills turn into mountains which challenge the playful, melodic drifter.
Though daunting and vast the mountains were, the breeze bows to the would-be challenger,
And the rage begins: Against the mountain the breeze crashes and slams its competitor.
Until finally, the once young, playful, carefree little breeze lies stiller and quieter,
A last breath whispers its lament: The Mountain was too strong."

Luc finishes and looks at Calley proudly.

"Well, that's just cryptic..." Calley says, slightly confused by the rhyme. "What is that supposed to teach?"

Luc sighs and answers, "It teaches that we shouldn't take on more than we can handle. That sometimes, there are things that are greater than ourselves that we should bow down to rather than fight against."

"Oh, I hadn't thought of that," Calley says, feeling slightly schooled. "I guess I can see that."

***

In the evening, when the caravan stops to rest for the night, Isabol instructs Calley that her duty will be to brush and feed the asimuns each night after they eat their supper and before she can go to bed.

Maybe she doesn't want to do it because she doesn't like their smell either, Calley wonders as she sticks her nose up at the vile creatures she must now care for.

As soon as she has finished her dinner, she walks over to the asimuns where they are all grouped together and tied to a long post. Isabol had given Calley a wiry brush to use on the asimuns. Although Calley doesn't really see the point in brushing them since they are mostly bald anyway. Then, the disgusting task must begin and Calley sets to it by trying to brush what little wisps of hair the beasts have.

Chapter Eight

THE DAYS BEGIN TO PASS seamlessly with the distraction of conversations with Luc each day. Calley and Luc become close friends. He even begins to help her with her chores in caring for the asimuns. Landscapes change as the caravan passes; from sparsely wooded, open field areas to a complete forest. In the thickness of the forest, Calley can hear several calls from wildlife she's never heard of before. She sees more vibrant and muted colors on the animals here than she had ever known were possible to combine into one creature. Squirrels are not only brown, but most have shades of red, orange, black and sometimes yellow and white. Red and pink does and fauns play exuberantly between the trees as the caravan passes; undaunted by the company's presence.

Although it is summer, the forest gives the feeling of springtime and even the temperature complies with the condition. Cooler mornings come with frost on the grasses and leaves. Then mild afternoons with cool breezes melt the frost and warm those same grasses and leaves. Everything here is some tint of green. Everything here is lush, vibrant and bursting into life. It is hard not to feel light-hearted in these woods. Like the deer she'd seen playing in the meadows, Calley cannot help but feel as though a weight has been lifted, even as she itches the spider silk on her wrist that holds her captive to the caravan. She'd almost forgotten that she was supposed to be a slave.

***

The caravan stops at midday and at night for rests. Calley is allowed out to use the restroom each time. As days have drawn on, they begin to allow Calley a little more freedom to wander some from the caravan. In a small meadow at the bottom of a little hill beside the dirt road where the caravan decides to stop one afternoon, Calley peers through the branches of a bush, spying on a pair of squirrels that energetically play among the trees. This particular pair of squirrels has complementary patterns of colors on their tails; one is red and tan while the other is orange, yellow and white. She watches as they take a huge leap from one tree and then they land safely on a branch in the next. They continue in this manner for some time, almost as though they are playing tag among the tree branches.

Then, a flash of color shoots passed her on the side and alights on a low-lying tree branch. Dazed, Calley looks up at what had so quickly zoomed through her view. It is some kind of butterfly with wings the size of a medium-sized bird. Beautiful hues of red, gold, yellow, green, blue and gray all decorate the wings of the mysterious creature in whirls with silver and black outlines, reminding Calley of a rainbow she'd colored once in elementary school with a black outline between the colors and along the edges of the rainbow. Mesmerized, Calley stands and begins to creep closer to the creature. With the urge to touch those magical colors, she reaches a hand toward the creature slowly and without the slightest hesitation. Calley's hand seems to be pulled toward the beautiful, hypnotizing thing as she reaches it out to touch the magnificent creature.

"Stop! Calley! Stop!" Luc reaches Calley just before she can touch the creature's wings. He pulls her hand away so fiercely that they fall back on the ground together. At the last second, a needle-like point shoots through the top where Calley's hand would have been a moment before had Luc not grabbed her away. At that same moment, the wings had snap around the body of the butterfly and wrap it like a cocoon, trapping anything within range and stabbing it through.

Eyes blinking as though awoken from some spell, Calley looks at the creature as it steadily unravels its wings from around its body to reveal a gigantic wasp! The size of a guinea pig—this deceiving creature with the beautiful butterfly wings and a poisonous, dangerous wasp body had almost caught its prey: Calley.

"Wha … what was that?" Calley asks drowsily, still lying on the ground. Calley's peridot pendant has fallen out of her shirt and dangles toward the ground now as she holds herself up on one arm.

"A *Vena Paplo*. They are very beautiful and very deadly. Had your hand been pricked by that stinger you would have fallen into a coma that you could never wake from. The insect stabs its prey, and then it injects the venom that immobilizes the victim. Then, while its victim sleeps, the *Vena Paplo* drinks its victim's blood until there is none left. It goes into a kind of hibernation while it drinks, but then it does not need to eat again for at least a month. There are many dangerous creatures here that you need to stay away from. Just stay with me so I can help you, okay?" Luc almost sounds worried as he says this. In fact, he is genuinely concerned, when something interesting catches his eye. Luc stares at Calley's pendant. It spins slowly as it dangles on its chain so the insignia can be seen.

"Okay, I guess I better be more careful," Calley says hesitantly. Looking back at the *Vena Paplo*, Calley adds, "Unless I want to become dinner for some vampire butterfly." Calley tries to smile, but it just won't come to her face. Realizing that Luc is staring at her, Calley follows his gaze to find that her pendant has fallen out of her shirt, and he is staring right at it. Calley tucks it safely back inside. Then, she looks up and sees that just outside of the meadow and watching her and Luc are a couple of the men in the caravan.

Of the two men, one is short with a stocky, rough build while the other is, albeit not much taller, lanky and thin. The stocky, rougher one of the men rushes up to Calley and Luc and says, in a low, rusty voice, "Is she all right? It didn't sting her, right? We have to protect our investment. Just think what Scyn would have done to us if any harm had come to this mortal!" He grabs Calley's arm and drags her back up to the caravan. Searching the area, Calley realizes that the other man who had been standing on the hill a moment before had disappeared.

***

That night while Calley sleeps, others in the caravan plan.

"I saw her, *Magistre Duz de Comitas*, she was almost stung by the *Vena Paplo* she was! That's when I saw it! The pendant! She's Majori! She wears the crest of the Majori family around her neck aside her own *Qui* stone! That was the proof I needed to come to you with this information. I had overheard them talking; her with that boy, Luc. I think he knows!" The gruff-voiced speaker is all but convinced of his assertions.

Scyn sits silently in her cushion of a chair at the center of her tent. Arms folded to her chest, eyes' concentrating on the flap of her tent opening, Scyn remains silent for a moment.

"Say you are right. Say she is truly a Majori. How would you suggest we retrieve her from Luc's protection? He has taken a particular liking to her. It would not be easy to separate her from him," Scyn asks; she had not moved much other than her lips as she spoke in a low tone, just below whispering.

"We take him out first, of course," the speaker says, as though it were some menial task to be accomplished.

"Luc is no trifle. And, I cannot be ruining my reputation among the people's trade routes by participating in this sort of *nigre veniculim* deal. You must use your own men and none of you may ever return to my caravan. I will require a hefty fee for allowing you to do this within my caravan. I imagine that my client would have paid well for her, even without knowing her heritage. So, you will pay me what he would have plus 70% of what you get from her once she's sold to the highest bidder on the *nigre veniculim*," Scyn says, narrowing her eyes at the man.

"And, before anything may be done toward Luc or the girl, I need to see proof that she is a Majori. You must test her tomorrow, first thing in the morning. Then, if all goes well, and she is in fact Majori as you claim, then you may have her in the evening if you can subdue the Lipus." With that, Scyn dismisses the man from her tent.

Chapter Nine

IN THE MORNING, CALLEY doesn't feel quite herself. A bit nauseas and blue in the face, Calley leans her face through the bars of her cage as she rides in case the nausea decides to become something more. Calley moans as a bump in the road brings stomach acids into her mouth. She'd been too ill to eat anything at breakfast and for that she is thankful now.

"Are you ok, Calley?" Luc asks, worriedly.

"Yeah, I think I just ate something bad last night is all. I'll be fine," Calley says smiling weakly back at him. She isn't completely sure it was something she'd eaten or if it is the smell of those asimuns, but she knows she is definitely ill.

By midmorning, Isabol takes a look at Calley. She burns with a fever and her lips have turned blue. Her breaths are shallow and short. The caravan is forced to take their lunch break early so that Calley can be cared for.

Isabol calls others to help her with Calley. A small, stoutly, gruff voiced man and a lanky, thin, nasally voiced man are to be Calley's attendants while she is ill. All afternoon, Calley rides in the back of the wagon lying down while Isabol rides alongside her son on the asimuns pulling the wagon. Calley spends most of the time in and out of delirium. Finally, evening comes and the caravan stops to rest for the night.

Calley can keep down a little water and some food, but is still quite a bit queasy. She still burns with the fever, though it has reduced since they had stopped at lunch. Although Calley would have gladly passed on supper, Luc forces a bit of food into her mouth. He promises that it will give her strength back to her by morning if she will just swallow it. Calley gags as the chunks slide awkwardly down her throat. Whatever Luc is feeding her, it tastes like gasoline with the same greasy feel of it too.

But morning never seems to come. Nightmares of monstrous, poisonous insects haunt Calley's mind. Sometimes they have the faces of some of the men from the caravan. Particularly the faces of the two who'd been attached to her as her attendants while she was sick made their way into her dreams quite a bit. Every time, they are a new form of monster, beast or insect. She dreams that she is being carried away.

She bounces on the back of a huge bald, black bear. Its scratchy skin feels sweaty beneath Calley's weight. She swings in the clutches of a creature that has the body of a cat, but feet, claws and wings of a hawk. Its wings are fur, with no feathers in sight. It has a beak where the muzzle should be. And in its eyes reflected back were the eyes of the short, stocky gruff-voiced man; the same one who was to serve as her attendant; the same one who had rushed to her aid when she was almost stung by the *Vena Paplo*.

***

When Calley finally opens her eyes, she does not see what she expects to see. She is on the ground beside a smoking fire-pit, the coals smolder under a blanket of smoke as if it had recently been doused with water. There is no sign of the caravan. Heaps of blankets lay scattered around the fire-pit with snores emanating from within some and shuffling sounds coming from others. Calley tries to sit, but is too weak. She knows she isn't feverish anymore and thinks that she may even be over whatever ailed her before. However, she is bound at the feet and wrists, with her hands behind her back.

Calley continues to try to free herself of the blankets that are smothering her by wiggling as quietly as she can so she will not wake any of her kidnappers. Once the blankets are on the ground, Calley tries again to sit. Slowly, strenuously, Calley sits up and looks around the camp. A single tent stands apart from the fire-pit with various packs strewn around it. There are horses tied up just a few feet away from that. If she could just get to one of the horses, then maybe she can escape.

Just then, Calley hears voices approaching her from behind. She lays back down quickly and closes her eyes, pretending to still be asleep.

"This had better be for real, Stephen! I've risked far too much for this to have been all for nothing!" Two men come and stand in front of Calley.

Please go away! Please go away! Please just go away and leave me alone! Calley thinks loudly in her head as she tries to maintain a steady pattern of breathing; an attempt at pretending to still be asleep.

"Don't worry, Rawger. Just see for yourself!" Stephen suggests proudly.

One of the men comes right up to Calley and reaches for her necklace. He pulls out the pendant as the two men lean in to read the inscription. Under his breath, Rawger whispers the inscription as he reads it.

"Ha! See there! I told you! You didn't believe me did you! Now you can see for yourself! She is Majori! We have hit the jackpot now my friend! Thanks to *Magistre* Scyn for allowing this! We'll have to remember her cut, but I'm sure there will be plenty to go around with this kind of catch!" Stephen says excitedly.

Clashing of metal and ripping of flesh distracts the two men and wakes the rest of the captors nearby. While most of the captors hastily jump from their blanket rolls and run to find the commotion, one captor stays to protect the prize. Calley opens her eyes in curiosity, remaining still and silent where she lies. Snarls, growls and screams reach her ears as she lies on the ground frightened to death with eyes wide open now.

"*Lipus Mutatie!* Run! *Lipus Mutatie!* It comes! Run for your lives!" A man, who sports a gaping wound across his left thigh and is splattered with blood from head to toe, yells as he runs back into the camp. He grabs a horse, climbs on with some difficulty, and takes off at a gallop.

Other men are right behind him, running back into the camp and screaming similar things. They all head straight for the horses in an attempt to flee. Right on their heels, however, is a shaggy brown wolf the size of a lion! Before one man can reach a horse, the wolf pounces on him and rips out his throat in one fluid movement. Then, the wolf takes aim at a man who is just mounting a horse and knocks him to the ground.

The man tries to get up quickly but the wolf is faster and attacks him, pouncing on his back and grabbing the back of the man's neck in its great, sharp teeth. In the blink of an eye, that man is throttled to death and the wolf drops him on the ground. The man lays completely still and lifeless on the ground. The wolf is again on to another victim, chasing one who has achieved his place on a horse and has begun to gallop away. Usually, you would think that the horse would outrun the wolf, but this wolf is abnormally fast. It attacks the horse like a lion attacking an antelope; reaching its paws, claws out, around both sides of the horse's rear end. With long, sharp retractable claws like those of a lion, the wolf is able to dig into the horse, maiming it and bringing it to the ground. Before the man can even get to his feet, a leg is trapped underneath the horse, he is made of short business when the wolf rips his throat out and then turns to search for the first of the men who ran back to the camp.

The first man who had returned to the camp after realizing his fate, is fortunate enough to be far enough away on his horse that there is no way the wolf can catch him now. It points its nose into the direction of the man, sniffing the air. Then it just stands there staring, as if calculating the distance to run or making a decision about whether to even give chase. The only ones left are Calley and Stephen who had stayed to protect his 'fortune'.

Calley was still bound and bundled on the ground; completely helpless. Stephen stood at the ready as if he thought he could take on this magnificent creature that had just run down and slain the rest of his comrades. With a short, double-edged broad sword in his hands, Stephen stands in front of Calley, trembling but ready to defend his treasure.

Snarling, baring its teeth and foaming saliva from its clenched jaws, the wolf draws nearer to the two left at the camp.

"You shall not have her, demon! She is mine! I found her! I took her! This is my treasure you foul *Lipus Mutatie*! I've worked too hard for this chance to have it taken away by some stupid animal!" Stephen yells, trembling violently from head to foot.

He's either brave enough to hold on to me for some special reason or he's too stupid to run away, Calley thinks as she lays there waiting for her own devastation. She had given up trying to free herself from the binds that keep her hands and feet together.

The wolf jumps at Stephen and he blocks it with the flat of the wide blade of the broadsword, knocking the wolf back to the ground. Before Stephen can recover his own blow backwards, the wolf is back at him again. And in one fluid movement, the wolf grips the man's throat in its teeth and tears it apart. Spraying outward, the blood covers everything in reach, including the wolf which is now drenched in blood.

Dripping blood from its mane around its head, panting heavily and dripping blood mixed with saliva into the dirt, the wolf takes a moment to stare at Calley. She stares back daringly, now passed fear.

"Well? Am I next?" Calley asks. "I'm trapped, I can't get loose. So, go for it. Take your final kill." Calley closes her eyes and waits.

When nothing happens, Calley opens her eyes again to find that the wolf has gone. She looks around and cannot see the creature anywhere. She starts wriggling around, trying to loosen the binds on her wrists. Then, Calley hears a noise come from the tent across the fire-pit from her. *Maybe there is still another of the captors at the camp that is alive?* Calley wonders momentarily.

Horrible groans and moans erupt out of the tent, bursting out of some wretched, miserable soul within. Suddenly the occupier thrashes wildly inside the tent, knocking down the poles and effectively collapsing the tent on top of him. Then, whoever occupies the tent pulls apart shreds of the tent, freeing himself and collapses on the ground with a thud, landing on hands and knees. Calley watches as the man, with clothes that are tattered and torn and which barely cover his nakedness, musters his strength and stands. His body is filthy; covered with blood, bruises, cuts and dirt mixed with sweat that's acts as a paste on his chest and face.

The man slowly begins to approach Calley. His head is full of wavy, brown curls the length of his shoulders which seems familiar to Calley. Fuzzy, crisp curls mount the man's cheeks, chin and neck. The pure wildness of his eyes is enough to send shivers through Calley's whole body; sending shockwaves of fear and excitement together. Once he reaches her, their eyes lock and Calley is certain she has seen his before.

Chapter Ten

JUST AS THE ANSWER DANCES on the tip of her tongue, the man speaks, "Are you all right, Calley?" The baritone of his voice assures her, and she smiles back at him.

"Luc?" Calley asks, bewildered and amazed. "How are you?... What did you?..." Calley attempts to finish a thought but cannot seem to connect the dots for herself. Luc connects them for her.

"When I woke up this morning, and saw that you weren't there, I confronted Mother. She admitted to drugging you with the *lacrima solmo* from the Tears of Eva flower that puts its victim into *caman solmo*, the crying sleep. It gives you nightmares and prevents you from being able to wake. I had suspected something like this when you got sick yesterday. That's why I slipped you some *acum viritas* in your dinner last night and forced you to eat as much as I could. It's an herb that would prevent or shorten any sleeping drug you'd been given. I just didn't count on my own mother slipping me a sleeping potion too!" Luc reaches out and pulls the heavy blankets off of Calley. Then in his fluid-like way, he cuts the binds from her wrists and feet. He holds her hand to steady her as she stands up. "We should head back as soon as possible."

Calley stops short and pulls her hand from Luc's. "I'm not going back there! I don't want to be somebody's slave! Besides, that man who was..." Calley allows her eyes to drift toward Stephen, "the one you saved me from said that Scyn gave them permission to 'take me'. They wanted to sell me on the '*nigre veniculim*'. They said she was getting a cut. Does this happen often to mortals in this place? They called me one of the 'Majori'. Do you know what that means?" Calley asks impatiently.

Luc frowns. He eyes Calley's bruised wrists where they had been bound as she rubs them.

"Sometimes this happens." Luc looks at Calley's neck where her necklace hides underneath her shirt. As if lost in thought, Luc just stares at the spot.

"Hello? What did they mean by that?" Calley says, waving her hand in front of Luc's face.

As if coming out of deep thought, Luc blinks and looks at Calley in the face. "So, we must take what we can and head out on our own. We must find a way to get you back to your own world, where you will be safe," Luc says as he empties a water canteen onto a cloth and begins cleaning himself with it.

He's coming with me? But, what about his mother? What about his home? Calley thinks while Luc walks over to one of the packs near the tent on the other side of the campfire. He riffles through it in search of something.

Remembering the wolf from before, Calley suddenly thinks, *Wait a minute, what happened to his clothes? Where did that wolf go? What just happened here?* Calley begins to wonder, realizing for the first time that Luc is unharmed by that mysterious wolf that ripped to shreds all of her captors only moments before Luc appeared.

Calley looks around and views her surroundings. There is the campfire at the center of the whole scene. Bodies lay strewn around here and there, mangled and covered in their own blood. Eight men lay around the campsite; a few near the remaining horses that are still tied up, a couple on the road leading away from the campsite and the one name Stephen who lay just before Calley. *What was that creature? It was certainly no ordinary wolf I've ever seen,* thinks Calley.

Luc walks back toward Calley, now fully dressed in complete clothes that are not torn and ripped to shreds. His face is again clean-shaven as it had been when they first met.

"How did you get here so fast? How did you get past the wolf that attacked these men?" Calley asks skeptically and looks at him suspiciously.

"I didn't get past the wolf—I am the wolf." Luc stands before Calley, looks her directly in the eyes and waits while she stands there and gawks back at him.

"You are... the... wolf?" Calley repeats slowly, not willing to believe what she has just heard. "You...are the... wolf.." Calley says again, raising one eyebrow at Luc and still struggling to make the connection between words and meanings.

He stands firm and continues to patiently look her in the eyes while she processes the information.

"Isabol adopted me. She found me as a wild, young pup playing just inside the *Coctili Silvestre,* the Burning Woods. They're a place that no child should be; they're dangerous. Although she hated children, she loved animals. She found me in my *Mutatie Lipus vere corpus,* my true wolf form; she didn't know I would turn into a man. She cared for me, kept me, fed me and even clothed me when I did begin to change. I don't know who my real family is or where they are," Luc says as he crosses his arms and tilts his head, still watching for Calley's response.

"So, that was you, who came and tore those men's throats out and ripped them all to shreds?" Calley asks, still not willing to let herself believe.

"Yes. And, we really should be going. I think I know how you can find your way back to your world. We need to find the *Duz de Prundencum.* He's always been a legend, but this is a world where legends are real. So, I think if we follow the legend, then we should find him. If anyone will know how to open the portal back to your realm, he will," Luc states and uncrosses his arms, shrugs his shoulders and lets his arms fall at his sides in an 'I-don't-know' sort of way. "It's worth a try at least. As far as I know, it's your only hope. Otherwise, there will be others who want you as their slave or who think you are some treasure to win."

"What does the legend say about him?" Calley asks.

Luc then begins to sing a low, heavy toned song that sends shivers down Calley's spine.

"A Majorus and more, the Majuscule Intellego, Discerner of all,

Truer words none other ever will speak, for a lie he cannot abide,

Loyal to everyone, for everyone, mortal and Essent Medei alike, he does love,

With aid and comfort he cares for his children and creations,

Never ceasing, always blessing both day and night those children he calls his own,

If ever he is needed, one must travel afar, and find him in his sanctuary,

The Libania Fretum, For there is his refuge, so there can he be found..."

Luc's song is interrupted by Calley's impatience.

"Well, then I will find this *Duz de Prudencome* or whatever you called him. But, I don't need your help; I can take care of myself, you know. Just give me a map and I'll find my way," Calley says, trying to sound convincing as she starts walking toward the downed and torn tent with the remaining packs on the ground next to it.

"I won't let you go alone. And you need to find the *Duz de Prundencum,*" Luc over-annunciates the title, "so you may learn how to return to your home. I will go with you and be your companion and guide. You would not last one day out in this world on your own." Luc says, and then he scurries around the camp gathering provisions and supplies, moving faster than Calley could even measure. She stops short of the fire as he moves fluidly, like a wolf, around the campsite. He loads two horses with the supplies he gathers and then returns to her, leading the horses by the bits.

"We must leave now, Calley. Before Scyn gets word from that one that got away." Luc holds the reins of one horse toward Calley. She looks at the reins and then snatches them up.

"Okay then, let's get on our way!" Calley says as she mounts her horse. Luc does the same and they are off heading west.

Chapter Eleven

WHEN THE SUN BEGINS SETTING, Calley and Luc
stop for the night and set up a small camp near a creek
that they have found. Fearing that they could have been
followed, Calley and Luc put their dinner fire out before
the sun completely sets and they settle in for the night.
There hadn't been any signs that anyone had followed
them, but they couldn't take the chance.

"To be honest, I'm not incredibly familiar with
this area. I've never gone to the *Libania Fretum* before.
But, I have seen many maps of this area. When Mother
was teaching me the nursery rhymes she insisted that I
study the maps of those areas as well. Every story about
the *Duz de Prundencum* claims that he wanders along the
beaches of the *Libania Fretum,*" Luc assures Calley the
next morning as they begin their trek anew. "I am confident that I can lead you to it though. And, what's more, I
believe that we will find him there," Luc says flashing a
cheesy grim at Calley. Each day, Luc and Calley continue
heading west, hoping to see a sign of the ocean soon.

One day, as the two are beginning their trek for
the day, Calley says, "You never did tell me what those
men meant when they called me 'Majori'," leaving the
actual question unasked.

"It means to be part of the Majori. They are our
elders who created this realm and yours along with all of
the creatures in both. They are *demideum*; part gods, almost perfect beings with almost unlimited power," Luc
answers reluctantly, knowing that he can't keep putting
off Calley's questions about it.

"But, why is their crest around my pendant?" Calley asks, frustrated. "Those men said this is the crest of the Majori…"

"Where did you get that pendant?" Luc responds to the question with a question cryptically.

"My mom gave it to me. She said it was from my grandparents. My dad's parents, that is. I've never really met them," Calley says, looking down at the pendant for a moment.

"You never knew your father either?" Luc asks, slightly confused.

"No, I mean, I never met my grandparents," Calley says, looking up and over at Luc. "I lived with my dad practically me entire life," Calley answers. Feeling the need to further elaborate, she continues to say, "My parents divorced when I was little and my dad and I moved up to New York."

"But, it was your mother who gave you the necklace…"Luc starts. "Where was your father then?" he asks.

"He disappeared about a month before I wound up here," Calley says and watches the ground as they pass over it. "I don't know what really happened to him," she adds quietly, reminded of how much she misses Dad.

"What is your father's name, may I ask?" Luc asks.

"Jethro. Why?" Calley answers looking back up at Luc again, puzzled.

"Oh, it's nothing. I was just curious is all," Luc says, brushing it off.

The rest of the day is spent with Calley listening as Luc sings various nursery rhymes and tells Calley the stories that accompany them.

> **"A tale of jealousy, a tale of hatred,**
> **A tale so fearful its validity is still debated.**
> **The beautiful Lady Anngora was esteemed by all,**
> **Honored by her peers until she did fall,"**

Luc begins to sing as they ride in the warm afternoon.

"A beautiful *Amata* she was desired by many,
But none could entice her, only one did she
    deem worthy.
She pursued the love interest, but her feelings
    were rejected,
There was another with whom he was complete-
    ly affected,"

Luc pauses briefly, allowing his eyes to linger on Calley as he begins again. Calley looks up at him momentarily and then directs her eyes back to the ground that passes beneath her horse, embarrassed slightly; though she doesn't know why.

"Scorned by jealousy, enraged by his choice,
The once beautiful *Amata* fell far from grace.
Hatred had consumed her, darkness she be-
    came;
She was engulfed in the void, devoured by the
    Nigre Odiaem.
Across the land of Calueria, a plague was
    spread,
Which drained the *Essent Medei*, and left them
    for dead.
Many claim it was the magic of the *Striga*
    Anngora,
Serving her vengeance across all of Calueria.
The origins of the plague none do truly know,
Though many have conspired, it is only going to
    grow,"

Luc finishes singing the nursery rhyme and all falls silent but for the falls of the horses hooves on the ground.

"That's horrible," Calley begins after several minutes have passed. "I mean, that she was so filled with hatred that she was devoured in the... *Nigre Odiaem*... What is that anyway? I'm guessing it's pretty bad."

"The *Nigre Odiaem* is the darkest of places where only the most hateful, most murderous and most vile of creatures reside. It is believed by many that the most loathsome magic was created there," Luc answers, slightly embellishing on his details. He looks over to Calley who continues staring at the passing rocks and small plants on the ground. "Should we stop for the night?" Luc asks cautiously.

"Sure," Calley says plainly. Luc leads her off the trail to a spot next to the creek.

After dinner is caught, cooked and eaten, the two are ready for bed. Together, Luc and Calley sit beside a fire, silently staring into the flames; both lost in reflection. Calley watches as the flames dance along the logs and sticks she'd found. She notices that closer to the wood, where the flames burn hotter, they are blue instead of orange. While staring into these blue flames, Calley realizes that she sees tiny little people dancing in the flames. No, that's not right, the more she stares, the more Calley realizes that they aren't dancing in the flames, they are the flames. Getting up, Calley moves in closer to the fire.

What are they? They're so pretty! Like tiny little belly dancers, Calley thinks as she tries to figure out what she is seeing on the logs in the fire.

She watches as the little men and women take partners; the blue flames mix with the orange in twirls and twists. Soon, little red flames appear around the dancers, outlining them like an aura. The way the dancers flicker in and out as they go makes it hard for Calley to determine what kind of dance they are doing. Slowly, Calley inches closer to the flames, entranced by their alluring dance.

"Hang on there!" Luc says as he pulls Calley away from the flames. "I should have warned you about the *Igni Sprites.* They can be enchanting and beautiful; when they're hungry," Luc says as he points back to the logs again.

This time, Calley sees only furious flames ripping and tearing apart the flesh of the logs.

"Greedy little imps," Luc says, shaking his head and placing another log onto the fire. "They lure you in with their vibrant dance and before you know it, you're engulfed in flames," he says as the little men and women appear once more as they pounce onto the new log, voraciously consuming it.

"Yikes..." Calley says, sitting back a little further from the fire now.

"They're perfectly harmless..." Luc says, "Unless you get too close," he teases.

Calley rolls her eyes at him, smiling as she does. "Well, I'm going to sleep. I don't know about you, but I'm exhausted," she says as she slides herself into her bedroll. Luc follows her example and also gets into his own bedroll.

Rolling over, Calley closes her eyes and tries to concentrate on letting her body relax so she can drift off to sleep.

Softly, Luc begins to sing:
**"I could write all night long, but where would that get me?
I would sleep all day long and write the whole night through!
And when would love's reverie save me from the wild world's fury?
I could write all night long, and sleep the day away.
But when would I find her? The one to whom my heart belongs...
When in the torrent of night and day would my love's heart
Beat only for mine, if I locked my heart away,
Writing throughout the night and sleeping all the day?
Oh, but where would I be without my dreams and fancies?
So, when do I write and dream if I must rest at night and wake in day?
Why, when, of course, the sun is full and mid-morn gives its glee,
The dreams come into view more clearly then and**

**Write I will the fanciful things that my heart
sees.
For when the sun rises o'er the clouds and dust,
o'er this mundane existence,
If I will but cast my eyes upon her heart, I will
see the pureness of her love.
Then I will know that my dreams and my rest
are not two but spiral into one,"**

Luc finishes singing and falls silent.

Calley can't help but turn towards him in reverence. "That was beautiful… What does it mean?" Calley asks quietly.

"It means that one may think that to have one love would be to give up another. But, the truth is both are possible," Luc sighs, exposing his exhaustion from the day's events.

"Did you write it yourself?" Calley asks curiously.

"I did," Luc affirms. "Good night, Calley," he says and he rolls over in his bedroll.

"Good night," Calley says as she lays her head down on the blanket again.

Chapter Twelve

Days begin to blend into nights, which blend into days as the two continue along their path. Although Luc continues to share nursery rhymes with Calley, she begins to grow weary of the same old thing day after day. Together, Luc and Calley fall into a routine of getting up in the morning, rekindling the fire from the night before, cooking some animal (a rabbit or squirrel) that Luc catches early in the morning, eating, cleaning up the camp, mounting back onto their horses and taking back off onto the road again.

At midday, it is much the same. Calley pulls out the cooking pot they had gotten from the packs they took from her captors and begins building a fire while Luc goes and hunts down something for them to eat. They save what little water they have in the camel pouches which they also had gleaned from Calley's captors. The creek they have been traveling alongside so far has all but disappeared into the ground as the terrain gets drier and drier.

Each day, Calley notices that Luc wanders off for a while every time they stop to rest and eat. She decides to follow him one day when they stop at midday. Once she is sitting and eating, like she normally would do, she waits until Luc gets up and leaves. Then carefully and slowly, she follows him at what she hopes is a good distance so that he can't smell or hear her.

Calley peers over a bush that she bends behind to try to see Luc better. There, she can see him crouched near some green, stringy plants. He's singing softly and stroking the plants along their stems. As he lifts his finger along the stem of one, going from the bottom to the top, it almost seems to stand up on its own. Luc continues singing as he strokes the plant, alternating between the stems. After a few minutes pass this way, the plant begins to change. A white, threadlike puff ball begins forming at the top of each stem that Luc touches. It reminds Calley of the puff balls people put on top of crocheted and knitted beanies; with all the strings hanging out everywhere.

These strings seem to be weightless the way they sway along with Luc's song; probably driven by his breath. They float from side to side easily. Finally, when what Calley assumes to be blossoms of some kind reach the size of a small peach, Luc's song changes. Calley shifts her weight where she crouches behind the bush. She accidently brushes against it and causes the bush to shake slightly. Fortunately for her, there just happened to be a little chipmunk also in the bush which she scared and it ran up the tree. Luc watches the chipmunk scurry up the tree trunk. Then, he turns back to the plant and begins to sing again.

With this new tune that Luc sings, the plant seems to reach its stems up as high as it can reach. At last, the puff ball blossoms pop right off the top of their stems and seem to float in midair. Luc hurries and gathers them all into a pouch he wears across his chest.

So, he sings to plants? Calley thinks as she sits back and down onto her rear end. *Who the heck sings to plants? And, what kind of plant is that?*

Calley leans forward again to peer through the bush. But, as she looks over the bushes branches, she realizes that Luc is gone.

"Hey, you!" Luc says from behind Calley, startling her enough to make her jump noticeably.

Calley screams and twists around quickly. "You jerk! You scared me half to death!"

"Serves you right for spying on me," Luc says and he chuckles slightly. "If you wanted to know what I was doing, you just needed to ask. I don't mind, you know," he says, trying to ease Calley's mind.

"Okay, so what were you doing?" Calley asks, gathering her confidence again.

"*Provenio.* It means, grow. I was commanding the *Andil* to grow so I could harvest its blossoms. They are great for seasoning stews and fish! Now, I will let them dry in my pouch. And when they have dried, I will crush them into a powder and it will be ready to use," Luc says, tapping on his pouch which now rests at his side with its strap across his chest again.

"It was beautiful, and peaceful… almost kind of sad though…" Calley says, staring into space blankly as if lost in thought.

"Well, shall we get back to our camp and our horses?" Luc asks and he starts walking back to where they had left their horses and belongings. "If you wanted, I could teach you about the various herbs that grow here," Luc offers.

"I'd like that," Calley says, smiling at him as they walk back to the camp. "Mom has a garden back ho… back in Texas. I always have wondered how she keeps it looking so beautiful."

***

Awake with the sunrise, as usual, Luc captures and cooks breakfast before Calley has even begun to stir. The smell of sizzling meat is carried with the breeze and over to Calley. She pokes her head out of the bedroll and looks over to Luc.

Getting up, Calley walks over to the fire and sits next to Luc. "You didn't wake me to help with breakfast," Calley says while curiously looking into the pot.

"I wanted to surprise you," he says as he stirs the pot.

"Surprise me with what?" Calley asks, even more intrigued than before.

"Here, taste this," Luc says, holding a spoon of whatever is cooking in the pot out for her to try. "Tell me what you think it tastes like."

Calley hesitantly and somewhat awkwardly leans forward and opens her mouth around the spoon. The hot, spicy liquid fills her mouth with chunks of stringy meat and bits of small vegetables.

Where did he get vegetables? We're in the middle of nowhere with no one around... Calley wonders as she swallows her mouthful.

"Well? What do you think it tastes like?" Luc asks excitedly.

"If I didn't know any better, I'd say you found potatoes, carrots, celery, onions and beef chunks and cooked them all into a beef stew. But, that would have taken hours, and we don't have any of those things with us," Calley says suspiciously.

"So, your favorite food is beef stew? I'll make a note of that," Luc says mysteriously, leaving the answer to Calley's question hanging in the air.

Exasperated, Calley huffs out a sigh and says, "Well, are you going to tell me what's in it? Or should I start guessing?"

Chuckling to himself, Luc says, "You would never figure it out yourself! I found some *delicata* grass a little while ago, before you joined the caravan," Luc answers. "I just thought it would be a nice way to introduce you to herbs in Calueria."

"*Deli-cata?*" Calley asks, glancing at Luc sideways.

"Yes, *delicata*. It means, favored. It has the ability to transform anything it's cooked in into the partaker's favorite dish. It's very rare and highly valuable," Luc says as he slurps up some of his own breakfast.

"Wow! That's amazing! I've never heard of anything that could do that!" Calley says, amazed at the thought of an herb that can do all that. "Wait a minute, are you telling me that there are no potatoes, carrots, onions, or any of that in there?" she asks.

"Nope, not a single one. The only two things in that pot are water and the herb," Luc says between slurps.

"So, what do you taste when you drink it?" Calley asks.

"Veal steaks cooked to rare over a seasoned rice pilaf," Luc answers.

Calley just stares at him for a minute, trying to remember to blink, in complete astonishment and utter disgust.

Snapping out of her thoughts, Calley asks, "So, what does this herb look like anyway?"

"Almost like your everyday variety of grass actually. It can be hard to determine it apart from other grasses," Luc says, finished with his bowl of *delicata* soup. Seeing that Calley was not satisfied with his answer, Luc continues, "The best way I can describe it to you is that if you take one of the blades of grass and nibble on the end it will taste like one of you favorite foods."

"That's the only way to tell the difference between it and any other everyday grass on the ground?" Calley asks, perturbed.

"Yup," Luc answers. "Thus the major reason it is so rare. Could you imagine having a job where you go around tasting blades of grass in hopes that you'll come across just one blade of *delicata*?" Luc chuckles and shakes his head slightly, while staring into the sky.

***

As the days pass, the landscape changes drastically from dense, lush forest to a barren, dry, desert waste land. As the trees become fewer and fewer, so too do the rain clouds. Calley looks up at the sky and realizes that it has also gotten darker. Even during midday, there is little sign of the sun. Looking up, Calley cannot see a cloud in the sky, but then she realizes, she can't see the blue of the sky either. It is as if some huge, grey blanket covers the world, blocking out the sun and moon and stars.

"Luc, are you sure we're going the right way? Things only seem to be getting darker... and colder." Calley shivers; a breeze of frosty wind swathes her in icy, bitterness. "We're almost out of water and food. What are we going to do? There doesn't seem to be a river or any source of water around here for miles," Calley whispers as they sit around a camp fire, having stopped for lunch at what they only assume is midday.

"I know we are going in the correct direction. I would bet my life on that. The problem is that I didn't know how far away we were from the ocean when we left the caravan or how far we have traveled since leaving." Luc glances at Calley to check that she is listening.

Calley sits with her eyes on the ground, her arms around her knees which are lifted up to her chest. She shivers impulsively as a breeze picks up.

"Well, you could be wrong though, right? What if we're going the opposite direction than we need to be?" Calley asks, shivering involuntarily as she holds her legs as tightly as she can.

"We are going in the right direction. West. That, I know for certain," Luc snaps at her. Then, hanging his head and shaking it slightly, Luc says, "I'm sorry, Calley. I fear I'm a poorer guide for this area than I thought."

"Then, I guess we don't have much choice other than to push on and hope that we find some food and water soon. Or maybe a town or village where we can get some more supplies." Calley says as she stands and gathers her things. It is nearly evening, but Calley wants to keep going in hopes of finding some small town or village. Without argument, Luc helps Calley pack their things, and they mount their horses once more.

"Maybe we should stop for the night?" Luc asks wearily after trudging on a few more hours.

"Not yet, I want to go a little further for today first," Calley insists as she leads the way on her horse; now doggedly pressing forward.

All the stories had been told, all the songs had been sung, and all the energy left in Luc had been spent. The lack of food and water was taking its toll on the Lipus. His kind was not meant for deserts; they were meant to live near enough to water to drink whenever desired. The Lipus was a species that lived in mild temperatures, with lush forests, and a water supply nearby; while the Kinsfolk, with whom Luc had been raised, were accustomed to their knolls and grassy hills, they too lived very near a water source and seldom stayed far from it.

As the two trudge on, the evening sun slowly lowers on the horizon behind that thick grey blanket that seems to cover the entire sky. Calley draws her horse to a stop as she gazes at a gleaming beneath the setting sun as if a reflection off of something. She hadn't seen it there before, but as the sun bows beneath the horizon, there it is. The reflection soon changes into a corporeal image. Calley blinks hard to ensure that there isn't any sand in her eyes causing her vision to distort. She isn't sure if she can believe what she is seeing.

Am I hallucinating? Has the thirst gotten to that point? The point to which I would imagine the thing I want most even though it's not really there? Calley wonders as she stares blankly in the direction of her supposed hallucination. *But, if I were creating the image from my own mind of the thing I desire most, wouldn't I be seeing a huge lake right now? Instead, I see… a wall with castle spires and towers sticking out of it…"*

"Why have you stopped, Calley? Are you ready to stop for the night now?" Luc's horse has wondered up to Calley's lazily. Luc is barely able to keep his eyes open for sleepiness.

"Luc, look! Don't you see it?" Calley points toward the town with its castle spires that mark the center.

Luc lifts his head with a sigh and looks in the direction of Calley's finger. With his mouth open in awe, Luc says, "Calley, I think I know that town. It looks familiar. Where did it come from?"

"What do you mean, where did it come from? It didn't come from anywhere of course. It is just there. One minute, the sun was in the sky and it wasn't there; the next minute the sun was sinking beneath the rim and there it was!" Calley says shrugging her shoulders. "Isn't it a relief? Maybe we'll find some food and water. Maybe we'll even find someone who knows the way to *Libania Fretum*. Come on! Let's go!" A second wind hits Calley as the prospect for water lies within reach and she pushes her horse into a trot. She tries to urge her horse into a gallop with all her excitement but the horse is just as tired and dehydrated as she is.

"Calley, I'm not so sure about this. There's something oddly familiar and foreboding about this town, and that castle..." Luc says as he catches up to Calley at the entrance to the town. "If we go in there, we need to be very careful. Be vigilant and stay with me, okay?" he adds nervously.

But, Calley isn't listening. She is so thrilled at the thought of a warm meal, a cool cup of water and maybe a guide, that she doesn't hear what Luc is trying to say to her. Into the small town that surrounds the great wall Calley rides. Every street seems as barren as the desert through which they had just spent weeks traversing. Every house is empty and quiet. Calley and Luc ride through the town, around the houses and down the alley-ways.

Looking up at the foreboding wall as they ride, Calley feels utterly small and insignificant.

"Calley, I think we should go around. Perhaps there's another entrance." Luc leads his horse alongside the wall and they begin to traverse the length of it. They follow the outer wall as far as it will go only to find themselves back where they started at the huge, heavy gates. This appears to be the only entrance or exit into or out of the walled-in castle.

"Well, let's see if we can get in here then," Calley says and then starts toward the gates. Just as she reaches her hand to touch one of them, it swings ajar slightly. "There you go. It's not locked. Let's see if we can find someone to help us out or who we can trade with for supplies."

Behind Calley, Luc pauses at the heavy metal gates and reaches a hand out to feel them. "Alloy?" he says and looks up and around at all of the wall that he can see. "It's a city... made of Alloy..." Luc rushes to catch up to Calley, now certain that he knows where they must be.

Chapter Thirteen

THERE IS NO SIGN OF LIFE anywhere. Like the empty houses outside the wall, every building within is still and dark. Finally, Calley thinks she sees smoke coming from the chimney of a building not far from them and Luc follows her in that direction. They come upon a blacksmith's in which a fire is lit and produces the smoke Calley had noticed trickling from the chimney. Calley dismounts and enters the blacksmith's out of curiosity. Luc is distracted by a glow from inside anther house and leaves to investigate it.

Inside the blacksmith's, no one can be seen. But, someone has lit the fire. And, someone had been fashioning a blade which now rests in a steaming bath of water.

So, there must be someone around here somewhere, Calley thinks curiously.

As Calley peers into a large circular room that makes up the entire building, she sees a little, scrawny, scaly, greenish-grey creature cross the room. It grabs the blade from the water with its bare hands and returns to the work bench where it sits and examines the workmanship of the blade. If Calley didn't know better, she would think that this was some kind of gigantic gecko; except for the fact that it walks on two feet like a person. It is the same shade of gecko green with tiny, little, shiny scales all along its back. It wears only a pair of torn brown trousers that tie at its waist with a piece of rope. One distinguishing feature is the large, round head that sits on narrow, thin shoulders which makes Calley wonder why it doesn't fall to the ground.

This creature's head is twice as round as its body and makes up almost a quarter of the creature's complete mass. The rest of it is skinny bones with tiny scales stretched over the entire length.

Forget how the creature is able to lift the heated blade, how is it wielding the heavy hammer? Calley wonders. Unsure of what to do next, Calley just hides behind some shelves and watches as the creature works.

Lost in thought, Calley leans forward, lifting herself slightly in order to get a better view of the sword when the creature lifts it from the water. She accidentally bumps into the shelf and knocks down a tin cup. It clatters on the floor, clanging an alarm to her presence. Calley shrinks down and slowly moves backward toward a dark corner behind the shelves.

The strange green creature hears the cup clanging on the ground and looks at it suspiciously. Freezing in place, it watches the cup on the ground. Then, a long, thin tongue whips out of its mouth like the flick of a snake's tongue when it's smelling the air. It begins to walk in Calley's direction when another sound, much louder, comes from outside. Some kind of horn is being blown. The creature stops in place again, still watching the cup on the ground. There's another flick of the tongue just before the bell rings again. It seems to be a summoning of sorts, because the creature hurries off out the door, leaving the sword where it lay on a cloth next to the water basin.

"A cobalt. I thought they were only a legend," Luc says, startling Calley. He'd slipped in while Calley watched the cobalt work silently. Only now did he make his presence known to her. "Sorry, that's what that is. It's a cobalt. You might know it as a goblin, I think that's what the mortals call them. But, I thought they were all extinct. There's a legend of a queen who saved a few of them during their extinction and who bred them and raised them as her servants and guards."

"So you think that this guy might work for that queen? Is it the same queen from that story you told me about with the prince who was forced to stay in the castle?" Calley turns to look at Luc.

Has he grown paler than before or is it the lighting in this place? Calley wonders. *He doesn't look quite like himself.* Calley watches sweat drip from Luc's forehead and can't help but notice the darker, gray circles beneath his eyes. *He looks exhausted...*

"They are one and the same story. I never would have dreamt it to be true though. But seeing that now, and in this town..." Luc pauses a moment, looks around suspiciously and then continues, "Now I know why this town is so familiar to me. We are in Baghad, the city made of Alloy; the one from the nursery rhyme. And we must leave here immediately!" Luc grabs Calley's hand and drags her back to their horses.

When they reach the gates they had entered through, they are shut soundly. There would be no exiting through them. Having already circled the wall from the outside, Luc and Calley already know that this is the only way in or out.

"Well, now what?" Calley asks as they sit before the gates. "Should we see if someone in the town knows how to get out? Maybe someone has a key that can open the gates for us," Calley suggests.

"Doubtful. I didn't see anyone in this place aside from that one cobalt. Besides, there wasn't anyone here before when we came through to have shut and locked the gates. Chances are there's a spell over this town that serves to lock in the inhabitants and trap any wanderers. If this town is the one from the tales, there is a good reason for the spell. The only way out now is to find the person holding the spell in place and hope he or she will take kindly to our plight and allow us to leave," Luc says even though he doesn't sound hopeful.

"How do we find him or her? I mean, the town isn't exactly bustling, and how do we know if we've found the right person?" Calley asks.

"He will have the key," Luc says matter-of-factly. "It won't be like any key you've seen before, however."

Luc takes in a deep breath as in preparing for a speech, "Most binding spells like this have 'keys', and it may or may not look like a traditional key. Don't be on the lookout for a key, only for the reason this place has been bound," Luc says and looks to see if Calley understands. Her blank stare tells him that she is confused and he decides to further elaborate, "Once we find the cause for the spell, we can determine the likely spell castor; whom will have the key or spell needed to open the gates," Luc says patiently.

"Well, we'll get more of the town covered if we split up to search it. I'll be on the lookout for everything. Does that work?" Calley says sarcastically and rolls her eyes.

"Yes, that will be fine," Luc says, ignoring the comment, and he turns to look around the town. "I'll go west, you can go…" As Luc looks back at Calley, he can see her wandering off in the direction of the castle at the center of the town. "Anywhere but there…" Luc says to himself, sighs and he sets off after her.

***

When Calley comes upon the massive castle doors, she is reminded of a dollhouse she'd made once as a child out of paper and crayons. The castle has the same kind of texture, almost like it isn't even real; like it is made from paper. Even the gray coloring on the walls looks more like crayon strokes than it does actual stones.

But when Calley raises her hand to use the gilded door knocker, everything becomes solid, branching away from where she has touched. Rippling across the building, crumpled paper walls become solid, gray granite stone walls, white paper Mache windows become smooth, shiny glass, and the tip on each pinnacle radiates a new golden hue.

A shadow casts over Calley and lands above the doors, which draws Calley's attention. Although the sun has set long ago, a faint glow seems to lighten the sky. It appears to be neither night nor day. This is why the shadow draws Calley's attention. She looks up to see gargoyles flying in and landing atop the doors, alighting on window sills and marking every corner of the castle. Upon landing, they turn to stone.

Is that music? Calley thinks as she listens. Music seems to have begun playing inside the castle. Calley knocks three times and waits. After only a second, the door jerks open slightly like a loose door does when opening from a breeze in the house. Pushing it open further, Calley takes a step inside.

Chapter Fourteen

Inside, a grand hall opens up, exposing a giant chandelier hanging from the ceiling, a stair case on each side of the room that climbs the walls to a second floor, and a balcony walkway that connects the two stair cases. Huge, heavy, scarlet tapestries, elegantly embroidered in gold, hang from the balcony in bundles which reach all the way to the ground floor. At the center of the grand hall stands the statue of a woman holding a ruby-topped scepter. Though made of marble, her sapphire eyes seem to scan the room.

Calley doesn't even notice the tumultuous throng throughout the room until one person bumps into her, knocking them both over.

"Oh, I'm sorry. Are you all right?" Calley asks as the little girl gets back up. Without replying, the girl reenters the mob of bodies, bouncing and dancing the whole way. "What the heck?" Calley asks aloud. She observes as the girl begins to move in particular steps as though dancing. Actually, everyone moves in some rhythmic pattern as though their steps are guided. It is some kind of dance they are all performing. No one sits in any of the chairs that line the walls. No one misses a beat of the silent music to which they dance.

"It's an enchanted castle. I wouldn't be surprised if they are all bewitched. We need to hurry and get out of here, Calley." Luc has come up behind without a sound and stands just inside the door way. "I don't like it here one bit, Calley. I don't have a good feeling about this place. If what the legend says is true, then we don't want to be here," he says as he nervously looks over the throng of dancers and then back out over the town.

"How else are we going to get out of here? Do you have any ideas? Because I think that if we need to find a key to get out of this place, this is most likely where it will be. I'm going in with or without you." With that, Calley turns and strolls into the group of rhythmic swaying, bowing and mindless people.

Looking around the room from the center now, Calley realizes that there are groups of people spread out around the room that simply seem to be talking and laughing. Other groups are spread about the room too, groups of cobalts. They are dressed up just like all of these supposed party guests.

No one even seems to notice that she stands smack dab in the center of their dance. They just dance around her as if she's just a piece of furniture. The music Calley had thought she heard cannot be accounted for either. There are no musicians or vocalists. And, now that Calley stands inside the hall, she doesn't hear the music anymore either.

Where did the music I heard from outside come from? What keeps these people dancing? Calley wonders, looking around at all of the clueless people as they bow and twirl around the room.

Luc follows Calley into the castle only to watch her disappear into the crowd. He decides that she probably has a point and tries to keep up with her but loses her to the tumultuous throng. Not long after entering, Luc is swept away with the dancers.

Calley meanders toward a stairwell on the right side of the room. She thinks she sees something up on the balcony walkway. It was just a flash of something, but it was the only freely moving thing in the room that didn't seem to have a predetermined path. Climbing the stairs, Calley eyes the people in their dance on the floor. While being elegant and beautiful, the dance is creepy and gives her goose-bumps.

There is definitely something weird going on here. Enchanted, or whatever! Calley thinks as she looks over the crowd from midway up the staircase. Then, she sees him. Luc is dancing in the crowd!

Calley hurries back down the stairs and heads straight for Luc. She is bombarded by dancing people as she tries to reach him. It is almost as if they are keeping her from him on purpose.

"Get out of my way!" Calley yells and forces her way through a few dancers who seem to have chosen that particular spot to become immovable in just as Calley needs get through. Dancing methodically, without expression or emotion, Luc waltzes with a partner right passed Calley. Luc's facial expression is blank and his movements are stiff, almost like he is a puppet being led about the room. His normal fluid-like movements are turned into stiff, mechanical processes.

Lurching forward, Calley grabs Luc by the arms and shakes, yelling at him, "Luc! Luc! Come on! Wake up! Break out of this stupid trance! Luc!"

Despite Calley's best efforts at shaking Luc out of the spell, he begins to dance with her as if she is a partner to be led around the room. He holds her wrist in one hand and lifts her with his other around her waist. She is helpless as he twirls her around the room, his grip tight in her hand and at her waist.

"No! Luc! Stop it! Let me go and WAKE UP!!" Calley shouts, pounding her fist on Luc's chest.

The dance must be over because Luc stops and sets Calley down. He then, begins speaking in some form of gibberish to the other dancers and laughing at gibberish jokes that make no sense at all to Calley.

Tears begin to well up in Calley's eyes and she fights them back. *I do not cry. I do not cry. I do NOT cry!* she reminds herself mentally.

"Do you love him?" a voice whispers in Calley's ear. She turns to see who, but there is no one around besides the dancers who have begun a new patterned ball room dance. This time they are all dancing around each other as a group, weaving in and out, with males going one way and females another. Calley watches Luc as he mixes in with the dancers as if he's been there all along and in fact belongs there.

"Do you love him?" again the voice whispers in Calley's ear. She whirls around, this time furious, feeling as though someone is teasing her; like this is someone's idea of a sick joke.

"Who is that?" Calley yells spinning around, searching for the possible culprit. All she sees are the blank faces of the dancers as they twirl passed her. "Stop joking right now and show yourself!" she commands angrily.

"If you want to break the spell, what do all the stories say? True love's kiss will break the spell." The words seem to float on the air, aimed straight at Calley.

Suspiciously, Calley glares at the mob; allowing her eyes to linger on each individual for only so long as she is sure it cannot be him or her that is playing this horrible joke.

"Okay then, you want to play games. Fine. What do I need to do then?" Calley asks the crowd and crosses her arms.

"Do you love him?" the voice asks once more, this time with a hint of superiority in his voice.

"I... uh.. I barely know him..."Calley says into the crowd. Standing still, just outside of the prancing circle of bodies makes Calley feel isolated, shy; and this kind of intimate question is definitely not the kind of thing she wants to talk about to an invisible joker in an enchanted castle at a time like this.

"Won't know until you try," the voice teases and chuckles.

Calley rolls her eyes. "Whatever," she says and strides toward Luc. She nearly has to jump to reach his face, but she lands a kiss right on his cheek.

She waits. Nothing happens.

"What now, oh, all-knowing, mystical one?" Calley scoffs, with a tone of irritation raising her voice a pitch at the end of the question.

"Oh come on, you call that a kiss? Haven't you ever heard of 'True Love's Kiss'? Do you think they mean on the cheek when they say that?" Although the voice now is louder in Calley's ears, she still cannot place it with a person. "You have to kiss him, for real," the voice insists.

Calley searches the room again, trying to find the being to whom that seriously annoying voice must belong. Everyone in the room is either dancing in the same methodic, patterned rhythm or is a cobalt passing out refreshments throughout the room or is a cobalt standing at-the-ready beside the doors and stairs and at every corner of the room.

For just a moment, Calley views the room entirely: the circling, swirling figures, pairing then parting, then pairing, then parting again; the flowing grace with which they float around the room in never ending blissful engagement. For just that moment, it reminds Calley of a music box her father gave her when she was a little girl. The characters in it had moved in a similar fashion, ever twirling in pairs, round and round and round the confines of the music box.

Luc dances passed her just in time for Calley to remember what she is supposed to be doing. She takes the place of his partner, leaving a fleetingly confused woman to find herself a new partner. Without hesitation this time,

Calley reaches her hands around Luc's head, bringing it down to hers.

She kisses him fast and hard. When she releases him, he stops dancing and stares at her for the briefest of moments before again resuming his dance with a new partner; leaving her behind again.

"Oh well, it was worth a try, right?" The voice taunts, "I guess your love isn't true after all." The floating voice chuckles a bit before appearing in the form of a boy not much older than Calley dancing in place just before her.

Chapter Fifteen

"Who are you? Why aren't you like everyone else?" Calley asks, bewildered. Right on cue, the boy spins in place just like all of the other dances do. Standing a few inches taller than Calley, the boy isn't quite 'tall', but is certainly not short. His short, straight jet black hair is combed back; kept there with some kind of hair gel, or whatever they use in this realm. Here and there little chunks of it stick out at odd angles. The boy's pale skin and emerald green eyes are sharply contrasted and complimented by the darkness of his hair.

Wow, he's cute! No, bad Calley! Luc! Must save Luc and get out of this situation! Calley thinks before the boy asks her another question.

"Everyone else?" the boy asks.

"You know," Calley says, glancing back at Luc and his current dance partner, "everyone else under this enchantment that makes you dance like a mindless fool?" Calley explains, looking away from Luc reluctantly.

"I might ask you the same thing," the boy counters. "But, I'm pretty sure I haven't seen you here before."

Crossing her arms, Calley can feel fumes begin to rise from her ears. "If you're not going to be helpful, then leave me alone and let me figure this out by myself," Calley shouts abruptly.

"Oh fine. I was just having a little bit of fun," he says, raising his shoulders slightly and then dropping them. "I'm immune," the boys says looking around to the Cobalts.

"Immune?" Calley asks skeptically.

"Yeah, or something like that," the boy says, suddenly nervous and he changes the topic, "My name is Jaxson. I live here. I pretend to be entranced too. That's why I've been dancing, so that they," he points to the cobalts, "don't realize I'm actually awake." He's still dancing and motions for her to follow suit and dance with him, which she does, not truly convinced that there is even a need.

It can't hurt, right? Calley thinks, looking suspiciously at the Cobalts around the room who don't seem to have even noticed her presence in the slightest.

"Are there any others who are awake?" Calley asks, allowing Jaxson to lead her in a waltz like the rest of the crowd has just started doing.

"So far, no; it's just me. I mean, not until you two came knocking. You don't belong here. Why are you here?" Jaxson asks, leading Calley around the room at a dizzying speed.

"We came into the town looking for supplies; we're traveling and need food and fresh water." Calley falls silent as she sees the little girl pass by dancing with a little boy. She asks, "What happened to all these people?" Calley asks, referring to all the bodies filling the room and dancing robotically.

"They're entranced. The queen keeps them prisoner for her entertainment," Jaxson says and he shrugs his shoulders, talking as if this is common place or acceptable.

"That's horrible! How can I free Luc of the spell?" Calley asks, getting straight to the point.

"You can't. Why do you want to anyway? Is he a close friend? Family perhaps? He's obviously not your true love..." Jaxson flashes a cheesy grin at Calley. Suddenly, her cheeks are rushed with hot blood to show her embarrassment, and she quickly inhales, bolstering up her shoulders and chest in protest.

"He's my friend; the only friend I have at the moment. He's helping me find a way home..." Realizing what she was about to say, Calley quickly adjusts what she is saying, "I'm lost. Please, can you help me free him?" Calley looks up into Jaxson's eyes pleadingly.

"I suppose I could do that. I know where the queen resides within these walls. I could take you to her and perhaps you could argue your case and she just might free him. But, what would be in it for me?" Jaxson asks in a calculating manner.

"What do you want?" Calley asks with mounting annoyance in her voice.

"Oh, the same as everyone else: adventure, mystery, a miracle, a quest, a journey, something beyond the tedious, lackluster of this," Jaxson says and waves a hand around the room. "Take me with you when you leave and I will help you free your friend."

Calley considers the offer and her current situation for only a few moments before responding.

"What other choice do I have?" Calley asks rhetorically, sighing and watching Luc twirl another partner around the room. "Okay, you can come along then."

"Brilliant! Let's go! We have to get something from a room up the stairs first. We'll need a weapon. The turret over on the left upper corner of the room is filled with gadgets, gizmos and cobalt constructed weapons. Among them is the one that will help us defeat the *Lamia Dominitri*," Jaxson says leading Calley's gaze to that corner of the room with a finger.

The left staircase is blocked by a large group of people talking and laughing; there are only a few cobalts at the bottom of the right staircase though. So, Calley and Jaxson head toward the right staircase.

"We'll have to take the other staircase and then cross the balcony," he tells Calley as they dance across the room. "I'll cause a distraction while you get up the stairs and into the room. Look for the weapon shaped like an 'L' that fits into the palm of your hand. It will have a large ruby attached to it somehow," Jaxson says, letting go of Calley's hands and disappearing into a flock of people gathered at the bottom of the staircase.

Calley waits behind a table and potted plant that are right next to the bottom of the right-hand stair case until she hears some clatter from across the room and the cobalts guarding the staircase leave to investigate. Calley hurries up the stairs. She crouches as much as possible while still being able to run across the balcony to the left-hand turret.

Just as she reaches the room, a tinkling sound floats from it to greet Calley. Shining metal bounces sunlight onto the walls and ceiling. Crystals, hang from a wooden beam that crosses the room, and sends bits of rainbow everywhere. There is only one window in the room. Beside the window sat a telescope looking kind of thing made of metal tubes and leather straps. Benches and tables set up around the room are covered with bolts, screws, washers, nails, and various tools and odd little items that Calley can't put a name to. Little sheets of metal, balls and rounds of rubber, and blue print sheets lay strewn all around the room. The walls are covered in bookshelves which are loaded with books. There isn't an empty spot in the room.

Some of the things Calley sees look like kinds of guns. These draw her eye because they each have some kind of gem stone in place of where the hammer would be. One has a thick, grey barrel about two inches in diameter. It looks bulbous and round. Another one looks like it is mostly made from bones. Little spiny bones protrude from around the tan barrel and down the pistol grip; there is an indentation of a small four fingered hand around the pistol grip which Calley assumes is for gripping the weapon.

A glimmer catches Calley's attention; it is the sun reflecting off of something metallic near the open window. She walks over to the window and picks up a jewel-encrusted sword hilt that has no sword attached. Calley recognizes the jewel as being a peridot, like her pendant. It sends shivers through her arm and down her spine. She feels powerful and strong all of a sudden; energy seems to fill her entire being. Calley puts it into her bag that she took from the traders' camp when Luc rescued her.

Scanning the tables, Calley sees another weapon that looks like a fat round gun that is mostly barrel and hardly any trigger. Beside it is a more regular type of gun that she's used to seeing. On the gun lay a huge ruby with edges sharp enough to slice her fingers when she touches it.

That must be the weapon that Jaxson was talking about, Calley thinks, while nursing the cut on her fingers. She carefully puts the gun in her bag and turns toward the door.

Before leaving the room, Calley picks up the first gun she saw and begins examining it once more.

What if this is what Jaxson was talking about though? The jewel that took the place of the gun's hammer was a ruby after all. Calley examines the weapon more closely and notices that just under the jewel and just above the handle, there is a little propeller blade with three spokes that spin like a pinwheel.

What in the world could that be for? Calley wonders as she peers into the tiny little space for a better view of the pinwheel-looking propeller.

A cobalt steps into the room and freezes when he sees her, widening his eyes and dropping his jaw. Calley looks up startled and when he starts to call out, Calley pulls the trigger on the gun she's holding without even thinking about it and aims it at the cobalt.

The propeller begins spinning and a rush of wind blows out of the gun, towards the cobalt. It turns into two huge hands which clasp the cobalt completely and suck him back into the gun with them. Calley stands there, frozen in place, in complete disbelief at what just happened; what she'd just done.

Jaxson appears at the door just in time to see the cobalt disappear into the weapon. "I take it you found one that likes you? That's one of my favorites! The *Duco Ballistae*. Did you find anything else?" he asks eagerly.

"It cut me, but I think so," Calley says as she opens the bag and shows him the gun she'd taken that had the huge sharp ruby on it.

"That's it, the *Ultrices Ballistae* let's go. She's going to know we're coming by now." Jaxson holds out his hand for the weapon, and Calley holds the bag open for him to reach in and take it, not willing to risk another cut.

"It cut me the last time I touched it," Calley explains as he takes the weapon.

"Now, we can go and find the *Lamia Dominitri*. Then, you can try to reason for the freedom of your friend downstairs." Jaxson leads Calley out of the room and together they crouch and run back across the walkway above the large ball room. She follows him into the room positioned at the top of the right staircase.

Calley follows Jaxson through a closet with a hidden door in the back that leads them through a maze of hidden walkways and staircases. They travel up stairs and down stairs; they turn left, then right, then left again. On his heels, Calley follows Jaxson through a maze.

What kind of a place is this? Someone's idea of a fun house? Calley thinks as she tries to keep up with Jaxson who speedily lowers himself down narrow twisting staircases and easily climbs through constricted hallways.

Finally, they reach an open alley way. Stepping out of a grandfather clock, Calley looks around. It looks like an avenue, with pavement and everything, but it's indoors.

"Her quarters lie at the end of this avenue. That's where we will find her," Jaxson says pointing to the end of the avenue. As he leads the way, Calley continues to follow closely behind Jaxson down the dimly lit avenue.

Dark purple velvet tapestries, with thin straps of black crepe material here and there between them, drape down huge windows which line the walls on both sides of the avenue. The windows reach almost two stories high; almost all the way from the ceiling to the floor.

So many windows! They are spread out at about one every ten feet and then they take up over half of those ten feet! Calley notices as they walk down the avenue.

You can see that the daylight is starting to show and the sun will soon be rising. Cobalts stand like statues alongside the walls at regular intervals, one between every window.

Wearily, Calley eyes the cobalt statues as they walk. "What about them?" Calley asks nervously.

"They won't bother us, nor will they sound the alarm. They're mute. Their only responsibility is to stand there and look fierce," Jaxson assures Calley without a doubt.

At the end of the avenue, two black granite doors are closed, blocking their access to the *Lamia Dominitri*. Just before the doors, Jaxson stops, looks at Calley, and asks with a smirk on his lips, "Ready?"

Suddenly, Jaxson boldly forces them open with a push and then announces their arrival as he strolls leisurely, as if he lived there, into the room.

Chapter Sixteen

"We have a matter to settle with the *Lamia Dominitri*! You have a new prisoner named Luc, this girl's friend. He does not belong here. I demand that you set him free at once or you will forfeit the kingdom to me immediately!" Jaxson booms as he strides into the *Lamia Dominitri's* chambers.

Surprised, Calley begins to worry that she's made the wrong choice by trusting Jaxson. The room has a couch, a dresser, a table, and even an armoire. But, the focus of the décor in the room seems to center around an elegantly carved and very tall mirror which stands on a platform raised just a couple of feet off of the floor. Beside the mirror, another Cobalt, slightly taller than the rest, silently waits. There, standing before the mirror, is the most beautiful woman Calley has ever seen. As tall as the mirror and just as slender, the woman's sapphire blue eyes turn to Calley. The *Lamia Dominitri* eyes Calley carefully, measuring her up as she meagerly stumbles just inside the room after Jaxson. Calley waits just inside the door trying to stand firm and appear brave; although she feels as though she might faint any moment.

"Oh really? You dare disturb the powerful *Lamia Dominitri?*" she starts, then noticing Calley's posture and conviction, she says, *"And you dear? Are you here to take my kingdom from me as well?"* the *Lamia Dominitri* asks laughingly, her eyes lingering on Jaxson as she turns her face towards Calley. "Well, girl?" the *Lamia Dominitri* demands, turning her gaze fully into Calley now.

Calley nervously straightens herself and smoothes her clothes, and after clearing her throat she hurriedly says, "My friend and I only came into your town to find supplies that we could trade for. We were only passing through when we were drawn to your castle. It was some kind of trance because now Luc is fixed on that stupid dance that you have those poor people doing over and over again," Calley realizes that she's gotten a little off topic when she hears the *Lamia Dominitri* inhale quickly, obviously offended by the comment. She hurries to get the point out and says, "He wasn't supposed to be here, you don't need him. Please, if you could just release him then we will go and be out of your hair. I don't want your castle or your kingdom. I just want to leave with my friend safely," Calley begs, taking a few steps closer to the *Lamia Dominitri*.

Standing before the elegantly carved mirror, the *Lamia Dominitri* goes back to admiring herself for a moment. She gazes at the curves of her hips. Her eyes travel up to her long, black curls that fall evenly across her shoulders. The *Lamia Dominitri's* slender figure is covered by a cream colored sparkling, form fitting gown which touches the floor. Together with an umpire waist, which emphasizes her bust line, and the sleeveless aspect which exposes her shoulders, the gown does little to conceal the woman's pale, flawless skin. The attractively perfect ringlets of her hair bounce as she shakes her head and turns to look directly at Jaxson.

Beside the mirror rests a long, embossed golden staff with a large, perfectly rounded, smooth ruby perched on top. The *Lamia Dominitri* takes it in hand as she turns toward Jaxson.

"I suppose it is you whom I should thank for this interruption and nuisance then, my son?" the *Lamia Dominitri* asks as she faces him, twisting the staff in her hand and looking down her nose into the smoothed ruby.

"Son?" Calley asks, looking at Jaxson in complete bewilderment, suddenly terrified and furious all at once.

"Yes, mother," Jaxson begins without looking at Calley, "It is my doing. I want to be free of this hell you have created for us. I want to explore and learn new things, find new places, and meet new faces. It was fun and all when I was a boy, but really, mother? Did you seriously think that it could last forever? Isn't it about time we moved on and let those people go? Have they not suffered through their penance enough by now?" he asks her, growing slowly closer to the *Lamia Dominitri*.

"Suffered enough? Have they not suffered enough!!" the *Lamia Dominitri* says significantly, bringing her hand over her chest as if taken aback. "Did I not suffer far greater than they when their king bedded me, made me heavy with his child, his heir to his throne and then threw me to the gutters once he discovered it?" the *Lamia Dominitri* throws her free arm down by her side dramatically and crashes the staff on the floor as she begins to pace angrily back and forth. "His queen I could have been, but no, he could not have a bastard child be the heir to his throne. Even though his own queen could not bear him an heir, he still would not acknowledge his own child in my womb," the *Lamia Dominitri* nearly screams until coming to a stop with her back now to Calley and Jaxson, neither of whom has dared to move while the *Lamia Dominitri* raged on.

After a moment of silence the *Lamia Dominitri* continues with her face down, looking at the ground, "Perhaps I will consider freeing the town people, but the Majori family will be mine forever." The *Lamia Dominitri* looks up and to her side where she reaches her hand up and fondly caresses the tall cobalt standing next to the elegantly carved mirror. Shivers race down Calley's back as she realizes who the cobalt must truly be.

"If what you say is true, then it was awful of the king of this land to do what he did to you, but it's not the people's fault that they had a ghastly king," Calley says stepping forward and attempting to empathize with the *Lamia Dominitri*. "I just want my friend back so we can be on our way. So, if you please, would just release him, then we will leave and…" Calley tries but is interrupted by the *Lamia Dominitri*.

"Silence, swine! All of this squealing is getting on my nerves. Son, leave and take this wretch with you. Be gone and leave me in my despair," the *Lamia Dominitri* says as she waves them off and turns back towards the mirror.

"I can't do that, mother. I'm done. I want out, and if this is the only way to do it…" Jaxson lifts up the ruby-jeweled *Ultrices Ballistae* and points it at her; she sees its reflection in the mirror but doesn't turn back around.

"Surely you don't truly believe that I would be so dull as to leave my own tool of destruction laying around my castle for anyone to pick up?" the *Lamia Dominitri* asks dryly.

"There's only one way to find out," Jaxson says and pulls the trigger on the *Ultrices Ballistae*. A red string of electrical current waves away from Jaxson and reaches the *Lamia Dominitri*. She holds her staff with both hands, turning toward Jaxson and holding it out front of her. Electric vines burst out from the *Ultrices Ballistae* in Jaxson's hands and seem to be pulled straight into the ruby on the *Lamia Dominitri*'s staff, like being sucked by a vacuum.

The *Lamia Dominitri* laughs, "You see? I have created a new weapon for myself. It's much more efficient than that and much better suited for a *Lamia Dominitri*, don't you think? The staff itself is made with pure silver; it is only painted yellow gold on the top for the color. How do you like my ruby? Isn't it just marvelous? It took my workers many years to completely smooth its surfaces into this perfectly rounded shape." She admires the *Qui* stone and staff, smoothing her hand over the top of the ruby as she speaks, pausing momentarily and causing a break in the red electricity.

Jaxson breathes heavily, almost panting like a dog. He stumbles and catches himself on a table, still attempting to hold the gun on the *Lamia Dominitri*.

"Oh, my son! Just look at you! You've tired! You know better than to use my *Qui* stone! You know how it drains you of your energy! You must truly want to leave this place.....", the *Lamia Dominitri* frowns and watches Jaxson struggle to stand and aim the *Ultrices Ballistae* steadily. "I'm sorry to do this, but I just can't allow you to leave me here all alone," she says as she closes her eyes and then begins whispering some language, holding her staff up and waving her free hand in the air. Crimson clouds begin forming around Jaxson and he is frozen in place.

"Calley! Quickly! Get the staff away from her!" Jaxson blurts out. Although his entire body is frozen in place, essentially turned to stone, Jaxson's head is still very much alive and conscious.

Calley hesitates, evaluating the situation in her mind. Jaxson is standing as still as a statue. The *Lamia Dominitri* is beside her mirror still whispering words Calley doesn't understand. Calley is already half way towards the staff before she even realizes it.

"Oh, not so fast young lady!" The *Lamia Dominitri* aims her magic at Calley with a blast from her free hand, still holding the staff firmly with the other as its power is focused on Jaxson. But Calley dodges behind an armoire, escaping the shot. Wood explodes outward from the armoire as Calley takes cover, shielding herself with her arms and crouching low to the ground.

"Oh come, come, dear. Once you join the others, you will never want to leave!" Calley peeks on the other side of the armoire. Red electric magic veins shoot passed her as she pulls her head back behind the armoire again, just missing their target.

Fiercely whispering strange but powerful words, Jaxson causes the magic smoke coiled around him to turn darker, turning into a burgundy, almost purple, shade. He can move more freely and frees his arms.

Free now, Jaxson sneaks up behind the *Lamia Dominitri* who has turned slightly to follow Calley who has run from the armoire to hide behind a couch. "Mother! This has gone on long enough!" He grabs the staff and they begin struggling for control over it. Both spout out words which cause the staff to shoot magical smoke puffs and electrical strikes all about the room.

Calley sees the ruby-powered *Ultrices Ballistae* lying on the ground not far from her. She grabs it, points and shoots at the ruby on the staff. Jaxson and the *Lamia Dominitri* both freeze, watching the staff as it floats in the air, collecting all of the magic pouring out of the *Ultrices Ballistae*. It begins to vibrate with power.

"No! You'll overload it! Stop! You little wretched swine!" She starts toward Calley, but is tackled by Jaxson who holds her down.

"Calley, full blast! Switch on the accelerator!" Jaxson yells as he struggles to hold the *Lamia Dominitri*, his mother, on the ground.

Calley finds the button near the trigger on the left side of the *Ultrices Ballistae* and switches it on. Suddenly, the magic bursts in a torrent of force, completely engulfing the ruby on the staff. The vibrations in the staff become faster and faster, until it finally implodes, first into itself and then explodes back out. Jaxson and the *Lamia Dominitri* are blown away, the walls and ceiling of the room are blasted away. Calley is thrown back to the farthest wall; the only wall still standing. She is knocked out.

***

"Calley? Get up!" Jaxson shouts as he shakes Calley's shoulders.

She is unresponsive so he hefts her onto his own shoulders. He takes a moment to look at the crumbled building around him. Underneath some of the rubble, he sees the *Lamia Dominitri's* arm, still and lifeless. Not far from where the *Lamia Dominitri* lays buried beneath a ton of rubble, Jaxson can see tiny shimmering remnants of that huge magnificent ruby; now, crushed into a thousand tiny shards.

Shifting Calley's weight on his shoulders, Jaxson heads back down the long avenue. He won't be able to take her back through the passages they had used in coming here, so he carries her the even longer distance through the avenues and large royally carpeted staircases. Walls crumble around him as he walks as fast as he can while carrying Calley around his shoulders.

Once in the great ballroom, Jaxson sees that the people are waking. They drowsily come to and take in their surroundings. Disoriented and confused, none of the people have any memories of who they are, where they are or even when they are. How long they had been there or had been entranced for would remain a mystery to them all.

Fortunately, Luc hasn't been under the spell long enough to have lost his memory yet. When Luc sees Jaxson carrying Calley, he takes Calley from Jaxson. After setting Calley gently on the ground, he punches Jaxson in the face, knocking him back onto his butt.

Rubbing his jaw and still sitting on the ground, Jaxson says, "You know, I saved her life." But, Luc turns and kneels down next to Calley.

"I saved your life too! You ungrateful, unworthy piece of garbage!" Jaxson yells at Luc's back while standing up again.

Just like that, Luc sets Calley on the ground, rushes Jaxson and throws a punch so hard it knocks Jaxson out completely. Then, Luc turns his attention to Calley. He bends down and lifts her easily into his arms, cradling her gently.

Calley stirs slightly, but is still unconscious. Luc carries Calley outside and lifts her onto his horse, mounting it just behind her. He ties the end of the lead of Calley's horse to the saddle of his own so it will follow. He holds her in one arm while the other guides his horse and they take off at a trot.

Luc leads Calley's horse back to the gates which have now swung wide open; the spell binding them was broken when the *Lamia Dominitri* was defeated. Once outside the town's boundaries, Luc slows the horses pace so as to go easier on Calley's unconscious body as it is jostled with every one of the horse's steps. After a few hours, Calley begins to wake up.

"Where are we?" Calley asks, looking around and realizing where she is.

Luc brings the horses to a halt and dismounts. He helps Calley down and says, "We left that wretched place as soon as the spell was broken. I don't know what you did, but it drained you of all of your strength and you have been unconscious for the last couple of hours.

"Mind if we stop for the night early?" Calley asks groggily, sinking to the ground where Luc had set her down.

"Yes, of course. I've been following this creek west. I think the creek began back there from within some underground caves beneath that city because it flows away from it. I found a map in a pack I took from that terrible castle. If I am correct, this feeds into the *Alace Lac* where the *Flu Lumens* originates. Then we follow the *Flu Lumens* until we reach the *Aurura Mons*. Once we've reached the *Aurura Mons* we will travel through the

Aurura Crena. It then opens to the ocean and the *Libania Fretum.*" Luc brings the horses closer to the little creek, where there is a small sandy beach-like area. He leads the horses to the water to drink.

"I'll get some wood and start a fire," Luc says as he ties the horses up to a small tree nearby. "You sit down and rest." Luc brings Calley a bedroll and lays it out next to Calley on the ground. She eases herself into it and lays her head down. Signing exhaustedly, Calley closes her eyes and falls fast asleep.

Chapter Seventeen

WIND WHIPS DAMP HAIR around my head, back and forth, slapping me in the face, stinging where it lands. I open my eyes, against the force of invisible weights that fight to keep them shut. Water splatters against my skin. It's raining, I realize. Tiny grains press against the tender places between my toes and I look down to see sand. I flex my toes in it, feeling the grains rub and crush against the skin. A roaring wave crashes up onto the shore, washing sand up to my ankles. I don't even flinch at its oncoming. The heaviness of the clouds lets loose all around and rain pours down in sheets. I lift my hands, palms up to feel it as it lands. As if everything is slow motion, I watch the drops each fall, land and bounce back up and out, breaking apart into several smaller drops of water.

"Peaceful isn't it?" A man stands above a shelf of culling waves preparing to bombard the shore. I tilt my head and stare at the man; trying to remember. Remember something. What should I be remembering?

"I love it here. It's my sanctuary. The wind, the waves, the rain, the grains of sand between my toes. Perfect bliss!" He says while still floating above that wave that has yet to release. Time seems to have gone from slowed to stopped. Nothing moves now. "Is there a better place for recuperating anywhere else in the world?" He asks while waving his arms to include the entire scene.

"Well, no, I suppose not," I answer. There it is! Right on the brink of exposure, something tickles the back of my mind; something wavers on the tip of my tongue…

"Dad?!?" I yell and look straight at the floating man. He smiles at me.

"Hi, Pumpkin Face," he says.

"How..? Where are we? What happened..(to you)?" I mean to say 'to you' but it never leaves my lips. I don't know what to say, what to ask first. I stand frozen in place, watching him watching me.

Pitch black. All the lights go out in a blink. Then, the cackling starts. Wretched, awful, screeching cackling breaks the peace. Flashes of lightning are the only source for light. Flashes that snap right in front of you and then crackle away, leaving veins of electricity that stretch out through the air from the point of impact. Dad is still floating above the water, that culling wave about ready to burst.

"Dad!!" I scream. He looks worried, but keeps his eyes steadfastly on me.

"We don't have much time, Calley. You must find the Libania Fretum. You are not safe in this world. You will be hunted by many; any who know of your true heritage. Some will guess at it when they see your pendant. Keep it hidden! Never take it off! It can protect you some..." Cackling fractures the message; ghostly masses of dark energy swarm around the man, slowly encompassing him wholly.

"Dad! No!!!" I scream, immobilized. Although frozen in place, I don't stop trying to fight against the darkness, the swirling, whirring masses of dark energy that attack my father. Inside, I am screaming, aching, fighting to get out, to break free, to save him.

"I love you, Calley!" he says and then his face too is gone; covered by the masses of dark energy. Cackling again crackles through the air, fracturing it in mimicry of the lightning veins; though there is no lightning close enough to hear that loudly. The cackling grows louder and louder just as the mass of dark energy that encompasses my father grows larger and larger; that wave still

mounting and culling into a massive tsunami bound to break out at any moment.

"He's mine now!" High-pitched, nasal screeches echo out of the dark energy. "Don't worry, my dear! You will see him again! You too will soon be mine! I will have you, Regina Alleynia! You too will soon be mine!" More cackles that screech on notes completely unnatural, causing the ear drums to bleed, echo out of the dark energy.

Furious anger urges me to move; every ounce of willpower is exerted, begging for movement, aching for control, longing for freedom. And then, release! Sweet release, my body relaxes and I again feel the sandy grains between my toes and the rain falling, slowly at first, on my outstretched arms. I breathe in deeply in preparation to jump into action to save my father, if it's not too late. Just as I look back up in his direction, the tsunami hits. At once I am dragged under the water. I can feel myself whirl around, being churned in the perpetual tumbler created by this wave. My lungs cry out for breathe, forcing my mouth open under the weight of the water; which then rams my throat like a bull rams a red flag. It floods my mouth, washing through my throat into my lungs. As they begin to fill with water, I can feel myself gagging, trying to breathe, and taking more and more water into my lungs.

"Calley! Calley! You must wake up! You must wake up now!" Luc is yelling, holding Calley's limp head and shoulders. He shakes her shoulders, he touches her face. She is cold and drenched in sweat. She isn't breathing. Suddenly, she inhales deeply and starts coughing, spewing dark liquid into the dirt.

"Oh thank *Deus*! You scared me half to death! You were screaming and thrashing around. And, then you went still, and the next second you were gagging, struggling to breath and thrusting your chest outward wildly; you were convulsing." Luc holds Calley's head in his arms, smoothing her damp hair away from her forehead and back behind her ear.

The struggled, heavy breaths slow and begin to steady. Calley sits up slightly, puts an arm around Luc and hugs him. She begins to sob, turning her head into his chest, hiding her face from the sky, and air, and earth. The sobbing flows like the culls and ebbs of the waves of the ocean; sometimes heavy and fast, other times slow and soft. Luc simply allows her the privacy to mourn and remains a fixed comfort on which she can lean. No words are exchanged as the two rest in each other's arms.

After a while, Calley's tear ducts are dry as the desert, there are no more tears left to be shed. Still, she holds onto Luc as if her life depended on his stable, firm grasp; to keep her tethered to this world, to keep her from drifting off into nothingness, to keep her from being encompassed by the massing dark energy that had taken her father.

"You should try to get some sleep, Calley. Sleep can be very healing. Blissful, dreamless sleep." Luc begins to pull away from Calley and she sits up, staring at the ground.

"I don't want to sleep if that's what I'm going to have in my mind." Then, a thought crosses Calley's mind as Luc gets onto his knees to shuffle away from her. "Stay with me?"

"I'm not leaving. I'll be right here, all night." Luc answers, a bit confused as he lowers himself into his large bedroll.

"No, hold me? Please? I can't face those dreams again alone." Calley looks from the ground up to Luc with pleading eyes.

"Of course," he says simply and turns to invite her into his arms. He lays on his bedroll, where he had been sleeping before Calley's nightmare, and he holds the blanket open invitingly.

With relief, Calley scoots in, up next to Luc. He wraps his long, thick-boned, muscular arm around her waist, pulling the blanket over the two. Against his massive chest, Calley feels tiny, petite, fragile; and safe. Every breath Luc takes, long and deep, feels like the waves on the ocean rocking Calley peacefully.

"Will you sing me another song?" Calley asks quietly.

"Of course," Luc says and then thinks for a minute before deciding which to sing. Then, he begins,

"In that place where sleep yet has no hold, but waking seems only in dreams,
In that place where comfort is all you know and yet noises still pierce your mind,
In that place where everything stands still while the world continues to wildly spin beyond,
In that place where eyelids close and dream lids open, hoping for another sweet escape,
In that place where fears and hurts all disappear and hopes and wishes are manifested anew,
In that place between asleep and awake where we lose ourselves,
In that place all our wishes and dreams can come true,"

Luc finishes and silently rocks Calley to sleep with the steady rhythm of his long, deep breathes.

Chapter Eighteen

THE NEXT MORNING, THE SUN rises, kissing the earth with its warmth. The creek spills giddily along its merry path. Fluffy, white puff-ball clouds drift lazily in the baby blue morning sky. Luc has already risen and startled the fire into life. Calley looks at him and sighs, sitting up and smiling to herself.

Am I falling for him or was it just the nightmare? Calley wonders as she wraps her arms around her knees, resting her head on them.

As if he heard her thoughts, Luc looks up from the fire at Calley, causing a flash of red to appear in her cheeks. "Good morning! That was a rough night. I hope you are feeling better now?" He watches her carefully, and asks genuinely; not the way people ask, nonchalantly, back in Calley's world; sarcastically, like people do when they're trying to make light of a situation either. He wasn't making fun, he wasn't taking advantage, and he wasn't abusing his new control over the situation. He was genuinely concerned. Calley sees all of this in his eyes and feels assured of it.

"If you ever feel like telling me about it, I am great at listening to long stories," Luc says and then turns back to the breakfast he cooks over the fire. The smell wafts up and rushes Calley's nostrils.

"What smells so good?" Calley asks out of curiosity, creeping towards Luc and the campfire.

"I heard some red coy swimming in the creek just before sunrise and thought it sounded good for breakfast. So, I got up and caught some." Luc says matter-of-factly.

"You *heard* them swimming in the creek?..." Calley waits for a response, but doesn't get one. "Right!

Of course you did!" Calley says, slowly remembering his Lipus heritage.

Luc simply turns the four fishes slowly on his wooden, make-shift picket on which the scaled, deboned fish are speared through and roasting over the fire. "Wait, how did you catch them? We don't have a fishing pole, or spear, or anything to catch fish with." Calley, puzzled, raises an eyebrow as she watches Luc. She'd never stopped to consider how Luc has caught their food to that point. It also hadn't ever come from water before.

"I'm Lipus, remember? My keen sense of hearing is from that power within me. And, I caught them using the art of *Atitilio*. If I'm careful to mask my own scent before going into the water, I can *titilo* them into one hand using the other." Calley still looks confused as she stares blankly at Luc. In another attempt to describe the effort to her, Luc uses his hands to imitate the action of *titilo*. "I keep one hand very still in the water while the other comes up behind the fish and …." He waves his fingers individually, as if tickling the air. He hands her one of the fishes and begins munching on another one.

"Oh! You tickle the fish!" Calley says with en-lightenment brightening her features as she giggles slight-ly at the thought of tickling a fish.

"Yes! Exactly! I tickle them into my other hand and then close the first on top and, wha-la! I've caught a fish!" Luc says and flashes a toothy, open-mouthed grin at Calley; unable to help being a little bit proud of himself. Calley is impressed too and shows it by returning the smile.

"Well, at least now we don't have to worry about water anymore," Calley adds, looking at the creek. "Hey, would you teach me to *Atitlio* like you?" Calley asks, looking at Luc.

"I suppose…" Luc answers with a mischievous smile. "But, it would require getting wet…"

"Oh, that's no problem! It's hot out here anyway!" Calley says as she starts pulling off all of her outer clothing, leaving on only her underwear.

Shocked, Luc sits and stares in amazement at Calley's brazenness.

"Well? Are you coming?" Calley asks as she takes a step into the creek.

Luc blinks once and then takes off his own shirt and follows her into the water.

"The first thing you should know is to never urinate in the water when you're trying to fish. They don't like it and they'll swim as far away from you as possible. Not to mention that it alerts them to your presence, which will also drive them away from you," Luc says as he lowers his body into the water up to his shoulders.

"I wouldn't dream of it!" Calley says, half joking and half appalled at the idea anyway. "So, what do we do first?"

"Well, first we have to identify a good spot where there might be a nest or a school of fish," Luc says as he moves cautiously and fluently in the water, almost as if he belongs there. "Here, Calley, come here, just like you saw me do," he says, motioning for her to join him.

Calley follows his command and slowly, cautiously, just as he had moved, joins him at the other side of the creek, close to the bank. Luc's eyes focus on a small cloudy pool between a large rock and the bank of the creek. Standing down river of the pool, Luc lowers himself into the water, completely submerging himself this time. A few minutes pass by and Calley begins to get nervous; though she doesn't dare make a noise or call out for him in case he is fine and she should scare away any fish he might catch.

After a time that seemed like forever to Calley, Luc finally emerges from the water, taking in a deep breath and holding a large, glimmering red, orange and yellow fish. The fish has whiskers, like a cat fish and even has the same kind of flat bill-like mouth. But, this fish glimmers in the sunlight as it wiggles in Luc's hands. With the changing positions of the fish, its color changes from red to orange to yellow and back again. This makes it difficult to determine individual scales from each other. Calley moves in closer to get a better look at the fish. She notices that on the bottom of each miniscule scale, there is a slight lightening of green! She hadn't noticed that from a distance.

"What kind of fish is that?" Calley asks Luc while reaching a hand out to stroke the fish scales.

"It's a *Magne Ora*. They don't have a big fishy taste like most fish do, and they don't have a lot of bones to deal with either. They're one of my personal favorites," Luc says as he lowers the fish back into the water and lets it go. After a second to realize where it was, the fish quickly swims away.

"So, what did you do to catch it?" Calley asks, watching the place where the fish had swam away.

"I place one hand inside the nest or at the back of the school, and then I place the other hand at the entrance of the nest or front of the school. Then, I slowly wiggle my fingers like this," Luc says and he shows her how he wiggles his fingers, holding them in the air for her to see. He brings his hands together gradually, wiggling his fingers all the way. "And, the fish think I'm just another part of the water life and follow my hands until I have it trapped and can lift it out of the water."

"That's awesome!" Calley says, very impressed, her smile spreading from ear to ear. "Can I try?" she asks.

"Sure, there's another one in that same nest. It's not as big, but it should be easier to catch for you," Luc answers and he moves aside and motions for Calley to take his place. "Now, first you need to lower yourself under the water. There, you must wait at least a minute for everything to settle after your entry. Your movements must be as fluid as the water so the fish don't get frightened or suspect danger," Luc says while Calley moves into his old spot. "Carefully, you reach one hand to the back of the nest while leaving the other one at the front. Lastly, you wiggle your fingers like I showed you and bring your hands together. Before the fish knows what is happening, your hands will meet and it will be caught," Luc says, matter-of-factly, as if he did this kind of thing every day. *Which he probably does,* Calley realizes.

"Okay, I think I'm ready," Calley says just before lowering herself completely under the water. After just a couple of minutes, she emerges from the water, empty handed; coughing and gagging for breath. "How do... you... hold your... breath for... so long?" Calley asks, taking breaks between words to take in large breaths. Once her breathing slows, she continues, "And, I couldn't even figure out how to move my fingers while I was down there. How do you do it?"

"Let's try something else," Luc says and he comes right up behind Calley, close enough that they are skin to skin. "Just follow my lead," Luc says and he takes her hands in his, sending warm shockwaves throughout her body. "Deep breathe in, and down we go," he says just before dipping them both beneath the water.

Under the water, Calley tries opening her eyes to see her surroundings to no avail. The water here is too cloudy and murky for her to see anything clearly enough. Fortunately, Luc is still holding onto her hands, and he crouches beneath the water with her practically in his lap. Beneath the water, they are weightless, floating peacefully. Luc guides Calley's hands to the positions he had specified before, with her fingers intertwined with his. His strong and steady arms keep them moving fluidly, with the water.

Then, she feels his fingers moving, wiggling back and forth with the rhythm of the water. Slowly, their hands move closer together. After another minute, their hands meet in the middle with something smooth, scaly and slippery between them. Quickly, Luc raises their hands and bodies up out of the water. Calley looks down at her hands as they are mixed into Luc's and she sees a smaller version of the *Magne Ora* Luc had caught earlier.

Calley smiles brightly at the fish and then looks up to Luc behind her. He smiles back and while they momentarily stare at each other, the fish slips out of their hands and back into the creek; startling the two back to reality. The fish swims away as fast as it can, but Calley doesn't seem to care.

"Shall we try again?" Luc asks, more than willing to maintain his hold around Calley.

Shakily, Calley responds, "I think I better sit down. Besides, look at the sky." Calley looks up to the sky. "It's almost midday and we haven't even gotten on the road yet," she says as she begins moving out of Luc's embrace and towards the shore.

"I'll catch us some of the *Magne Ora* for lunch so you can try it then," Luc says and he turns back to the creek and ducks underneath the water once more. Calley carefully guides her feet over the slick stones in the water back out and onto the dry ground.

When Luc returns to the fire, Calley has rekindled the embers into a nice flame for cooking the fish over. Taking some spices from his pouch, Luc sprinkles them over the fish. They roast the fish instead of boiling it in the pot this time. As soon as it is finished, Luc hands Calley a fish and takes another for himself.

All at once, Luc looks up in the direction they had traveled from the night before. Although there had been few trees along the way on the dirt road, closer to the creek, trees are much more abundant. Luc eyes the path along which they'd traveled, and follows it to a patch of low-lying branches that hang partly over the creek. He sits perfectly still, staring at the location until it is quite uncomfortable and becoming somewhat eerie for Calley.

"What? What is it?" Calley asks, squinting her eyes in the same direction Luc's eyes are focused on.

"I think we've been followed by someone or something from *Baghad*," Luc says quietly, lowering his gaze back onto his handful of *Magne Ora* fish. "It could be a spy from that Lamia Dominitri, sent to find us and report on our location. You are not safe here. She will want you, if she doesn't already." Luc glances at Calley and sees that she hasn't taken a single bite of her lunch yet.

"Are you feeling ill?" He asks her, using his eyes to gesture toward the fish in her hands.

"Oh, no, I'm fine," Calley chuckles nervously and then raises the fish to her mouth. Truthfully, Calley had hated fish all her life. But, the ache in her stomach and angry growl it made reminds her of just how hungry she is and she bites into the fish. Sweet, tangy juices flood Calley's taste buds. Although the fishy taste was still just barely there, it was different than how Calley had remembered it. This fishy taste was sweet, tangy and delicious!

"We need to get back on the road. The sooner we get to *Libania Fretum* the better," Luc says and he gets up and begins packing up the camp and putting out the fire.

"Tell me about it," Calley says as she finishes the last of her fish. "I saw my dad last night; in my dream I mean." Calley thinks about the dream, the nightmare, and remembers what Jethro had said about her pendant. "He told me to keep this hidden so no one can see, but to keep it on me at all times. He said that it could help to protect me." Calley says, pulling out the pendant and holding the chain so that the pendant spins from front to back. "How in the world can a simple little trinket help to protect me?" Calley asks, dumbfounded.

"May I look at it?" Luc asks, sitting next to Calley on the ground and holding out a hand.

Calley holds the pendant out for him to take and look at it. Turning it over in his hand, without taking it off of Calley's neck, Luc examines the pendant, front and back.

"In this realm, many people use a stone known as their *Qui* stone to channel their magic. This is one of those kinds of stones. The silver is usually used to connect the stone to the person. It enhances their abilities and smoothes the flow of magic from the person to the *Qui* stone. When the Majori began mixing the mortal and Essent Medei blood lines, magic became more difficult to use and the stones provided a convenient conduit for it," Luc says, pausing briefly.

And then pointing to the markings engraved into the silver, he says, "This insignia molded into the silver that surrounds the pendant is the crest of one of the Majori. I can't remember the specific one." Luc turns the pendant over and reads the inscription. "Alleynia…. You are Alleynia?" Luc almost whispers as he says this and he looks Calley in the eyes with an expression of respect and reverence. "Yes, you must keep that hidden, safe. We must leave immediately." Suddenly rushing, Luc sets to work, busying himself with packing up the camp and readying the horses.

"Who is Alleynia? Why is she so important?" Calley asks the buzzing Luc who is rushing to pack up.

"I will tell you once we are on the move. We must leave now," Luc says hurriedly.

Without another question, Calley gets up and helps clean up their camp site.

Chapter Nineteen

ONCE ON THEIR HORSES, LUC continues to evade Calley's questions, however.

"You said that once we were on the road again, you would tell me who Alleynia is and what is so important about her. Now, stop avoiding my questions and give me some answers," Calley says, becoming frustrated.

Luc sighs heavily and reluctantly answers the question, "The *Dea Regia* Alleynia is another nursery rhyme, told to primary children from infancy. The legend says that the *Dea Regia* Alleynia would bring the destruction of all magic and all magical creatures. It was based on a prophecy foretold by the *Saga Spectare;* basically she's a witch whose power is to bare the record of all that has, does and will come to pass," Luc explains.

Luc glances over to Calley to look for a reaction. When she simply continues to look to him with curiosity, he continues, "Soon after the Majori created the mortals, the *Saga Spectare* approached them with a vision she had had of one of the Majori falling in love with a mortal woman. And it was not just any mortal woman, but Eva, the mother of all mortal women that the Majorus would fall in love with. It was foretold by the *Saga Spectare* that the two would bear a daughter; and it would be that child that would end all magic and bring this world to destruction. Ever since then it was forbidden for any essent medei to fall in love with any mortal. It had already been forbidden for any Majorus to bear children let alone to fall in love with a mortal. Although many thought this prevented the prophecy from coming to pass, others believe it to be true and so communicate a warning in the form of the rhyme." Luc stops and looks over at Calley who stares back at him in awe.

"Will you tell me the rhyme?" Calley asks, blushing slightly.

Luc considers this a moment and then begins,
"There once was a Majorus, so mighty and fair,
He was held in high regard by his peers, on a pedestal there;
In that great home of the Majori, the great city in Caelestis,
Together they governed Calueria, home of various species;
When mortals were born, all in the land rejoiced,
A solution was found and the people had a choice;
A price they would pay for offspring they could bear,
For their gift of magic, finally a child could be theirs;
At last the races would not die,
For Abram and Eva's power they could buy;
Until one day when Eva disappeared,
Along with the Majorus whom all had revered;
The rumors of an affair spread far and wide,
Heavy with the Majorus' child, together they would hide;
A prophecy foretold of the forbidden love affair,
And of the destined child Eva would bear;
A child of destiny, a child of power,
A child who could love unconditional every hour;
With a magic far stronger than even the Majori,
With this child's life, all magic shall surely die;
The Dea Regia will bring an end to all magic and all magical creatures,
And at that last day, the only magic to survive will be hers."

Together they ride in silence for a few minutes. Calley thinks about all of this and tries to sort it all out in her mind. Luc wonders if Calley is that child in the rhyme, the one who would bring all magic to its end.

"Let me make sure I have this right: the Essent Medei cannot have children, the Majori created mortals who could to help the Essent Medei have children, but in doing so, they had to trade their magic…" Calley looks at Luc for confirmation, which he gives with a nod of his head.

"Okay," Calley takes in a deep breath, "So then this Majorus fell in love with Eva, the mother of all mortals, and she got pregnant with his child, and that child is supposed to bring the end of all magic." Calley pauses for a moment, thinking, "And, this *Dea Regia* Alleynia is supposed to be this child of destiny…. What does any of that have to do with me though?"

Calley worries: *It's not possible that I am this Dea Regia Alleynia! It's just not possible. Calm down, Calley! If it's not possible, then there's nothing here to worry about,* Calley tries to calm herself by concentrating on her breathing as she begins to feel herself hyperventilate.

"I don't know; but any who see that pendant will surely think that you are the *Dea Regia* spoken of in the rhyme," Luc says.

"That's just insane! I'm just a silly human girl who is lost in this crazy nightmare of a place!" Calley bursts out, certain that she must still be having some elaborate, never-ending nightmare.

***

A couple of hours pass in silent thought while the two trudge onward. Calley begins to take notice of the landscape they travel through.

This place is so weird! Calley thinks as she realizes that when she first got to this world, it was forests and hills and small, winding roads; everything was some tint of green and filled with warmth. Then, as they travelled, the temperature rose, the trees became sparse and the hills became taller and wider apart; beige became the fluent color. Just as they reached the city of Baghad, the land had changed to a smooth, flat desert plain. It was dry, windy, cold, and flat and gray there. Now, the scenes are once again changing. Patches of trees sprout up at the creek shoreline. Well, it started out as a creek, but as they travelled alongside it, it seems to be widening to the width of an average river.

As the evening begins with the sun dipping low on the western horizon, Luc and Calley stop to eat and water their horses. Calley notices that Luc is intently focused on some project and asks, "What are you up to?"

"Do you remember this morning when I told you that someone or something was following us from Baghad? They are still there. I plan to catch them. I'm setting a trap." Luc continues his busy work while Calley goes to the creek and rests her feet in the water.

A break would be nice, just for an hour, I guess, Calley thinks while she flicks her feet in and out of the water on the shore of the creek.

After a short while, Luc calls to Calley, "Come with me. We must make it look like we've left and are back on the road. We will go a ways farther and when I hear that trap, I will know we have captured our stalker." Luc retrieves his horse from where it is resting in the shade of a tree and mounts it. Calley follows suit with her horse and they again take to the road; however, much slower than they had that morning.

After an hour on the road, Calley asks, "Well? Anything yet?"

"No," Luc says, shaking his head and keeping his eyes forward on the road.

"How will you even know if your trap has been sprung?" Calley asks.

"I'll know. Lipus, remember. I'll hear or smell it. We are down wind; I will pick up that scent with no problem at all," Luc says confidently.

Calley giggles to herself and slightly shakes her head. *What a strange dream this is! I'm riding alongside the great ware-wolf of some romance-drama novel! I'm intruding on paper-Mache castles and breaking spells from wicked Lamia Dominitri. What's next? Prince Charming?* Calley giggles harder at the thought of it. Then, she remembers, *There was that nightmare; although nightmares aren't all that uncommon for me. I have them all the time. But, never like that... it was so real!*

Interrupting Calley's thoughts, Luc shouts, "Aha! We've got him! Follow me." Turning around and galloping now, Luc chases the path back to the spot where he had laid his trap. Calley follows behind at a trot. When Calley does catch up with Luc, he is standing next to a boy who is bound at the feet and covered in red goo that smells like he'd stirred a nest full of skunks, making them very upset.

I'm surprised I couldn't smell it on my way back here too! Calley thinks as she dismounts her horse and walks closer to the two boys.

"Calley! Tell your boy-friend who I am! We made a deal! I helped you defeat my own mother!" the boy yells from under the goo and stench.

"Jaxson?" Calley says, leaning in slightly closer, enough to see him better, but not so close as to get any of the nasty goo on herself. "Oh my goodness! I completely forgot!" Calley says, backing away from the nasty smelling red goo.

"Luc, this is Jaxson. I met him at the city of Baghad. He helped me break the spell that had you and all those people entranced; trapped there forever. The *Lamia Dominitri* wouldn't let you go when I asked, so we fought her. Jaxson actually saved you," Calley says, looking at Luc innocently and holding a hand over her nose.

"Thank you," Luc says as he pulls out a knife from a holster at his waist and cuts the bindings around Jaxson's wrists. "Now, leave us alone and be on your way; in another direction." Luc says while putting his blade away and turns to remount his horse.

"I'm afraid it doesn't work like that. We made a deal back in the castle that if I helped Calley free you that she would allow me to come with you." Jaxson smiles a mischievous, trouble-some smile; one side of his mouth is raised slightly higher than the other, and it is only slightly open. It makes Jaxson look like a prince and a drunkard at the same time. In spite of the rancid smell and red goo covering his face, something about that smile makes Calley's gut flutter and squirm with butterflies making Calley lose her balance. She looks up at Luc and feels steady again.

"He has a point, Luc. I did promise that he could come. At the time, I didn't see that I had another choice in the matter," Calley says dejectedly, crossing her arms in front of her chest.

A moment of silence passes between the three while Luc stares at the ground thinking it over in his mind. He studies Jaxson, who has sidled over to the edge of the creek to wash himself off, eyeing him up and down. He looks over at Calley, sighs and looks back at Jaxson.

"You take one misstep while travelling with us and it will mean your death. You remember your manners and keep your hands to yourself and we'll be just fine. I guess we don't have a choice in the matter." Looking at Calley now, Luc continues, "You made a promise, and you should keep it. He can come." Luc mounts his horse and Calley follows suit. "Come, we need to be going. We are in somewhat of a hurry."

"I just need to get my horse," Jaxson says as he disappears behind some tall bushes. A moment later, he comes out riding a tall, white stallion.

He almost looks like a prince! Calley thinks as she feels the butterflies come back. Thankful for the horse beneath her, Calley tightens her grip of the stern on the saddle to steady herself.

Then, Jaxson turns his face to reveal a patch of the sick, red stuff still clumped up in his hair above his ear! *Well, maybe just a boy after all?* Calley thinks while stifling a giggle and forcing away a smile. Luc also seems to have noticed as he too is hiding a smirk of his own.

"So, where are we headed off to anyway?" Jaxson asks casually as they start back down the road again.

"We're taking Calley home," Luc answers before Calley has a chance to even consider the question. "And you will leave it at that." Luc shoots Jaxson a look that could kill; just as a warning, but severe enough that Jaxson ceases that line of questioning.

"Okay, I'm not to ask about Calley's home, got it. Well, then, where are you from, Luc?" Jaxson asks, receiving a sideways glance of pure annoyance from Luc.

"Kinsland," Luc says sternly through clenched jaws.

"That's odd. You're much too tall for Kinsfolk. Were you born there? Or, did you just live there for a time?" Jaxson continues in a non-committal, separated kind of way.

It's almost as if he doesn't even realize that he's annoying Luc. He seems completely oblivious, Calley thinks as she listens to the boys' exchange.

"I was raised there," Luc's jaw seems set more so now, as if he's actually grinding his teeth.

"Tell us about you, Jaxson. How did you come to live in that castle? Your mother said something about the Queen not being able to bear the King a child; as if she wasn't the Queen then. What did she mean by that?" Calley asks out of curiosity, trying to change the subject.

"Well, according to mother, she was a servant to the queen when the king took her as a mistress. When she got pregnant with me, she told the king and he sent her away to live outside of his kingdom's boundaries to keep it hidden. He commanded that any who knew of the affair or the pregnancy to be either exiled as well or hanged. With pregnancy being so rare, it was imminent that the queen at least would discover it." Jaxson pauses for a moment.

"Wait. How did she get pregnant in the first place? I thought the Essent Med-" Calley begins to say and is cut off by Luc clearing his throat. Calley remembers that Jaxson doesn't know she is mortal and realizes she was about to tell him by referring to her supposed self in the third person by saying 'Essent Medei'. "So, how did she even get pregnant?" Calley says slower and more carefully watching her words.

Jaxson doesn't seem to even have noticed the pause and continues without missing a beat, "Mother is one-quarter mortal; although she can still wield magic through the use of her *Qui* stone. Her mortal part allowed her to conceive me, while the Essent Medei in her allows her to use magic," Jaxson says. "Of course, she wouldn't have needed the *Qui* stone if she were 100% Essent Medei, but there aren't many left who are," he adds matter-of-factly.

Chapter Twenty

WHEN THEY STOP FOR THE NIGHT, Jaxson offers to help Calley with everything she tries to do. Calley pulls out their cooking pot from one of the packs and goes to collect water to boil from the creek.

Upon returning, Jaxson takes the pot from her and says, "You shouldn't be lifting such a heavy pot. Allow me to take it," Jaxson brings it over to the fire which Luc has constructed while Calley gathered the water. "Where do I put this now?" Jaxson asks eyeing the fire.

"Here," Calley says and reaches to take the pot from him. Jaxson resists her, insisting that he do it himself, and he pulls the pot away abruptly.

The momentum of the pull away causes Jaxson to trip when he backs up. Covered in water now, Jaxson shouts, "For *Deus* sake! I try to do something nice to help out and this is what I get!"

After Jaxson storms off, Calley shakes her head, picks up the pot and fills it herself at the creek.

Luc and Calley had gotten so used to doing things, just between the two of them, that it leaves little for Jaxson to do. When Calley takes out a knife and begins cutting up left-over fish from the morning to put into the pot, Jaxson reappears, takes the blade and says, "Here, allow me."

Calley releases the knife immediately, worried she might get cut as he jerks it from her hand. She then goes and sits with her back against a tree, starting to get annoyed with all of Jaxson's 'helpfulness'.

He might be hot, but he doesn't know anything about being on the road or taking care of himself; like cooking dinner or surviving alone, Calley contemplates.

As they wait for the fish to cook into a stew, Jaxson asks, "So, where do we sleep?" looking obliviously from Luc to Calley. The two exchange glances and Luc answers, "You're sitting on your bed now," motioning to the ground as he speaks.

"On the ground? We sleep on the ground?" Jaxson says, appalled at the idea.

"Not on the bare ground. We have blanket rolls that we lay out to sleep on," Calley explains.

"Oh, well I guess that's not so bad," Jaxson says, stirring the pot impatiently.

"No, it's not so bad," Luc repeats sarcastically. "But we do only have the two blanket rolls," he says emphasizing the word 'two'. "Unless you thought to bring one before running away from your castle…" Luc offers, looking over at Jaxson and rhetorically daring him to pull one out of thin air.

"Well, no, I didn't actually…" Jaxson says, frowning and looking at the ground. "But, wait a minute!" he says, and getting up, he walks over to his stallion. Once Jaxson moves away from the stew pot, Calley slides up next to it, stirring it and breathing in its aroma. After rifling through the saddle bags for a few minutes, Jaxson comes back to the fire and announces, "Here we go!" He lays out the blanket roll to reveal plush fleece and a down feather-filled mat for sleeping on.

Annoyed at his dumb luck, Luc says, "Yes, good for you," and he adds some of his herbs to the stew.

Calley giggles quietly as she watches the exchange and then says, "Stew's done."

As Calley and Luc slurp their stew without a spoon in sight, Jaxson just watches in wonder for a minute. Then, Jaxson attempts to mimic them by bringing his own bowl to his lips, all the while watching Calley and Luc carefully.

"Ouch!" Jaxson squeals, jumping back and spilling his stew all over. Calley can't help but laugh at the sight.

"It's hot!" Jaxson complains while Calley and Luc just laugh at him. Looking between the two of them laughing and the whole mess of a situation, Jaxson says, "Yeah, I guess it's pretty funny," and he too chuckles a bit, lightening the mood.

As Calley cleans the pot out next to the creek, Jaxson walks up and offers to help.

"No, thanks. I can handle this," Calley answers. Jaxson shrugs his shoulders and walks back to the fire.

He really wanted to help with the clean-up, didn't he? Calley thinks sarcastically. *I guess the allure of the 'exploration' has passed. What happened to 'Mr. Helpful'?* Calley sighs and returns to the pot.

***

In the morning, Luc and Calley get up like they usually would; early with the sun rise. Jaxson is still in his blanket roll, snoring as they bring the fire back to life and begin cooking some breakfast. Luc pulls out a bag of oats from one of his packs.

"Where'd you get that?" Calley asks at the welcome sight.

"Back at the castle of Baghad. I guess I found the kitchen even in that trance-like state I was in. I must have been really hungry. When we first stopped after leaving there I found it in my pack," Luc answers pouring some into the pot, in which the water has come to a boil.

"Oh, that reminds me," Calley says and she gets up and walks over to her horse whereon her pack is strapped. After pulling something wrapped in cloth out, she walks back over to Luc. "Here, take a look at this," she says, handing it to him.

Luc opens the cloth to reveal the sword hilt she had taken from the cobalt workshop in the castle turret. He weighs it in his hands and looks it over, turning it over and slightly bouncing it on his palms. He balances it on the palm of one hand. Finally, he says, "It's good. Very well crafted. But where's the blade to it?" he asks, looking from the sword hilt up to Calley.

"I don't know. That's how it was when I found it," Calley says and Luc hands it back to her.

Jaxson stirs and sits up, yawning and stretching his arms. "Aren't you two early risers?" he asks mid yawn.

"We need to get back on the road," Luc tells him. "This isn't a trip of leisure. We need to get Calley home safely and as soon as possible," Luc says annoyed at Jaxson once more, and he turns his attention to the pot of oats.

"What's that?" Jaxson asks as he notices the hilt in Calley's hands. He gets up and slides in next to her on the ground.

"Oh, you have it!" he exclaims excitedly. "I'd thought maybe it had been destroyed with the castle," Jaxson says, holding his hands out as if expecting Calley to give it to him. Hesitantly, she hands the sword hilt over to Jaxson.

"It's yours?" she asks, somewhat dismayed. "It's beautiful," Calley adds, looking at it longingly, almost mesmerized by it. "But, it doesn't have a blade attached. I just liked it for the stone on it," she says, almost apologetically.

"That's not a problem," Jaxson says, getting up. He walks over to his saddlebags and pulls out something large, wrapped in layers of thick, ragged clothes. "Here's my blade," he says, bringing the parcel over to Calley and exposing the newly refined and sharpened blade that she'd seen the cobalt working on back in the forge in Baghad. "All I need now is fire," he says, eyeing the small blaze over which Luc stirs the breakfast oats. "After we eat I suppose," Jaxson says as he sets the blade down and sits next to Calley again.

Once breakfast is finished, Jaxson adds wood to their fire, creating much larger, much hotter flames. He takes the dull side of the sword blade and, using the thick clothes for protection as he grips the sharp blade, he holds it over the flames until it becomes red hot. Quickly, Jaxson jams the sword's end into a notch in the sword hilt. As soon as he does this, he mutters magical words which act to bind the two pieces and cool the hot metal all at once.

Finally, Jaxson lifts the sword, as a whole, into the air and swings it around. He shows off his skills with the blade as he dances around for a few minutes. Luc yawns and leans back onto his hands, while Calley sits up, fully interested and completely impressed by the show.

***

Back on the road again, Luc's usual songs and stories are replaced by Jaxson's tales of mighty knights and princes who save their villages from destruction by some wicked *Striga* or other. One that he tells seems to especially grab Calley's attention.

"It's like *Beauty and the Beast*!" she says after he tells the story, "except that in your story, Beauty saves the Beast from the village mob by using a *Qui* stone to summon all of the animals from the surrounding forest to her aid. Then, the animals ravish the castle invaders, I mean."

"I heard a different version of the story anyway," she says attempting to cover up the fact that this was all news to her.

"In the end of the story, *Gemma* and *Bestum* are left alone in the forest castle with only the animals for company. *Bestum* was a Lipus who had been hexed by the jealous *Dea Luna* because although she loved him, he did not return her feelings. He was to always remain in his *vere corpus* and to never be able to change back into a man," Jaxson concludes. "*Bestum* never did regain his human form, but that didn't matter to *Gemma*. Her power was with the animals anyway. She was able to talk to them and know what they were thinking. In a way, I guess you could say that they were perfect together," Jaxson says, cocking his head to one side and smirking at Calley.

Shivers spread down Calley's spine and throughout her body as he gives her that smirk of a smile; successfully awakening butterflies in the pit of her belly again.

Chapter Twenty-One

A FEW DAYS PASS BY WITH little to no proof of civilization anywhere. The countryside continues to change as they progress westward. Large, spread-out rolling hills appear on the horizon accompanied by fields of different kinds of crops. One field seems to be covered with something that looks oddly similar to clover, but is as big as a dinner plate. Another field is covered with a crop that grows on vines. *Pumpkins or squash maybe?* Calley wonders about the round green bulbs on the vines.

As they make their way to the top of a large hill, the view they find at the top takes their breath away. The sun is setting behind the mountains in the distance, casting a shadow over the valley. Calley can't help but stop her horse so she can take in the entire view. A large valley opens up before them, covered with more fields full of crops. There are a few houses all built closer together in the center of the fields. Smoke rises from their chimney stacks. In the distance, a chain of mountains make up the back-drop to complete the whole scene. Closer to them is a long, narrow lake that covers half of the land in sight. A long, thin snake-like dirt path boarders the lake and travels all the way from their current path past the houses, and on to the *Aurura Mons*.

"Those are the *Aurura Mons*. We must travel through them using the *Aurura Crena*. The *Flu Lumens* gathers there at the head of the *Alace Lac* and it flows west into the *Aurura Mons*." Luc points to a small lake not far from them, where they can see that various small creeks do empty into it. At the opposite end of the lake from where they now stand, you can see a small dam with water trickling over it, forming a large river that continues west into the mountains.

That must be the Flu Lumens! Calley thinks as she strains her eyes to see the river.

"We are running low on supplies again. Do you think someone there will trade with us for what we need?" Calley asks, thinking about the now empty sack of oats, her new favorite breakfast.

"I'm not sure, but I think we should try anyway," Luc says and kicks his horse into motion. Calley and Jaxson follow him down the hill, towards the little houses in the distance.

"It's awfully late," Calley mentions as she feels the coolness of the night breeze blow across her skin. A slight shiver runs down her spine. "Maybe we should just make camp for the night and approach them in the morning?" she suggests, yawning.

"We're too close already, we should push on. If they see our camp fire, they may think that we've come to intrude on their lands or to steal their crops. I think it would be best if we continue forward and make them aware of our presence tonight," Luc suggests wisely.

"I'm happy with whichever you two choose. It doesn't matter much to me either way," Jaxson adds from behind them.

The group continues on the path all the way to the group of houses. As they approach the first house, they see three children, looking about the ages of a preteen, a school age and a preschool child, playing in the front yard. They are chasing each other in turn, playing a kind of tag game. A few adults are sitting on one of the house porches watching. As the newcomers walk past the first house, the adults begin to take notice of the strangers.

Getting up, the adults walk to meet the group on the road. Two women and a man reach Luc, Calley and Jaxson just as they make it passed the first of the houses.

"Hello, strangers, is there something we can do for you?" the man says, stopping short and crossing his arms protectively.

"We are just passing through. We mean to make our way through the *Aurura Crena* in order to reach the *Libania Fretum*. We are in need of some supplies if you are willing to trade. We don't have much, but we do hope to be able come to an agreement with you," Luc says, looking directly at the man.

The man looks at the shorter of the two women and nods his head just barely enough to be noticed. "Mallory! Come here, child," the woman says and the littlest girl, the youngest of the children, comes running toward them.

"Yes, mama?" Mallory asks.

"Go inside and fetch me the *Vere Marmo*," the woman says and the little girl skips inside the house. After only a moment, she is back, skipping all the way back to the group.

"Thank you, *Puella*. Please tell your cousins that it is time to go inside and get ready for bed." The woman takes the small, white crystal from the child who then continues skipping all the way to the other children.

"You will hold this crystal while you tell us what you need and why you are here. If you lie, we will know." After the woman hands the crystal to Luc, the man then begins his line of questioning, "Why do you seek the *Libania Fretum*?"

"We are looking for a way to get our friend home," Luc answers straight away. "We seek an audience with the *Duz de Prundencum*," Luc answers with more information than he'd meant to share.

"What are your names and what do you mean to do while you are here in our valley?" the man asks.

"I am Luc, this is Calley and that is Jaxson," Luc says pointing to Calley and Jaxson one at a time. "We mean only to rest for a night, trade for supplies and then continue on our way," Luc says, keeping his face stern and sincere. "We will be on our way first thing in the morning if you want us to leave and will allow us to just rest here on your land for the night," Luc adds.

"Do you mean us any harm?" the man asks, turning his head slightly in doubt.

"No, we do not mean you any harm. We simply want to rest, trade and continue our travels," Luc says.

Luc's very diplomatic, Calley thinks. *They are not used to visitors, are they? I wonder what the Vere Marmo would do if Luc lied to them,* Calley marvels.

"What are you in need of, and what have you to trade for it?" the man asks, easing his stature slightly by taking the *Vere Marmo* and resting his hands down by his sides.

"We need food and healing herbs for the rest of our trip. And, we would ask your permission to make a camp for the night on your lands. We will be gone at first light in the morning if that is what you desire," Luc answers. "As for trading, we have some gold thrushes we could pay you in exchange for your food and herbs. We also have some other herbs you may like to trade for. I have a pack full of herbs I have collected along our way. We have come across many wild herbs in our travels so far," Luc offers.

The man sighs, "Very well, then. You may make your camp here in the road, between our homes where we may keep an eye on you. You may stay two nights. We have not yet harvested our spring crop yet, the *seligro*, and had planned to do that tomorrow. Once we have done that, we can trade with you for the food you need. In exchange for food, all I ask is that you help us in the harvest. In truth, our crops have grown more abundant than we expected due to very welcome, and yet unanticipated, rains that we have received over the last month. My name is Saunder," the man says. Then, gesturing to the women with him one at a time, starting with the taller of the two, he says, "this is my sister, Naomi, and this is my wife, Hazel; she may want to browse through your pack of herbs to trade with you; she is our healer," the man says, placing an arm around the shorter, more plump woman's shoulders.

"Thank you! We will not abuse your hospitality," Luc says, slightly lowering his head in respect. "We will make our camp here for the night and help in the harvesting come sunrise," he promises.

With that, Saunder, Hazel and Naomi split up and find their way into their separate houses; Saunder and Hazel go into one house and Naomi into the one across the dirt road from theirs. Calley remembers seeing the children split up likewise, each one into a different house. *I wonder who lives in that other house down there. If they are brother and sister, could it be another sibling? That older boy went into that house,* Calley considers it for a moment.

After a minute, Mallory skips out of her house, smiling and waving to Calley, and continues up to the last house on the little dirt road. She knocks on the door and waits. When an elderly man answers the door, she talks for him for a minute. He pats her on the head and shuts the door. Mallory then skips back to her own house and goes inside.

I wonder if that house belongs to their father then, Calley wonders to herself while helping Luc to ready a fire and lay out blanket rolls. While Luc starts the fire for warmth, Calley lays out the blanket rolls around it. As soon as she lays Jaxson's roll down, he flops down onto it, forcing a wave of dust and dirt to kick up into Calley's face.

Coughing, Calley says, slightly annoyed, "Jaxson! Really? Why don't you give us a hand?"

"It looks to me like you're already done. Not much for me to help with now anyway," Jaxson says as he makes himself comfortable on his plush, fleece blanket roll. He figures that he'd helped enough for one journey already.

Calley glares at him and says, "Some prince you are! I thought princes were supposed to be chivalrous and noble. You have been nothing but a spoiled brat so far though," Calley accuses, rolling her eyes. By now, Luc has got the fire started and is making himself comfortable in his own blanket roll. In no time at all, he is snoring loudly.

I guess it doesn't bother Luc, Calley thinks and rolls her eyes again. *Some prince! Try pig!* Calley watches as Jaxson wrestles around in his blanket roll, making strange noises. *He even snorts like one and shuffles in his blankets like a hog digging his snout in the mud in search of a truffle,* Calley thinks and smiles at her comparison and analogy, feeling proud of herself for making the connection. *So, if he is so annoying, why do I keep getting these feelings around him?* Calley wonders, remembering the butterflies in her belly. For some reason, they aren't there right now.

"I will never understand how anyone can find any sleep in these things, on the ground!" Jaxson complains, even though his blanket roll is far more comfortable than Calley's or Luc's.

"You didn't have to come along, you know. If you don't like it, then go back to Baghad." Calley wiggles herself into her own blanket roll and turns away from the fire and away from the boys. She doesn't want to have to face either of them; especially not Jaxson. She doesn't know what it is with him lately, but Jaxson has been acting more like a spoiled brat each day.

I guess the novelty of this little trip really has worn off. Now, reality is setting in for him. I don't know why he even stays with us, Calley thinks as she drifts to sleep.

***

The next morning, before the sun is even raised, Luc rouses Calley and Jaxson. "It's time to get ready to help with the harvest," he says. "They've already gotten started." He gets his shoes on and laced up and heads off into the fields.

Calley quickly gets up and starts getting ready to work. Jaxson, on the other hand, rolls over in his blanket roll and says, "Wake me in an hour or so."

"No, you're getting up now, your majesty!" Calley says harshly, finally reaching the limit of her patience, as she grabs Jaxson's blanket roll on the side and pulls up. The smooth soil makes the bag roll easily out from under the boy. "Get up!" Calley yells at him and stomps off leaving a dazed and confused Jaxson to shake off the dirt and make a decision. A few minutes later, Jaxson catches up with Calley and Luc.

"Good morning to you, too, young Magistre!" Jaxson says to Calley in a half-mocking, half-admiring tone as he sidles alongside her. He can't decide whether he likes her or hates her. But, he is sure that she is someone he wants to get to know better. She is someone to be around. He is drawn to her and he doesn't know why, other than something about her attracts him to her. Little does he know that she too has the same mixed feelings about him. Every time Jaxson is close to her, he ignites nervous butterflies in her belly. She's gotten used to them but they still cause a nuisance to her every time he comes too near to her.

This frustrates Calley because Jaxson can be so inconsiderate, conceited and even downright rude at times.

Calley, Jaxson and Luc follow the directions given by Hazel about how to harvest the *seligro*. Even the children are helping with the harvest. There are two other people helping to harvest that they did not meet the night before. Calley recognizes the elderly man she'd seen answer the door when Mallory knocked on it last night.

I guess they're the people who live in the last house, Calley thinks. There isn't time for introductions; all are busy at work, intent on getting the harvest in before day's end.

By midday, they are all hot and sweaty and ready for a break. Hazel brings out a couple of loaves of bread, a block of cheese and a pitcher of clear liquid she calls *podulce*. Everyone is offered a piece of bread, a piece of cheese and a cup full of the *podulce*. The bread is sweet, tangy and soft. The cheese is very similar to Gouda, and Calley can't help but ask, "Where do you get your cheese?"

"I made it from the milk I get from our *Bonamaru*, our cow. We have a few of them between our three families," Hazel answers. Noticing the awkward glances between the other residents and the group of newcomers, Hazel adds, "Oh, this is our father, Kaleb," Hazel points to the elderly man Calley had seen briefly the night before. "And, this is our brother, Kalen," Hazel nods at the oldest of the children, a young man, and then reaches out and grabs the hand of the younger of the two girls. "And these are the children: Mallory is ours." Lastly, Hazel nods towards the older of the two girls and says, "And, Miah is Naomi's daughter."

"How do you make this bread? It's delicious!" Calley asks, noting how sweet, tangy and soft the bread is.

"We call it *Triceres*. I make it from the *seligro* which we grow. It gives it the flavor. The *seligro* acts as both the sugar and the yeast," Hazel answers, flattered.

"Mama, can we play for a little bit before we go back to work?" Mallory asks Hazel. Calley can tell that Hazel is a loving mother because of the way she looks at Mallory and strokes the girl's hair as she answers her.

"Yes dear. Be careful to stay away from the water!" Hazel says and the three youngsters run towards the lake shore.

When Calley looks over to the children, she sees Kalen reach into the water of the lake and pull something the size of a soft ball out. Kalen then blows on the scaly, white object, causing the scales to ruffle with the motion of the air. They turn into fluffy, white feathers which start to bristle up and fan out. He smoothes the feathers to the sides and fans them out like two wings. Finally, Kalen stands up, takes aim, and throws the object like one would throw a javelin or paper airplane. The object soars into the air, still at first, and then the wings begin to flap like a bird's. Mallory is thrilled by the flapping and giggles and squeals as she watches it soar and dive around them.

Kalen mutters something Calley can't hear and the object returns to him. Once back in his hands, the object resumes its original form of a scaly, white soft-ball sized inanimate thing.

"My turn! My turn!" Mallory squeals as Kalen reaches into the water and pulls out another scaly, soft-ball sized object. This one is very colorful and grows feathers in shades of red, yellow, blue and purple. It reminds Calley of the Mardi Gras celebrations in New Orleans. Kalen blows on it just like the one before to puff out the feathers and then hands it to Mallory, who then throws it into the air as high as she can. The object whirls up and away from her, and just before falling back to the earth a gust of wind catches it and inspires the wings to take life, just like the first one did.

"They're *Pinundas*. They grow wild along the shore of the lake. One day, years ago, when he was younger, Kalen figured out that they could do that with them. The children certainly enjoy it. They are very delicious also!" Naomi says, speaking to them for the first time since they arrived.

"Well, I suppose it's time to get back to work," Saunder says as he stands up. "Thank you for lunch, my dear. It was delicious as always." All of the rest of the adults get up and walk solemnly back into the field in order to hopefully finish the harvest. Calley is the last to leave the lake shore where the children still play with their new toys. She is mesmerized by the amazing way in which the *Pinundas* take on a life of their own once they're in the air.

It's almost as if they were just playing dead before and once they feel the air on their wings, they realize they are free, Calley thinks, astounded by the versatile creatures.

Calley walks along the banks of the lake back to the part of the field she had been working in that morning. She is still not far from where the children play and giggle when she hears a whoosh by her ear and feels a slight brush of something as it flies by her. Mallory's *pinunda* zooms passed Calley and shoots off over the water of the lake.

Like a balloon that's being deflated, the *pinunda* fizzles and whirls in every direction until at last it comes to rest in the air and just drops into the water about ten feet into the lake. Without thinking, Calley jumps into the water to retrieve the *pinunda* for Mallory who comes running up to the side of the lake where Calley had entered it. She doesn't dare go into the water herself, so she waits at the edge of the water for Calley to return with her toy.

Before Calley reaches the *pinunda*, the water makes its way all the way up her thighs and almost to her buttocks. The *pinunda* floats on the water where it landed, again in its scaly ball state without any feathers. She grabs hold of it and trudges back out of the water, soaked to her waist now.

   With mouths open and eyes wide, the children on the shore stare as Calley returns to them with the *pinunda*. Calley hands the *pinunda* back to Mallory, smiling as she says, "Here you go."

   "Thank you. Are you okay?" Mallory asks Calley worriedly as she takes the *pinunda*.

   "Yeah, I'm fine. Why wouldn't I be?" Calley says reciprocally, shaking her head slightly.

   "Oh, nothing I guess. Thanks!" Mallory says and then skips back off to where they had first found the *pinunda.*

   Calley goes back to work in the field, helping in the harvesting of the *seligro*. The rest of the afternoon is uneventful as they harvest the *seligro*.

Chapter Twenty-Two

LATER THAT AFTERNOON, CALLEY BEGINS feel-
ing ill. She shivers although it's been warm all day, and
she feels dizzy, weak and nauseas. Although the harvest
isn't finished, Calley asks to be excused and she goes and
sits down to rest where they had all eaten lunch that day.

"Are you all right?" Mallory asks as she comes up
to Calley. Putting her hand on Calley's forehead, she says,
"You are burning up. I'm going to get Mama!" Before
Calley could object, Mallory was running to fetch her
mother.

"What's the matter?" Hazel says as she approaches Calley, who is barely managing to keep her head up.
Suddenly, Calley heaves forward, turning slightly, and
vomits into a patch of grass next to her. "Oh dear, we
have a problem, don't we?" Hazel says, laying the back of
her hand on Calley's forehead.

"Mama, she went into the *Alace Lac* when my
pinunda fell in the water. Did it do something to her?"
Mallory asks showing her concern. Hazel puts her hands
to Calley's face and forehead, feeling the temperature of
her skin.

"You're fevered, my dear," she says to Calley who
just manages to keep another upheaval attack from making its way out. "Saunder! Father! Come quickly!" Hazel
calls out into the field with a booming voice incompatible
with her petite frame.

The men, including Jaxson and Luc, jog out of the
fields and up to the women. "What's going on?" Saunder
asks on approach.

"She has *cercarciae* from the *Alace Lac*. Mallory
said that she went into the lake after her *pinunda* when it

went in. Now, she is fevered, vomiting and I suspect if I check her legs I will find welts where they have burrowed into her flesh." Hazel looks at Saunder, slightly annoyed at Calley's ignorance, but also genuinely concerned for her health.

"What do we need to do to help her?" Luc asks, stepping forward and up next to Calley. He kneels down so that he is eye level with her and places a hand on her shoulder as an attempt to comfort. Calley smiles at him weakly, then is overcome with another upheaval attack and is again lurching over the same patch of grass as before. Luc moves just in time to dodge it.

"Carry her inside and lay her on the table," Hazel commands and then goes into the house first. She starts opening cupboards and pulling out different items: clean strips of cloth, a tool that looks like a pair of tongs or gigantic tweezers, and herbs from a pantry full of them. As Luc brings Calley into the house, he is followed by the rest. Hazel is shuffling through her herb pantry, looking for something frantically.

"No, no, no, no, NO! It's not here!" she says as she holds each small glass bottle up, reads its label and sets it down to pick up the next one. Reaching in the back of the pantry, Hazel says, "Ah! Here it is! Well, what's left of it that is." Hazel looks down into the bottle which holds only a remnant of its previous contents.

"We will need more *jenabar,* a root that grows in the lake, if we're to save the girl. Mallory, do you remember what *jenabar* looks like? Do you think you could lead Luc or Jaxson there to pick some?" Hazel asks the little girl, who shakes her head, eyes watering and looking very worried. "It's okay, *Puella*. She's going to be okay." Hazel looks up at Calley, then over to Luc. "I will have to go gather some myself, then. While I'm gone, you will need to begin-"

"I know what *jenabar* is. I can gather it. How much of it do you need?" Luc suggests and asks, "Where does it grow in the most abundance here?"

"I will go with you. I can show you where it grows," Saunder says as he steps forward and holds out his hand.

"Fill this bag," Hazel retrieves a bag from the herb pantry and hands it to Saunder. "It grows most abundantly about 4 kilometers north-west of here, where the lake narrows and becomes the *Flu Lumens*. You will need to hurry. That root, the *jenabar,* needs to be crushed and inserted into every burrow they've made if she is to live and keep the use of her legs," Hazel answers and begins crushing what *jenabar* she has in a pestle.

Luc and Saunder leave immediately without a moment's hesitation. Luc mounts his horse. Saunder stops before an open field and whistles. After only a second or two, a wild mare comes galloping toward Saunder. He mounts her bareback and they gallop off in the direction they were given, leaving Calley in the hands of people Luc barely knows and is unsure of whether or not he trusts them. But, he realizes that sometimes faith is required when a miracle is needed. Besides, he doesn't have time to question it.

"Mallory," Hazel says, "go and get a pitcher of water from the well. Bring it and place it over the hearth to boil, okay?" Mallory leaves at once, immediately obeying her mother. "And, you," Hazel points to Jaxson who has been hiding in the shadowy corner of the room, "you have power. You will aide me. Bring that bucket there before she vomits all over my rug. Father, will you watch the children at the other house while we work here, please?" The old man nods his head and leads the other two children out of the house.

Jaxson hesitantly brings the bucket to Hazel at the table where Calley lays coughing and heaving about ready to spew onto the floor. He gets the bucket underneath her just in time for her to lean her head over the side of the table and vomit. Just as he sets the bucket down, she vomits and he is splattered with the vile, acidic liquid.

"Oh go clean yourself off! There's soap in the bath house you may use," she says and Jaxson begins to head out of the front door. "It's out behind the house, that way," she says, pointing in the opposite direction. "It's shared by all our families; we only have the one, so please be mindful of that when you're using it to clean up." Jaxson turns and disappears with a wave of his hand to signal thanks to Hazel.

Calley is itching terribly all over her legs. While Calley scratches at her legs, Hazel uses a knife to slice up the slacks Calley is wearing. Once the skin is exposed, Hazel calculates how many *cercarciae* have gotten into Calley. She sees the welts, the size of cherries, spread out along both calves and thighs. On Calley's feet, one is clear of wounds and the other only has one burrowed in. The higher up on Calley's legs the more there are it seems.

"My word, child! I never have seen so many take such a liking to one person before in all my years! Your flesh must taste to them like honey, I swear!" Hazel tells Calley as she inspects Calley's legs.

"Ugh," Calley moans and turns her head away from the older woman. *I sure hope she doesn't guess that I'm human! Could they have gotten to me so badly because I'm human? Oh, this is miserable! Luc, please hurry!* Calley thinks while cringing, bring her knees up and grabbing her stomach, eyes shut tight and face screwed up in agony.

***

"What will the *cercarciae* do to her?" Luc asks Saunder as they ride.

"The *cercarciae* are actually part of the *pinunda*. They start out in the blossom, or mouth. The *Pinunda*s grow in the lake. They are long and rope like, they're long enough to reach the top of the water. The *cercarciae* is born in the fruit of the *pinunda*. When it begins to bud, the *cercarciae* is in its egg state. Once the bud blossoms, the *cercarciae* hatches and is a larvae. It acts like a long, thin tongue of the *pinunda*, attaching itself to any living thing that passes close enough and holding on. If the animal or creature stays still long enough, which it doesn't take long, they can burrow into the flesh, pulling the rest of their bodies with them into the body of the animal or creature. Most of the time, you don't even feel it happening. Some have felt a slight tickling sensation when they first attached themselves to them, but nothing more." Saunder pauses for a moment and looks around them; they are at a crossroads. "This way," He says and leads Luc down one of the paths.

"I thought you said they were plants; like the ones the kids were playing with. They seemed harmless," Luc says, confused.

"It's not a plant. It's a parasite when it is in larva state. Once the larvae of the *cercarciae* becomes an adult, it leaves the *pinunda*. Then, they are safe to handle. That is why we tell the children to stay out of the *Alace Lac*," Saunder explains, staring straight ahead.

"So, what will they do to her?" Luc asks, holding back his own nausea at the description of the *cercarciae*.

"They'll continue to burrow until they reach her bones. At which point they will attach themselves along the outsides of the bones. Then, they will suck the bones dry of any nutrients, blood, and marrow. It's an agonizingly painful way to die. I've have many a dog die from them. We just can't keep those ridiculous creatures out of the water! The stupidest of animals, dogs are!" Saunder insists, shaking his head as he remembers the last dog he had.

"And, what happens if these *cercarciae* aren't removed in time?" Luc asks hesitantly.

"Well, obviously the worst case is death. But, depending on how long they've been inside the body, they can cause paralysis of part or all of the body. This can spread to the internal organs, which is what then leads to death," Saunder says automatically, without any emotion.

***

Jaxson washes his hair out and returns to the house where Calley lays on her belly, fighting the parasites. As he walks through the door, he notices that Hazel has undressed Calley from the waist down and has covered her with a plain white sheet which is lifted to expose her legs.

"Ah, good, you've returned. I need you to sit and comfort her. She's in agonizing pain and I need her to calm down and lay as still as possible while I attempt to extract the *cercarciae*," Hazel says as she is attempting to extract one as she speaks.

Jaxson saddles alongside Calley, lowering himself so they are face to face. "Hey! So, I hear the parasites are really bad this year and the *Alace Lac* is off limits for swimmers," he says, not knowing what else to say and trying to be funny.

Calley smiles at that and shakes her head, "Really? Is that all you can come up with? That's pathetic." Calley speaks weakly and stops frequently for short breaths of air. Beads of sweat roll across Calley's horizontal face and drip off of the tip of her nose. Her eyes are red and swollen and her lips are an unnatural shade of bluish-purple. "Hazel said something before you left about you having magic. What did she mean?" Calley asks, dryly.

"Well, you remember back at Baghad when we were fighting the *Lamia Dominitri* ? I was able to use the *Ultrices Ballistae*, wasn't I? So, obviously I have magic. But, that wasn't my *Qui* stone. So, that's why it tired me so much. I was trying to use mother's *Qui* stone and it drained me almost completely; like it did you when you used it at the end," Jaxson answers, reaching up a hand to brush some fallen hair out of Calley's eyes.

Like it did when I used it? Does that mean that I have magic too? Calley thinks and then another pang of nausea and round of cramps in her legs take all of her attention once more. She fights the urge to jerk her legs away and roll into a ball.

"Yeah, but how can you help me now?" Calley asks once the pain lessens.

"My *Qui* stone is the healing one: the peridot. My power is the power of healing. But, I've never really used it though; except for once when I was boy, by accident. It was before Mother had gathered enough of her *Qui* stone to increase her power enough to take control of Baghad. There was a little girl in our village who fell into the river that ran beside it."

Jaxson pauses and looks at Calley to measure her level of interest. When he sees that she's intently trying to focus on his story, he continues, "Well, the current was too fast for such a small girl and she couldn't swim in it. She was bashed against a few larger rocks before the water threw her back up onto shore. We had a saga lymph in our village and she had finally gotten to the river to help. But she was too late. There was water in the girl's lungs and her head was cracked open where it had struck the rocks. Her brain was swelling and she was going to die. At the time, I was wearing a ring with my *Qui* stone on it that I had been given," Jaxson says and looks at Calley again.

Jaxson shrugs and says, "I didn't even know what my *Qui* stone was or what it could do, but something inside of me took control of my movements and words. I ran over to the girl, put my hands over her head and chest, holding them up like this," Jaxson holds his hands in the air, flat, palms down as an example. "Then I just started chanting. I don't even remember what I said. It just came to me, like it was just inside of me, taking over control of me," he says, putting his hands into his lap and staring at the wall, lost in his memory of the event.

Leaning back slightly, Jaxson looks up at Calley's face to see tears rolling across her turned down face now. "Don't worry, the little girl lived, she didn't die," Jaxson says sitting up and moving closer to Calley.

"No, it hurts," Calley forces out, shutting her eyes tightly.

"Ah! That one is deep! And it's in a very tender place, so high on her thigh," Hazel says and looks up at Jaxson.

"Do you think you have it in you now, boy?" Hazel asks seriously, looking directly at Jaxson.

"I don't dare. I never received any official training or education in it. I don't know what I'm doing," Jaxson says cautiously, raising his eyebrows and opening his eyes widely.

"Can't you try again? I'm sure you can do it. I'll hold so still, I promise," Calley pleads with Hazel. Calley's never had any kind of surgical procedure before, let alone one involving a magical form of extraction. She was not sure she trusted it in the first place and with Jaxson's response to the invitation, she was even more uneasy about the prospect of him doing it.

Suddenly, Jaxson sits up straight and says, "I could place a stillness spell on you! I remember one my mother used to use at the castle." Jaxson hops up and begins muttering over Calley. After only a moment, Calley becomes stiff and still. She cannot move on her own anymore, though it doesn't keep her from breathing or moving her head.

"That will help with the moving, but will it do anything for her pain?" Hazel asks, looking at Jaxson.

"I'm afraid not. Mother wasn't much on compassion when it came to the pain her subjects felt when she used this spell on them," Jaxson says as he takes his seat once more.

Calley groans and closes her eyes just as another tear slips out from under her eyelid. A flash of light outside the window precedes a boom of thunder. Suddenly, rain pours down, pounding on the roof of the little house.

"More rain? This time of year? This is very odd. We have had such strange weather this year. It has been unprecedented how much rain we have received," Hazel says as she stares out the window in front of them that offers a view to the front of the house. "I do hope Saunder and Luc return soon. A storm this time of year is remarkable; in addition to your unusual presence and this dilemma," turning around, Hazel rolls her eyes over the scene that lay before her in her home, "I worry that this is a very bad omen." Another strike of lightning flashes above the house followed shortly afterwards by the booming thunder.

With the spell on Calley, Hazel attempts to reach the *cercarciae* again. She struggles with finding it. Although Calley cannot flinch for the pain, she moans and groans, and tears run down her cheek. Rain continues to batter the roof and ground outside, with the occasional flashes and booms of the lightning and thunder.

Hazel gets a hold on the parasite and pulls hard, but it will not relinquish its hold of Calley. "I cannot remove the *cercarciae*. It has burrowed too deeply for me to extract it with only these tools," Hazel says, shaking her head.

"Jaxson, do you think you could try?" Calley whispers weakly. He looks into her pleading eyes and sighs, defeated.

"I don't even have a *Qui* stone..." Jaxson starts to say and then he remembers something. Quickly, he jumps up and dashes out the door. A moment later, he reappears carrying his sword. "I guess I do have one, on my sword, that I can use."

"Yes, I will try," Jaxson says, as he reenters the room and walks around to the other side of Calley where Hazel has been working. From this point of view, he can see the various holes that now ooze blood mixed with green foamy goo to create a disgusting brown substance as they pool together on the table. The holes and substance cover the entire length of both of Calley's legs and drench Hazel's wooden table.

Hazel backs up, making room for Jaxson at Calley's side. Jaxson lays the sword down, hilt up, beside Calley on the table so he can touch it while he works. Taking a deep breath, Jaxson raises a hand over the spot which Hazel indicates as the one in which the parasite is, making sure to keep one hand firmly on his *Qui* stone on the sword hilt.

He begins whispering, nervously at first. As he slows his breathing and concentrates, the words begin to flow out of his mind and through his lips. Light blue power begins to poor from his hands and into the wound on Calley's thigh. Jaxson chants as the power floods the wound, seeking out and drawing out the *cercarcia*. Steadily, the parasite rises out from Calley's thigh, wriggling and squirming in the air. Hazel takes it with a pair of tongs and throws it into the fire.

Before Hazel can even say a word, Jaxson moves his hands over the next wound. He swiftly, fluidly moves his hands over every wound on Calley's legs, one at a time. He makes sure that the wound is clear of any parasite and cleans the foamy substances out of it using his power. Together, Jaxson and Hazel turn Calley onto her back so they can examine the front of her legs. There, they find more lesions where the parasites have burrowed and Jaxson continues his work to remove and clean each wound.

As the storm rages on outside, Jaxson and Hazel diligently work together to remove the parasites and clean all of the wounds. Just as they are removing the last of them, Luc and Saunder enter the house.

"At last! You had me worried!" Hazel chastises.

"My apologies, my love. The storm made it difficult to retrieve the *jenabar* from the river bed where it grows. But, we are here now, and it seems just in time." Saunder hands the *jenabar* to his wife, who then takes it to another table where she begins chopping it. He then goes over to the other house where their children have all been. Hazel prepares the salve to be placed into every wound by first chopping it into smaller pieces and then crushing it with a mortar and pestle. As she crushes the *jenabar*, she whispers. While Hazel works, Jaxson finishes removing the parasites and cleaning the wounds. Lastly, he removes the stillness spell so Calley can again move freely.

The salve is paste-like, orange and smells like mustard. It looks thick, but feels thin and watery to the touch; it reminds Calley of how corn starch feels when you add just enough water to it. As soon as the salve is ready, Hazel brings it back over to Calley and begins applying it to all of the wounds.

Finding that Luc has taken the seat next to Calley, Jaxson decides to find one at the corner of the room, away from everyone else. At once, Jaxson drops into the seat and falls asleep. Luc caresses Calley's face and holds her hand while the salve is applied.

"Why is she still so hot?" Luc asks as he feels Calley's forehead.

"She shouldn't be. By now, the fever should have broken if all of the *cercarciae* have been removed." Hazel feels Calley's forehead, which is still burning and producing beads of hot sweat. The stillness spell has already worn off which allows Calley to turn her head to look at Hazel worriedly.

"What if there's still one inside of me? What will happen if we don't get it out?" Calley asks. Her breathing is labored as she manages to utter the words. Hazel lowers her head and listens to Calley's lungs through her chest.

"This is not good. Her breathing is labored, her lungs are stressed. There is fluid building in them. We have missed a *cercarcia* that is beginning to reach her lungs. Jaxson! Wake up boy! You're not finished."

Jaxson jumps up at the sound of his name and rushes over to the table on which Calley lays. Luc looks up with a quizzical look on his face, "What's going on?" he asks. "How is Jaxson going to help? What can he do?"

With a sideways glance at Luc, Jaxson says, "What can I do?" in a sarcastic tone.

"There is still a *cercarcia* somewhere in the girl. You must find it and remove it, and quickly." Hazel moves aside and Jaxson fills her void beside Calley. Once again, he lays his sword beside Calley on the table. He raises his hand over Calley's legs, slowly holding it above her legs, moving it from feet to hips.

"I don't know, I'm not sure how to-" Jaxson begins when Hazel cuts him off.

"Feel the energy flow. You will feel the *cercarcia* disturb Calley's energy," Hazel instructs optimistically.

Jaxson nods his head once. He closes his eyes and again holds out his hand to hover across Calley's legs, moving them back up her legs from her feet to her hips again. Calley is still lying on her back as he does this. She lies as perfectly still as she can.

"I think I've located the *cercarcia*. It's in her left thigh, on the inside of her leg, very high up on the leg." Jaxson says and lowers his hand to his side. He is exhausted from the exertion of pulling out of the parasites thus far and it shows in his face and energy level.

Hazel moves to Calley's side and lifts the sheet from Calley's left leg. She turns the leg out so it is easier to view the inside of her upper thigh. Sure enough, just where leg meets torso, in that very sensitive region, is a lesion the size of a golf ball. Jaxson turns his gaze away and shudders.

"It will have burrowed far too deep for me to extract it surgically. You will have to do it. Do you have the energy, Jaxson?" Hazel asks, looking up at Jaxson.

"If I don't? What will happen to her?" Jaxson asks, looking back at Hazel.

"She will die, at worst. At best, she will be paralyzed for the rest of her life," Hazel replies frankly.

"Then, it seems I must, doesn't it?" Jaxson states and moves back in next to Calley once more. He holds his hands above the golf-ball sized lesion, in which the parasite begins to wriggle and squirm, causing Calley distress.

"It's moving inside me! It's biting me! It's biting me!" Calley tries hard not to move, but twists her leg unintentionally.

Luc stands and tries to grab a hold of Calley to keep her still. Jaxson reinstates the stillness spell so that Calley can be still and Luc looks at him in shock. "What did you do to her?" Luc asks, angrily.

"Calm down, boy! Let him alone, he's saving the girl's life!" Hazel scolds Luc, who lowers himself back into the chair at Calley's side, feeling humbled. Luc watches helplessly as Jaxson whispers fiercely and holds his hands above the lesion on Calley's thigh.

Jaxson begins to tremble as he chants. The *cercarcia* begins to emerge, fighting the entire time. Calley groans, and screams in a stifled, closed mouth as it rips her flesh on its way out. Hazel takes the parasite and throws it into the fire, like she did with all the others. Blood gushes out of Calley's leg where it had taken hold, and Calley loses consciousness.

"The damned *cercarcia* had taken hold of her artery! She's going to bleed to death if you don't stop the bleeding immediately. Jaxson, have faith in yourself. You must do this if you want to save your friend," Hazel says and places a hand on Jaxson's arm, looking at him with conviction.

Jaxson clenches his jaw and again lifts his hand over Calley's thigh, this time lowering it until it covers the wound. He feels her warm, wet blood as it gushes out and over his hand. The words come flowing out of Jaxson's mouth, quiet at first, but growing to almost a shout. This isn't a chant; instead this is more like a prayer that Jaxson offers over Calley's listless, pale body. Trembling turns to shaking as Jaxson speaks. Blood spills onto the floor. With an increased motivation, Jaxson prays harder, begging for Calley's life, begging for the artery to close up and repair. He commands the cells to rejoin and close the gap through which the blood escapes. Gradually, the bleeding slows while Jaxson begs and pleads. He can feel the current slow to a trickle and at last stop all together. As soon as Jaxson stops talking, he closes his eyes and collapses onto the floor.

Chapter Twenty-Four

A BREEZE SWOOSHES THROUGH the open window in the room and tickles Calley's face, rousing her from sleep. She opens her eyes and looks over to the window. Sitting in an arm chair beneath it is Luc, fast asleep with his head on his arms. He looks so cramped in that long-backed arm chair because his legs curve on the ground and his back is slumped and curved into the back of the chair as an effort to get comfortable while trying to sleep. Calley smiles to herself then yawns.

"Oh, you're awake," Luc says, rubbing his eyes and yawning also.

"How long was I asleep for?" Calley asks, looking at him.

"Just for the night. So not long really. I'm glad that you are back with us now though!" Luc says as he kneels down beside the bed. Even though he is kneeling, he still reaches Calley at eye level.

"What about Jaxson? Where is he?" Calley asks and Luc angles his head to point to the corner near the door of the room. Calley turns her head and looks. There, in a small chair, with his head leaning against the corner of the room and with his arms folded across his chest is a sleeping Jaxson. He snores loudly in response to the prying eyes in his direction as if in a conscious effort.

"He passed out while healing you. When we were moving him to a bed to rest, he woke and insisted on seeing you. Once in your room, he refused to leave. He hasn't moved from that spot since Saunder brought in the chair for him to sit in. For some reason, he wasn't comfortable in this chair," Luc says, motioning to the long-backed arm chair he'd been sitting in under the window. Jaxson snores loudly and rolls his head to the side, drawing their attention momentarily.

Calley tries to sit up, but Luc stops her. "You're not supposed to move for at least a day. Tomorrow you can try to get up, but for today, you need to rest and heal. Since we didn't get the harvest done yesterday like we'd hoped, I'll be going out to help with that again today. I'll go let Hazel know you're awake. Are you hungry?" Luc asks as he stands.

"Not really, but I am thirsty," Calley says, again resting in the bed.

"I'll let Hazel know. I have to go help with the harvest now that I know you're going to be okay," Luc says and bends over to kiss Calley on the forehead.

"Thank you, Luc," Calley says, smiling back up at Luc. Those same warm feelings from the night of her terrible nightmare swarm around her insides, warming her thoroughly. Luc turns and walks out of the room, shutting the door behind him.

"You can stop pretending to sleep now, Jaxson," Calley says knowingly.

"I wasn't pretending. Well, at least not until Luc mentioned going to help with the harvest again today," Jaxson says with his eyes still closed and still leaning his head against the wall. "Getting all hot and sticky with sweat just isn't my idea of a good time, you know what I mean?" he adds, bringing his hands up and resting them on his face which he has lifted up toward the ceiling. He leans his head back against the chair.

"Luc said that you were exhausted after healing me to the point that you passed out. I think they would understand if you didn't help with the harvest today," Calley suggests.

"Well, in that case," Jaxson begins and stands up. He strides over to Calley's bed and plops down in the chair next to the window. Just then, Hazel knocks on the door and comes in bringing a tray of food.

"I brought you some breakfast, my dear. Luc said that you weren't very hungry, but I'll have to insist that you try to eat something. You cannot heal completely without the nutrients your body needs in your system," Hazel insists and sets the tray down on a side table near Calley's head. "Would you like to sit up a little?" she asks and Calley nods her head.

"I would like to, yes," Calley answers and begins to try to sit up.

"No, let us help you," Hazel says and she looks at Jaxson, raising her eyebrows and tilting her head slightly. Jaxson gets up, rolling his eyes and helps Hazel lift Calley by her arms just slightly higher in the bed. While Calley still holds Hazel's arms, Hazel takes a pillow and places it behind Calley's back. "I'm not sure how long you will be comfortable sitting though. Some of those lesions were very high on your thighs which may cause some discomfort after a short while. Just let me know if you would like to lie down again." Hazel smiles at Calley then looks at Jaxson. While she picks the tray up and sets on Calley's lap, she gives Jaxson a stern, 'I'm watching you' kind of look and then leaves them alone again.

"Thank you, by the way, for what you did for me," Calley says, looking at the tray of food. She reaches for the cup and feels a pull in her thigh; just a reminder that she needs to rest and heal.

"Well, you know, what else was I going to do? Sit there and watch you die?" Jaxson says coolly, leaning back in the chair and putting his hands behind his head. "Besides, you're too interesting to just watch die; that's not interesting, that's just boring." Jaxson yawns again and closes his eyes.

"What humility! Wow!" Calley shakes her head in disbelief, giggling. "Thank you anyway," Calley says, attempting to look Jaxson in the eye by tilting her head forward. He looks at her for a moment, but then turns his gaze away.

"Oh, if you're not going to eat that, then may I? I'm starving and no one offered me breakfast in bed," Jaxson says sitting up and eyeing the tray on my lap.

"Go for it, the only thing I want is this," Calley says, holding the mug of *bonelac* up to her mouth. Jaxson jumps up and grabs the tray. Then he plops back down in the chair holding the tray up so nothing spills when he lands.

"Thanks, I'm starving," Jaxson says just before digging into something that looks like scrambled eggs with a piece of toast.

It's probably more of that Triceres Hazel had given as for lunch the day before, Calley wonders as she watches Jaxson fill his mouth. *I don't remember seeing any chickens around here. I wonder where the eggs came from.*

After finishing everything on the tray, Jaxson stands up and says, "I think I'll go ahead and go help them in the field. That was an energizing breakfast! I couldn't sleep a wink more if I tried!" He leaves the tray on the chair and dashes out of the room.

Calley sets the mug down on the side table and manages to pull the extra pillow out from behind her back and scoot herself down just enough that she can lay once more.

He seems lively now! I think I'm going to go back to sleep though. Calley turns her head to the side and settles it on the pillow into a comfortable position. She tries not to move her legs too much, but must move them slightly in order to get comfortable once more. As soon as she is still for more than a second, her eyelids shut and she falls asleep.

Chapter Twenty-Five

LAUGHTER AND GIGGLES FLOAT ON THE breeze through the open window, being carried all the way to Calley's ears from outside. Opening her eyes, Calley looks out the window. The sight she sees takes her by surprise.

Mallory and Jaxson are running in circles chasing each other. Actually, right now, Mallory is chasing Jaxson who pretends to run faster than he is and lets her catch him after a minute. She tackles him, giggling and smiling from ear to ear. He grabs hold of her and, with her on his chest, rolls over with her in the grass. They roll around for a minute and then stop and Mallory crawls out of Jaxson's arms. He is getting tired and lays there on the ground, breathing heavily.

"Come on Jaxson! Again! Again! Play with me!" Mallory has one of Jaxson's hands and is pulling it up and away to try to get Jaxson to get up.

"Give me a few minutes to catch my breath okay, Mallory?" Jaxson asks, smiling up at the little girl.

Mallory sees Luc sitting on the log seat, eating his lunch and runs over to him. "What about you, Luc? Will you play with me while Jaxson get's his breath?" Mallory asks, taking Luc's hand in hers and pulling on it.

"Um, I don't know," Luc starts.

"Oh, please? Please come and play with me?" Mallory begs. No one can say 'no' to that adorable little girl!

"Okay, I guess so," Luc says and stands up, letting Mallory drag him away from his lunch.

"Come on, chase me, Luc!" Mallory says and she begins running, with Luc trotting behind her.

Jaxson gets up and goes to sit on the log bench to watch and eat a little bit of his own lunch. Calley realizes as she looks at him that something about him has changed. He's just not the same; he seems happy, energetic, and full of life.

"No! That's not how you do it! Come on, Luc! Like this," Mallory yells at Luc because he doesn't seem to understand the gist of letting Mallory get him when she chases him back.

Calley giggles at him. Luc is awkwardly attempting to play with the little girl.

He's really not that much of a kid person, is he? Calley giggles some more as she thinks. *He's so shy, and he doesn't seem to know what to do.*

Jaxson gets up from cleaning off his lunch plate and goes over to the two. "Tag, you're it!" he says, tagging Mallory and pretending to run away again. Mallory takes off after him, leaving Luc in her dust.

Mallory sure seems to respond to Jaxson though, Calley thinks as she smiles at the thought. *He's not in the slightest bit shy.*

"He has changed since yesterday," Hazel says, standing just inside the room, looking out the window. She holds a tray of food. "This is for you. I know that Jaxson helped you eat your breakfast, but he is not allowed in here this time. You must eat if you want to get better sooner," Hazel brings the tray over to the bed as Calley scoots herself up into a sitting position. "Oh, look at you! Moving already! Well, then my *bonelac* did more good than I could have hoped it would! Good, you may be able to move on with your friends tomorrow if you continue to heal at this rate," Hazel says as she sets the tray onto Calley's lap.

Although moving still causes a little pain to Calley, she does feel much better than she had before. She has to admit that she is starting to feel stronger too. Calley eats as Hazel chats with her about the crops and the harvests and the weather.

"I need to take a look at those wounds, okay," Hazel says when Calley is finished eating. Calley scoots back down in the bed again so that Hazel can examine all of the lesions from the *cercarciae*. Hazel lifts the blankets and sheets and sets them on the side of Calley and Calley looks down at the nightgown that she's wearing. Noticing how Calley admires the nightgown, Hazel says, "It's mine. I made it actually. Do you like it?"

"I love it! It's so soft! I hadn't even noticed I was wearing anything at all, it's so soft and the fabric is so fine!" Calley claims as she admires the nightgown and caresses it with her fingers.

"I'm glad you like it! It took me many nights to finish weaving in all of the silk to make it. It's made of spider_silk," Hazel says while Calley pulls it up to free her legs for examination.

"Silk!? You made the fabric from spider silk? You mean you weaved it into fabric yourself?" Calley says, dumbfounded.

"Yes, I weaved into fabric every last inch of that gown," Hazel says as she looks over the various wounds on Calley's legs.

"No way! That's amazing! It must have taken you forever! That's incredibly impressive! You must be very talented for sure!" Calley praises, still feeling the softness of the gown and admiring it greatly.

"Well, as far as I can tell, they've all healed over like I'd hoped they would. Now, only time will tell if all of the venom has made its way out of your system. But, judging by the way you look and the way you are acting, I would render a guess that it is all gone," Hazel says as she lifts the sheets and blankets back up and over Calley.

"So, do you think I will be able to leave with my friends in the morning tomorrow?" Calley asks, excitedly.

"I don't see why not. However, I will be coming in to check on you again tonight after supper. We'll let that be the final say as to whether or not you will be well enough in the morning to leave with your friends, okay?" Hazel smoothes the blankets over Calley and says, "I couldn't help notice your pendant last night while I was dressing you. It's very unusual, isn't it? You wouldn't consider trading it for the items you need, would you?" Hazel asks.

Calley suddenly remembers the pendant and her hands flies to her chest where it should fall underneath her clothing. It's there, or at least, something is there. Just to make sure it is her pendant, Calley pulls it out and turns it over in her hand, looking it over thoroughly.

"No, I wouldn't. I'm sorry, but this pendant is very special to me. It has sentimental value, more than anything else anyway. It's only silver it's encased in; so it's not like gold or platinum or anything. And, it's not like it's a diamond, it's just a green peridot. Granted it's a rare shade of peridot, but it's also not a very highly de-manded shade either," Calley realizes that she is rambling and looks up at Hazel where she stands, watching Calley.

Putting the necklace back under her shirt and look-ing back up at Hazel, Calley says, "I guess what I'm say-ing is that it's not very valuable anyway and probably wouldn't even be enough to cover what we need. Besides, we already have a deal set up and we've held our end of the bargain. Aren't Luc and Jaxson out there helping to harvest the crops right now like we'd agreed on?" Calley asks.

"Oh don't worry, I was merely asking. I was only checking in case it was a possibility. Your bargain is still valid and you will receive the items you asked for to-night," Hazel says, almost stiffly. "You get some rest, all right?" Hazel says as she walks back out of the room.

That sure was strange. I better be careful with this, Calley thinks and holds her pendant tightly in one hand. *When Mom first gave this to me, I thought that the 'Princess' part was just a pet name; like parents will call their little girl 'princess'. I never imagined I would actually be a kind of real-life 'Princess'; especially not one foretold and prophesied about,* Calley thinks as she re-members the nursery rhyme Luc had told her.

Calley rolls over in bed toward the window before remembering that it was supposed to hurt. To her surprise, the sores only ached a little when she moved them and when they rubbed against each other.

I really hope we can leave first thing in the morn-ing. I think we've been here too long already. She looks out the window to see that the children and Luc and Jaxson have all gone now. *They're probably in the fields harvesting again.* Calley decides that it's time for a nap and closes her eyes.

This time, Calley finds it difficult to sleep. She feels restless. Thoughts about Hazel haunt Calley. Thoughts about Hazel taking her pendant, drugging her and taking the pendant away, play over and over in her mind. Calley replays the conversation in which Hazel ex-pressed an interest in the pendant in her mind. Something in the way Hazel had looked at it, something about the way she dismissed it when Calley said 'no' worried Calley. Maybe she was just reading way too much into it, and maybe there was something to be worried about.

Dad did warn me that people would want me, or did he mean they would want the pendant? He said they would guess at who I was if they saw it. Who am I to be so sought after? Am I safe here now that she has seen it? Will she try to take it? Calley rolls over again with her eyes open facing the door to the room. *No, she wouldn't do that. Not with Jaxson and Luc here with me. It's not like I'm here alone or anything. But, she's got Saunder and her father here to help her if they will.* Calley shakes her head. *I need to stop thinking like this! I'm acting like I'm paranoid!* She rolls over onto her back again. She barely even notices the ache in her legs this time. She is certainly healing quickly.

Calley finally drifts off into an uneasy sleep. She has dreams of Hazel coming into the room and taking the pendant while she sleeps. Then, she dreams that Hazel sends Saunder in to take the pendant and he has to force it off of her. Lastly, Calley dreams that Mallory comes into the room to talk to her and play a game with her. She brings a card game into the room with her. As Mallory explains the rules, Calley discovers that the game is about chance; you have to gamble something to play it. When Calley realizes this, she refuses to play the game and when Mallory gets upset, she turns into some kind of scaly, clawed monster which swipes at Calley's chest trying to take the necklace.

Finally, Calley opens her eyes and looks around the room, breathing heavily. She is alone. They were just dreams after all. But she knows that there is no way they can stay there another night. Dreams or not, Calley does not feel safe there and there is a real danger that Hazel may desire the pendant badly enough to try something.

Calley sits up in the bed with little discomfort in her legs. Slowly, cautiously, Calley puts weight onto her feet. Amazingly enough she can stand. It's very painful to put her full weight on her legs, but she can stand. In truth, she probably should stay and rest more, allowing the *jenabar* to continue to heal her wounds and kill the venom from the *cercarciae*, but she cannot take the chance of being discovered by Hazel.

As soon as they give us the supplies, we need to get away from here! Calley decides anxiously.

Looking out the window again, Calley realizes that the sun has become very low in the sky. She gets back into bed and waits for Luc and Jaxson to come to her. Luc is the first to enter, followed by Jaxson. Smiling at her when their eyes meet, Luc goes straight to Calley's side. She is sitting in the bed and pats it for him to sit next to her. Gladly, he sits down. Jaxson takes the seat next to the window on the other side of the bed, putting his feet up on the bed and leaning his back against the chair.

"How are you feeling?" Luc asks as he carefully sits down on the bed next to Calley.

"Much better! It hurts to stand, but I can still move around in the bed. I just can't put my weight on my legs yet," Calley says looking down toward her legs, which were covered by blankets.

"Does that mean we can leave this place soon?" Jaxson asks, almost reading Calley's mind.

"What's the matter? Too much work for your liking?" Luc teases.

Jaxson shoots Luc a look of annoyance and Calley joins in, "Yes!" Both of the boys stop and look at her. "I mean, yes, we can leave soon. Actually, that's what I wanted to talk to you guys about. I think we-" Calley is interrupted by a knock on the door and she falls silent.

"Hello, it's just me. I've brought your dinner." Miah enters the room carrying a tray with three bowls on it and a basket full of freshly baked *Triceres*. Mallory follows behind her carrying a tray with three mugs of *bonelac* on it.

"Mmm, that smells delicious! I'm famished!" Jaxson says, sitting straight in the chair.

"Thank you," Luc says as he takes the tray from Miah and she turns and leaves the room.

"I think we should leave immediately! As soon as they give you the supplies we asked for, we need to leave," Calley mutters out all together.

"Hold on, what is going on? What happened?" Jaxson says scooting to the edge of his seat.

"Just after lunch, Hazel came in to examine my wounds and she asked me about this," Calley says and grabs her pendant through her shirt, looking straight at Luc. "She wanted to know if I'd trade it for our supplies or something. She was really upset when I turned her down."

Knowingly, Luc drops his eyes to the tray of food in his hands. Jaxson, confused, speaks up, "What are you talking about? What did she want?" he asks, looking from Luc to Calley.

Calley and Luc exchange glances and Calley pulls out the pendant and shows it to Jaxson before Luc can say a word. "She wants this," Calley says as she turns toward Jaxson and holds out the pendant, careful not to take the necklace off. He leans in and looks at the front, which she holds out to him. Squinting his eyes, Jaxson studies the design etched along the frame of the peridot. Then, Calley turns it around so he can read the inscription on the back.

"She saw this when she was dressing me last night," Calley says as Jaxson finishes reading the inscription; which he did by mouthing each word. When he finishes, he looks up at Calley, eyes wide with wonder and jaw on the floor.

"Well, that's maybe the first time I've seen you lost for words, Prince Jaxson," Luc jeers.

Jaxson closes his mouth and slightly leans back in the chair again, thinking intently.

"At any rate, that explains our dinner tonight. It's laced with *caman solmo*. They mean to poison us so we can't leave in the morning. As for the trade, they already gave us the supplies we asked for," Lu says without missing a beat.

"Wait just a minute here," Jaxson says, sitting up once more and shaking his head, "let me get this all straight. First, how it that you know the food has *caman solmo* in it?" he asks, looking at Luc. "It looks fine to me. And, it smells great! I'm just famished!" Jaxson finishes, licking his lips and intently eyeing the tray of food.

"Because I can smell it. Look, in the heart of full disclosure, I'm Lipus, okay?" Luc reveals reluctantly, looking Jaxson directly in the eyes for probably the first time since they met. He does this purposefully to show Jaxson his proof. Because in that instant, Luc's eyes change from their normal chocolate brown hue to a blood red. His pupils enlarge, fangs begin to poke up in his mouth and he opens it to bare them. A deep, low snarl escapes Luc's throat.

"Okay, okay! I got it, Abram and Eva!" Jaxson says, blinking wildly to remove the image from his mind. He rubs his eyes and he adds, "So, you're Lipus, and our little missy here is Majori. I knew you were special, Calley, but the *Dea Regia*?" He says looking at her now.

"Yeah, well now Hazel knows it too. Or, she at least suspects it after seeing my pendant. We need to leave as soon as possible," Calley starts, slowly at first, feeling a little self-conscious at the mention of her being a *Dea Regia*. That fades when she's reminded about Hazel's interest in her pendant.

"But, you said you couldn't walk yet," Jaxson starts but is cut off by Luc.

"That doesn't mean she can't ride. We still have our horses," Luc reminds Jaxson.

"Yeah, but how is she supposed to get to them? Are we just going to carry her out of here?" Jaxson asks a little annoyed.

"Why not?" Luc asks and looks at Calley. "If they poisoned our food, then they mean to rob us in our sleep. Which means that waiting until they are asleep to sneak out will be to no avail. We must leave immediately if we are to escape." Luc seems to be talking directly to Calley, which annoys Jaxson even further. Calley nods her head in agreement.

"Fine, then we leave immediately, without even eating any supper!" Jaxson says defiantly and stands up. "Do we just sneak out the window? Or are we going through the front door?" Jaxson watches as Luc and Calley exchange glances and then both look at him together.

After a few minutes, Jaxson walks out of the room and back into the front of the house carrying the tray, an empty bread basket and three empty bowls. "Thank you graciously for the meal! Your hospitality has surely been incomparable! I'm off to sleep for the night, I just feel so sleepy all of a sudden. I guess it was all that hard work in the fields today. Anyway, we plan to be off first thing in the morning. Thank you so very much for all of your hospitality," Jaxson says, walks into the kitchen, hands Hazel the tray and then turns to leave. He was speaking too quickly and worries when Hazel steps in his path that she may have seen through his guise.

"Will Luc be spending the night with Calley?" Hazel asks, gesturing toward the room where Luc still hasn't exited.

"No, of course not! They just wanted a moment alone is all," Jaxson says and then hurries out the front door before more questions can be asked of him.

A minute later, Luc walks out of the room. "Good night, all! I'm just exhausted. Thank you for all of your help and generosity!" Luc takes long strides so that he covers the length of the house in no time and is out the door before anyone can say anything to him.

Outside, Calley is already mounted on her horse; still wearing the nightgown and riding side-saddle; with both her legs off to one side of the saddle. It's much more difficult, but in a dress and with all of her wounds, it is better than the alternative. Jaxson is just mounting his horse when Luc strides out of the house.

Quickly and effortlessly, like all of his fluid movements, Luc mounts his horse and the three of them take off at a gallop down the dirt path toward the *Aurura Crena*.

"Do you think they suspected anything?" Calley asks, worriedly.

"I think Hazel might have," Jaxson answers.

"All the more reason for us to get as far away from here as fast as we can," Luc adds.

An hour or more passes silently; the only sound being that of the horse's hooves beating against the dirt. Finally, they pass the last of the family's lands and can breathe a sigh of relief. At last, they have made it to the *Flu Lumens*.

"That was the border of their lands there." Luc points to the mouth of the river where it begins at the *Alace Lac*. Then, he continues saying, "Saunder was telling me, when we went for the *jenabar,* that their land extends only until the river forms and no farther west. We should be safe here until sunrise," Luc says as he dismounts his horse. The others do the same, mechanically.

Without much discussion, they each unroll their blanket rolls, climb inside and fall asleep.

Chapter Twenty-Six

CALLEY FEELS A HAND COVER HER mouth, rudely waking her up. She looks over where Luc and Jaxson lay and sees that both of them are fast asleep. The moon hangs high in the sky.

"Shhh, one word and he'll kill them," Saunder whispers and Kaleb reveals himself. Kaleb stands just over Luc with a short dagger in his hand.

Calley's eyes grow large as she sees this and becomes terrified.

"Now, you come with us quietly and easily and we won't hurt the boys," Saunder says with his hand still clasped over Calley's mouth. She nods her head in agreement hastily.

"Good. Now, slowly get up and hold your hands behind your back," Saunder commands.

Just as Calley begins to get to her feet, Luc kicks his legs up into the air above him, knocking the dagger from Kaleb's hands, effectively disarming the old man. Luc jumps up, grabbing the dagger off of the ground and pointing it at Kaleb, who now stands trembling and weaponless. Jaxson stirs, and seeing what is happening, he too jumps to his feet.

Saunder has grabbed Calley and now holds her in front of him, threatening her with a dagger of his own. "Try anything and she's dead," he says to them while Kaleb slowly backs away from Luc and joins his son.

With Calley in his arms and the blade at her chest, Saunder begins backing away from the boys toward his horse not far away. Kaleb turns and mounts his horse, waiting for Saunder to do likewise. Luc and Jaxson exchange glances and a second later, Jaxson has his sword out and points it at Saunder. Simultaneously, Luc shifts into his *Mutatie Lipus* and pounces Kaleb's horse, tackling it to the ground and injuring it.

"As you can see, we are perfectly capable of defending ourselves if needed," Jaxson says, taking a step closer to Saunder.

Kaleb recovers from his tumble off the horse and runs away. Luc's wolf lets him go and turns to snarl at Saunder.

"We don't want to hurt you," Jaxson continues, "but we will if you give us no other choice. Let her go and we'll forget this ever happened," Jaxson finishes, taking another step closer to Saunder. Luc, still snarling and baring his fangs, also moves closer to Saunder and Calley.

"What guarantee do I have that you won't just kill me as soon as I let her go?" Saunder asks, shifting his weight nervously from one foot to the other.

"We let Kaleb go, didn't we?" Jaxson answers, again taking a step closer.

Saunder looks from Jaxson's sword to Luc's wolf. He looks back and forth a few times, still nervously shifting his weight between his feet. Finally, Saunder makes a decision and pushes Calley away from him and onto the ground. He turns and mounts his horse and is gone before Calley even has time to stand back up.

Luc begins his transformation back into a man, while Jaxson drops his sword and falls to his knees beside Calley on the ground.

"Are you okay?" Jaxson asks, touching her face and lifting it to see it from different angles. "He didn't hurt you, did he?"

"No, I'm fine," Calley assures him and she stands up.

Now, back in his form as a man, Luc walks over to them, barefoot and still pulling on a shirt over his head.

He reaches out for Calley and she leans into his hug. A moment later, Calley giggles and pulls away.

"What's so funny?" Luc asks, not quite seeing the comedy in the moment.

"Your beard! It tickles!" Calley answers, giggling some more. Jaxson even starts laughing at this.

"Yeah, I get one every time I change. My hair grows longer each time I change too," he says apologetically, running a hand through his hair, which now reaches passed his shoulders, and suddenly feeling self-conscious.

"I know," Calley says as she reaches a hand up and runs her fingers through some of the lowest locks of his mousey brown, curly hair.

"Anyone up for getting some more sleep tonight?" Jaxson interrupts. "Or, should we mount up and be on our way?"

Unanimously, they pack up their blanket rolls and mount their horses. Sun rise comes all too soon and the group finally stops for some rest after having ridden all night. No one wanted to risk another ambush from Saunder and Kaleb.

***

After a few hours of sleep and a cold meal of *Triceres* and *Bonecase*, which they'd traded for with Hazel, the group once again takes to the road. The main goal at this point is to put as many miles between them and Saunder and Hazel as possible.

Still days away from making it into the *Aurura Crena*, the group continues on steadily. Each day, they start at dawn, stop at midday to rest the horses and eat, and then continue through the afternoon until dusk. Calley begins to warm up to Jaxson. He reminds her of her father in the way that he jokes and teases; not always appropriately, but always in his own style. Little flirtations begin to make their presence between Jaxson and Calley. Luc watches in dismay but says nothing.

After a few days on the road, and away from Hazel and Saunder, Calley relaxes enough to really start having fun and laugh again.

One morning while eating a breakfast of oats, Calley and Jaxson sit side by side on the ground next to the river. They joke back and forth, rubbing shoulders as they do.

"No, you didn't! That can't be real!" Calley squeals as she nudges Jaxson's shoulder with hers.

"Oh? And how would you even know, Dea Regia Alleynia, who grew up in the mortal's realm?" Jaxson teases back, bumping into Calley's bowl and dropping some onto her legs.

Calley scoops up the fallen oats from her leg and puts it on Jaxson's nose, laughing full-heartedly all the while.

"There!" she says, "Finally an improvement!" she exclaims while laughing hysterically.

"You think so, do you?" Jaxson asks and then he reaches over and tickles Calley's sides.

Calley squeals in delight and laughs uncontrollably, grabbing her belly and squirming in place on the ground.

"We should get going," Luc interrupts. "That is if you're finished eating," he adds as he packs up their camp by himself.

Jaxson and Calley mostly sober up. But as they help pack up so they can get back on the road again, they continue to poke and prod each other, sending out giggles and laughs each time.

***

"You've changed, you know," Calley says to Jaxson as they sit around a campfire finishing their supper late one evening. "You're not the same as when we first met. You were kind of weird, and I wasn't even sure I could trust you. But, you didn't give me much of a choice." Calley says teasingly, as she smiles at Jaxson who sits on the ground right next to her.

"Well, now you had your own secrets too, didn't you? *Dea Regia*.." Jaxson teases back, cocking his head to the side and narrowing his eyes playfully.

Calley lightly punches Jaxson in the shoulder, "Shut up!" She smiles at him and her cheeks take on a shade of rosy pink, which reveals her reticence. Although he calls her that frequently now, she still hasn't grown any more comfortable with it than she was the first time he said it. Every time Jaxson calls her 'Princess', even in a different language, she feels giddy inside. Those butterflies have now taken up permanent residence in her abdomen. Every time she looks at him and meets his eyes with hers, they take flight, fluttering around in circles in that cramped up little space inside of her belly.

"We should think about putting out the fire and getting some sleep," Luc suggests from the other side of the fire, watching the two dance their twitter-pated jitter hop.

"Tomorrow is the full moon," Luc says to no avail. He rolls his eyes to the back of his head and plops his head onto his mat. "Tomorrow is the full moon," Luc tries again.

After a few minutes of continuing to be ignored, Luc sits up abruptly and almost shouts, "Calley! Tomorrow is the *Antequia Luna Mensie in Armis* moon. I must change and run come the moon rise. It is unpredictable, much like a lunar or solar eclipse are, and I will not have a choice but to reside in my Lipus skin for those three days, until it passes." Luc has finally gotten the attention of the two. Calley feels ashamed that he'd had to shout to get her attention. Embarrassment flushes her into complete sobriety.

"I'm sorry, Luc. I didn't mean to ignore you. I just," she starts out, meaning to apologize and then can't find the right words to say. "I understand. So, you will have to leave us for a few days?" Calley says, and then remembers something. "Wait a minute, I thought that werewolves," embarrassed that she's called him something so mundane, Calley blushes, "err, I mean, Lipus..es.. um, only change during the full moon? The full moon has come and gone since I met you and you didn't have to change then."

"You are mistaken," Luc states abruptly, hinting at his annoyance. "That is the mortal version of a Lipus, commonly called in your realm, a werewolf. Lipus' never HAVE to *mutatie*, change, if they do not choose to. However, I have never heard of one that didn't long to run in his or her own true skin, our *vere corpus*! We do enjoy running in the full moon, and we are granted extra blessings by the *Dea Luna* on those nights of the month. However, during this particular phase of the moon, the Lipus are requested to remain in *vere corpus* by both the *Dea Luna* and the *Celestia*. It is out of respect that we do this, and in return, often, but not always, the *Celestia* too will grant a Lipus his or her greatest desire. He often chooses one to bless. It is always the hope of every Lipus to be the chosen. This phase of the moon usually only occurs once, or rarely, twice a year. This is the first *Antequia Luna Mensie in Armis* moon to have occurred this year and will likely be the only one this year," Luc says as he stares into the fire.

"Seriously? You Lipus' are all a bunch of morons. The *Celestia* doesn't care what you do or who you are. He hasn't cared about any of his people here on Calueria for millennia. Why do you think the elders have all disappeared? I heard that most of them got lost searching for him," Jaxson chimes in looking cross-eyed at Luc. He realizes that he's staring, and that Calley is staring at him and decides to end on a lighter note. "At least the *Dea Luna* is still around, somewhere. I've heard similar tales of what you said where she 'blesses' lowly people like us with her gifts."

Calley shakes her head with a slanted brow and a crooked smirk thinking, *What in the world was that about? So, okay, Jaxson doesn't believe in his god?*

"So, what does this *Antequia Luna Mensie in Armis* look like anyway?" Calley asks, changing the subject and turning to look at Luc. She smiles at him sincerely and ignores Jaxson when he gets up to leave and walks over to the river alone.

"At the beginning and ending of the *lunae*, the lunar month, the moon is nothing but is sliver in the night's sky. But sometimes, the world's light will reflect back onto the part of the moon which is hidden by the earth from the sun; illuminating the rest of it. This is called 'the new moon in the old moon's arms' or the *Antequia Luna Mensie in Armis* as we commonly call it. It can be seen day and night. Lipus are most often drawn to the moon; it was the *Dea Luna*, Goddess over the Moon, who helped create our race in the beginning after all. She blesses us; she is the source for our transformative powers. But, it is on these occasions that we are given the privilege of appearing before both her and *Celestia*, the God over the Sun. It is an honor, really."

Jaxson, standing not more than a stone's throw away, scoffs and turns to walk upstream a little further away.

He must have heard that comment Luc just made. I wonder what his issue is what this Celestia, Calley thinks.

"There is a song we like to sing to remind us of it," Luc says and then begins singing in his mesmerizing baritone voice,

"*Luna in Corpus*, the moon in all her glory, smiles
    in the nightly sky,
Bidding the shadows come out and play, mischief
    is to be found again.
But, where do the shadows run to, who hide and
    lurk ere morning bring the sun?
All of the arrow pointed streams which pierce the
    merry making of shadow and night,
Come swiftly, without warning, part the shadows
    and leave no heeding night.
Though night drifts away, the shadows secretly
    stay;
They wait for night once more to conquer over
    day,"

Luc finishes. "It's about the continuous rotation of day and night. We are born of *Dea Luna*, born of the moon and night. And, we are ever changing our forms; into our *vere corpus* and back into men and women."

"That's a lovely song," Calley says, and asks for clarity, "So, you will remain in your *vere corpus* for three days and two nights?"

"Yes. But, I do retain my mental faculties when I am *Mutatie Lipus*, so I will still follow you. You and Jaxson can continue the journey. I'll keep up with you."

Luc looks over at Jaxson where he now sits on the edge of the *Flu Lumens* some 15 yards away from them and sees scheming in his eyes. Whether it is truly there or not is beside the point. Luc worries about leaving Calley alone with Jaxson.

"But, one of you will have to lead my horse. I don't dare run with you or even come into camp for fear that I will frighten the horses," Luc says, looking back at Calley. "The moon will rise about an hour after the sun sets tomorrow night. Shortly after sun set, I must change in preparation. That is when I will have to leave you," Luc tells Calley.

Chapter Twenty-Seven

THE NEXT MORNING, THE GROUP loads up and gets on the road with little discussion. Although Calley feels guilty, she can't put a finger on why. She hasn't done anything wrong.

Why is he so mad at me? Calley can't help wondering as they ride in silence. *Luc hasn't spoken a word since last night. What did I do? Maybe it has something to do with last night, how I didn't hear him when he was trying to talk to me,* Calley hypothesizes as their horses trod along the dirt road.

That evening when the group stops for the night, Luc bids the other two "farewell" and takes off into the densest part of the trees. All throughout the night, Calley has a hard time sleeping because she keeps thinking about Luc; wondering what he's doing, if he's okay, if he's somewhere nearby.

A few times in the night, Calley wakes up to howling. One time, she wakes up to the sound of rustling in the bushes near her. Startled, Calley jerks awake lifting her head and shoulders straight up without completely sitting, and looks in the direction of the noise. A small rodent scurries out of the bushes and Calley settles back into her blanket roll, still watching the area where the rodent had emerged.

"Luc?" Calley whispers, hoping it's him.

Why am I so scared? Luc said he'd be around and that he'd be following us. Why am I so jumpy? Eventually, Calley falls back to sleep.

***

The next morning Jaxson is his usual bouncy, charming self. Once back on the road, he is joking and laughing as if nothing has changed and they aren't missing a part of their group. Although, Calley is fairly certain that they are being followed, and she hopes that it is Luc in his *vere corpus*.

At midday Calley and Jaxson stop for lunch alongside the river. The hot summer sun beats down on them from high in the sky.

"Hey, why don't we go for a swim?" Calley suggests. "The water looks great and it's so hot today!"

"Sure, I'm game," Jaxson says as he strips off his shirt. Calley can't help but notice Jaxson's broad, strong shoulders. She can't help but be attracted by him and blushes slightly when he catches her staring at him. Jaxson jumps into the river. Jaxson shakes his head upon emerging from the water. He runs his hands through it, causing the jet black strands to spike in every direction.

A moment later, Calley, stripped to her underwear, joins him in the river, splashing him and kicking up water into Jaxson's face. Jaxson dives under the water and before Calley knows it, she is dragged under by the feet. Resurfacing again, Calley wipes her eyes and looks around for the culprit. Before she can see clearly, Jaxson bombards her with splashes in the face.

"Oh really?" Calley yells and she lies on her back, floating in the water and uses her feet and legs to renew her attack on Jaxson with new fury.

Laughing, Jaxson grabs one of Calley's feet and begins pulling her to him. Calley pretends to try to get away, all the while creeping closer to Jaxson. She feels her heart racing as he brings her closer to him. Finally, right next to him, Jaxson drops Calley's foot so she can stand. Everything becomes suddenly serious and still as they both stay in the water, their faces only inches apart.

Jaxson leans in to kiss Calley, but they're interrupted by growling and snarling on the river bank.

There, they see Luc in his *vere corpus*. As if being snapped out of a trance, Calley looks at Luc and feels a pang of guilt in her chest. He stops snarling for the moment that his eyes focus in on her. Then, he turns his glare back onto Jaxson and the growling and snarling begins again.

Jaxson decides that it's time to stop pressing his luck and he gets out of the water on the other side of the river. He looks at Calley and she looks between him and Luc, completely oblivious to what is taking place.

From that point on, Calley can see glimpses of Luc running alongside them as they travel. He keeps his distance so he doesn't scare the horses, but he also stays in the open where they can easily see him and know that he is with them. The rest of the ride that day passes in awkward silence, with Luc making frequent appearances.

"So, what is the deal with you and Luc?" Jaxson asks as the two share a dinner at sunset. "Are you two a couple?" he asks with minor annoyance in his voice.

"No, we are not a couple," Calley starts uncertainly, "I mean, I don't know what we are. Other than that we are friends. At least, as far as I know, we are just friends." Calley stirs her bowl of rainbow trout she'd caught for their dinner, using the *Atitilio* technique that Luc had taught her. She even uses some of his spices to season it.

"Then, why is he so protective of you?" Jaxson asks watching her expression as she blushes again.

"I don't know. I didn't realize he was," Calley says shrugging her shoulders. The two look up and in the direction of a howl that emerges from somewhere east of them.

"I'd say he was in love with you, if I didn't know any better," Jaxson chances hurriedly.

"I don't know about that. Besides, I'm not really in any position for 'love' right now. I need to get home and get this stuff figured out," Calley says, bringing her knees up under her chin and setting her bowl on the ground, mostly uneaten. She wraps her arms around her knees and extends one hand to hold the pendant through her shirt at her chest.

Thinking of her father, Calley wonders, *What is all of this anyway? Maybe this is all some elaborate dream? No, too much has happened for that at this point. Right now, I'd give anything for this to just all be a dream. That way I could just wake up and be home again,* Calley thinks as she forces back a tear.

"Well, I'm off to bed! Good night! Sweet dreams, don't let the werewolves bite!" Jaxson says as he lays out his blanket roll and settles in, successfully snapping Calley out of her thoughts.

"Night," she says and lays out her own blanket roll, slides in and makes herself comfortable enough for sleep. *I wonder where Luc will be sleeping tonight. I hope he's not too far away. I'm starting to miss him,* Calley thinks as she drifts off to sleep.

Chapter Twenty-Eight

SALTY SEA AIR WHIPS MY hair all around my face. I hear the roaring of waves that crash against the shore. Pebbles shift under the weight of my feet as I stand; small and round pebbles, smooth and cool to the touch. A wave rushes the shore and sprays me with tiny droplets of salty sea water. Luc takes my right hand in his. He smiles at me. Jaxson appears on my left, taking my left hand. He too smiles at me. I am filled with joy that my two best friends are here with me, in my favorite place. I can feel the warmth in my hands that radiates from my friends' love for me.

Together we watch as the storm approaches over the ocean. Lightning strikes not far in front of us over the water. Veins of electricity spread out and away from the strike, reaching through the water for anything it may pass through, reaching for a victim. It crawls all the way to the edges of the water. We are not standing in the water or we would be electrocuted. The waves continue to crash into the rocks below us. We stand on a small cliff above the waves.

Looking down, I am amazed that we do not fall. The cliff side is thin, narrow and barely holding up the three of us. Above us in the evening sky the sun is setting. I watch it sink into the ocean in the distance, swallowed up by the sea. A short moment later, I see the moon rise in nearly the same place the sun has just set, given birth by the sea. Lightning continues to strike the water, shooting veins of electricity in every direction, still searching for a victim. Almost like a tree taking roots in the ground, the veins of electricity spread from their originating points outward. Multiple strikes of lightning leave several webs of these electric veins, taking root and searching through the salty water.

I am mesmerized by the crawling, searching electric veins. I do not realize that we are not alone in this serene place. I do not realize that Jaxson and Luc are slowly being pulled away from me. I do not notice the witch behind us until it is too late.

Sharp, nasal cackling begins and black smoky arms wrap around Luc and Jaxson, restraining them and lifting them over the cliff and above the crashing waves and jagged rocks that jut out of the ocean below. I spin around to see her enveloped in that smoky black energy. Before me stands a personage made entirely of the black energy that swirls and whirls around within the invisible frame of a body. Glowing yellow eyes with diamond shaped pupils like those of a cat glare out at me from somewhere in the head, appearing almost disembodied because they are not where eyes should be on a face but are rather smack in the middle of the face.

Eyelids shut out the yellow momentarily while the cackling repeats and echoes out of the swirling, whirling mass of black energy. The entire mass even seems to jiggle a little with the laughter like your chest will normally do when laughing. Again those yellow eyes beat down on me, narrowing and focusing.

"Which one will it be, my dear? Think quickly, for their fates lie in your hands now," that high-pitched, nasal voice echoes, shouting out from within the black energy.

"What do you mean?" I ask, confused.

"You care for them both, do you not? Choose, for only one will I spare, if I choose to spare any at all," the witch cackles hysterically again as if she's just shared a hilarious joke, in which she is the only one who got the *punch line. I stare at the black, whirring, whirling mass blankly.*

"I'm getting really tired of these stupid dreams. And, I've had about enough of you! I'm not choosing anything. You're not taking either of them!" I yell into the darkness between us.

Cackling grows to a roaring, thundering booming that echoes in waves, riding on the gusts of wind that now throw my hair around my face violently. The black whirring mass shifts out of its human form and splits in two, rushing passed Calley toward the boys behind her, who are still held in those big, black, smoky fists over the water. A huge face with yellow eyes takes shape in the sky beyond them.

"Make your choice, or I shall choose for you!" the witch screams through the air.

"Never! You cannot have either of them, not now or ever!" I scream back, clueless of what I could actually do to stop her, but knowing that she cannot win.

"Have it your way!" she says and the giant fist holding Jaxson opens, dropping the boy to the water and sharp, spiky rocks below.

Almost as if in slow motion, I see Jaxson glow, radiating sunlight, as he is swallowed up into the sea, just as the setting sun was swallowed up. I am screaming in dread as this antagonizing moment seems to move in slow motion. Tears stream down my face as I stare in the direction which Jaxson has drowned, helpless to do a thing to help him.

"Next," the witch says calmly and the other fist opens to reveal a wolf lying lifeless in it. Luc lifts his head enough to show he is still alive and then the fist closes around him, crushing and squeezing the life out of him. As Luc is being crushed, blood covers the moon, streaming down it like the tears stream down my cheeks.

I can't help but feel like my own tears are blood because of the synchronicity of it all; the ways the blood falls over the moon and the way my tears fall down my cheeks, the way blood starts seeping out of the clenched fist around Luc that still floats in midair.

"STOP!" I scream at the top of my lungs and a surge of white energy explodes outward from my chest where my pendant lies hidden. It heaves forward and outward in every direction away from me like a bomb has gone off and I am ground zero.

Everywhere my white energy burst reaches, the black whirring energy dissipates. Together they vanish leaving only the night sky in the background wherever they mix. As my burst reaches out and neutralizes the witch's black energy, the fist holding Luc is disbursed and Luc is dropped into the ocean below.

Laughter cackles again from all around in the air, "So much power and no idea how to use it! I look forward to our inevitable introduction! I can't wait to get you back in my lair! What power!" Lightning strikes everywhere, one strike every second. The water is lit up like a Christmas tree. Salty sea water splashes as the waves begin to reach the cliff on which I still stand. Tears flood my eyes, forcing them shut. I am thrown onto the ground on my hands and knees. I drop my hands and head down so that only my elbows support my upper body. My head rests on the ground as I sob. Lightning continues flashing all around me, now hitting the ground next to me, but I don't care. Let it strike me dead where I am; I have nothing left to live for.

Finally, resolved and more determined than ever before, I open my eyes, done crying and I look into the remaining hovering black, whirling mass that is positioned just over the water away from the cliff. As the lightning strikes the ground and water, I gather my re-

solve and stand up. At full speed, I break into a sprint, aimed at that whirling mass of darkness.

"Want me? Here I am!" I scream as I leap from the cliff...

"Want me? Here I am!" Calley screams hysterically, thrashing around in her bedroll.

"Calley! Come on! Wake up!" Jaxson yells, holding Calley's shoulders and shaking her. She has been screaming and flailing her arms and legs around in her sleep.

Opening her eyes, Calley looks up to Jaxson and says, "You're all right!" and she wraps her arms around him and puts her face into his neck, breathing in his scent deeply. "It was another nightmare. It was that witch again; the... um, Striga. This time, she killed you and Luc. She dropped you into the ocean to drown and she crushed Luc to death in a giant fist!" Calley blurts out, unable to contain the tears which now flow freely.

As Jaxson cradles Calley in his arms, they hear rustling in some bushes nearby. When they look in that direction, they see only the tail of a wolf as it disappears into them.

Luc must have been watching. He must be worried, Calley thinks. "Luc, I'm okay! It was just another nightmare," Calley says, hoping to comfort her friend, not knowing if he'd even heard her.

"Well, should we try to finish our night's sleep?" Jaxson asks and begins to pull away from Calley.

"Wait, stay with me. Please?" Calley asks and burrows her head into his chest.

"Okay," Jaxson says and slides himself into the blanket roll, lying on his back. Calley curls up into his side, keeping her head on his chest.

She can hear his heart beating, his steady breathing. She feels safe. With the attraction she feels for Jaxson, this all makes her tingle throughout. Even though he seems to fall asleep quickly, Calley lies in a half sleep; somewhere between awake and asleep. She can't help thinking about how being next to Jaxson makes her feel; how it makes her whole body tingle; how giddy it makes her stomach. It's almost enough to make her completely forget the Striga and the nightmare. Almost.

Chapter Twenty-Nine

WHEN THE SUN RISES, LUC SITS and kindles the fire into a blaze. Jaxson and Calley begin to stir as the smell of breakfast wafts up from the heat of the fire.

"Good morning," Luc says, not looking at the two, still lying in each other's arms.

Feeling a little embarrassed, Calley groggily gets up and goes to sit next to Luc at the fire.

"You had another nightmare last night," Luc states matter-of-factly. "What happened?"

"Well, this time I was able to stand up to her. I had some kind of power that exploded out from my chest," Calley explains, rubbing the sleep from her eyes. Jaxson begins to climb out of the blankets.

"You're growing stronger, more confident," Luc says glancing at Calley and smirking, as if he knows something she doesn't.

"She's always been strong. How else could she have defeated the *Lamia Dominitri*?" Jaxson says as he sidles alongside Calley on the ground by the fire.

"Well, whatever. It's all just really confusing if you ask me. Let's just eat and get back on the road. I just want to get home." Calley dishes herself a bowl full of the delicious smelling oatmeal and starts eating. The boys take turns dishing up and eating.

Back on the road again, Jaxson is back to his normal antics; teasing, telling jokes and singing crazy songs. Calley can't help but smile and laugh at every word Jaxson says. Luc rides behind the two, simply watching the ground and counting the surrounding trees as they pass by.

About noon that day, they finally reach the *Aurura Crena*. Calley takes in the view as she turns to look out over the valley they had just traversed. She can see the fields of *seligro* where they had stopped to rest and had almost been captured. She can see the snake-like river slither its way from the lake all the way to where they were now at the mouth of the *Aurura Crena*. Calley follows the river with her eyes all the way from the lake to where it disappears into the mountainside below her.

"It's so beautiful," Calley says to herself while the boys chow on their lunch. *If nothing else, this land sure if beautiful! I wouldn't mind living in a place just like this at all! It's too bad Dad isn't here to see it! He'd love this...* Calley thinks as she looks out over the valley.

***

By evening, the group reaches a town that is burrowed into the side of the mountain, right in the middle of the *Aurura Crena*. The road continues through the middle of the town, taking up the entire pass between the mountains. Houses and shops fill the area. People bustle in and out of stores; some carrying bags, some pushing carts, and others just laughing and skipping along. Flowers bloom in every window box and at the base of every tree.

Although the temperature is much cooler here than it was down in the valley due to their rise in elevation, it is still comfortably warm. Everyone wears light, loose-fitted clothing in various bright colors. Many of them resemble the petals of a flower or the flowers themselves. Banners hang across the road which are decorated in spring flowers of pinks, reds, purples, blues and oranges. They read,

BASCULAE ILLUMBAR MATCHING FESTIVAL
Week Long Celebration!
Find Your One True Love

On several shop doors, posters are displayed which further outline the weekly events taking place. Jaxson stops at one shop door to read it.

"Ah, welcome to Amobem! Are you three here for the *Basculae Illumbar* Festival? Our little town hosts the *Basculae Illumbar* Festival every year when the *Basculae Illumbar* blossoms! People come from all over for it every year! What am I saying, of course you are!" an elderly woman in a long, bright orange-pink frock talks to them quickly as they stand outside the shop.

"What a wonderful time of year! Yes, indeed! Have you a place to stay while you're here?" the woman asks.

"No, we've only just arrived in town," Luc answers flatly.

"Oh, well follow me! I know just the place! I have an inn, you know! I'll give you a good rate seeing as it's celebration time and all!" the woman says as she begins walking further into town.

"Well, money isn't really a problem," Jaxson says. When he left Baghad, Jaxson didn't leave empty handed. One of his saddlebags is filled with gold thrushes and platinum senines.

"Oh that's good too!" the woman says absent-mindedly. "Well, it's not much farther up this road here," she says as she turns, leading them onto a side road off of the main road. Here, there are more shops and businesses and a few inns.

"Here we are," the woman says as she stops in front of a building with a sign that reads, '*Basculae Illumbar Inn*'. The two-story building shares a wall with each of its neighbors. Huge tan and beige bricks make up the building. "We're pretty full up, but I might be able to find you a room." They follow the woman inside. "By the way, my name is Philomena and my husband is Philip. He's the caretaker here. I just run the place for him," she says smiling as she leads them to a sort of bar that is set out a ways from the wall; it looks like a very tall desk. She goes around behind it and brings up a large book.

"Write your names here on this page," Philomena says as she opens the book to a specific page. "It'll be 15 gold thrushes for the room."

"Do you have two rooms available?" Calley asks, hopeful for some privacy from the boys at last. "I just really need to clean up and would like some privacy if possible," she says, blushing.

"I'm afraid we don't. I'm sorry, dear," Philomena answers, frowning.

"That's fine, we have our payment here," Jaxson says fishing out 15 gold thrushes from a pouch he had pulled from his saddlebags before entering.

Calley looks at him surprised. "I didn't know you had so much money!"

"Well then there are still a few things that I have up my sleeve, aren't there?" Jaxson says and smirks at Calley, elbowing her in the ribs.

Luc rolls his eyes and asks, eager to get cleaned up himself, "So, where is our room then?"

"Oh, just up those stairs and all the way at the end of the hall," Philomena points up a staircase not ten feet from where they stand to the right. "We serve breakfast and dinner in the dining hall just there," Philomena points to an open area with tables and chairs set up not far from them on the main floor.

"Thank you! Let's go get settled in," Luc says as he takes a key from Philomena and heads for the stairs.

Once in their room, the three friends take turns cleaning up in the wash tub. There is a large wash tub in the corner of the room which is surrounded by curtains to provide privacy. When it is Calley's turn, the boys leave the room and go down stairs in order to give her privacy.

Almost as soon as Calley finishes her bath, the door bursts open and the boys stroll inside excitedly.

"We should stick around here for a few days! Luc and I were talking to a few of the locals and some of the people who have come for the festival downstairs in the dining hall, and they have tons of great activities planned for the next few days," Jaxson says, brimming with excitement as the boys walk back into the room where Calley is just drying her hair with a towel.

"Really? I don't know. I really want to get home..." Calley starts. "Well, what do you think, Luc?" she asks, looking at him.

"It could be fun. I guess. I'll stay if you want to stay, Calley," Luc answers, flashing his eyes in her direction briefly.

"Oh, Calley you have to see the *Basculae Illumbar*! It's beautiful! It will take your breath away! And, tomorrow they're having a carnival with various booths selling different handmade items and different kinds of foods. Apparently, they do this kind of thing once a year. They first settled here around the *Basculae Illumbar* over 200 years ago," Jaxson goes on enthusiastically.

Jaxson settles into a chair by the window and glances out. Then, he continues, "By that time, it was already hundreds of years old. The first person to discover its magical abilities was Amos Shatworth when he and his new bride came here from *Atsu Damscence* that is by the *Lax Acore*, the Open Sea. They say that when he and his new wife were picnicking beneath the *Basculae Illumbar* they shared a kiss. That was when the magic happened," Jaxson pauses and looks over to see if Calley is still listening.

She looks back at him, smiles and nods her head. So, he continues, "The petals from the newly bloomed *Peonies* began to fall all of a sudden and surrounded the couple. They were encompassed by them so completely in a whirlwind that they couldn't even see through them. Then, as the couple sat watching the events unfold, the petals began to turn into fairies. The fairies all kissed the couple, one at a time until each had given it's kiss to them. After gifting their kisses, each fairy took flight into the night sky," Jaxson says and gets up from the chair and walks over to the bed where Calley has been listening from.

He sits down next to her, takes her hand in his and says, "They say that Amos and his wife were blessed by the *Basculae Illumbar* when they kissed underneath its bows. The fairies' gifts of kisses blessed them with long life and health. They were together the rest of their days. They both lived to be over 100 years old. When Amos' wife passed away, he was so completely ridden with sorrow at losing her that his own heart gave out within days of her death." Jaxson finishes the story while looking into Calley's eyes. Calley feels those familiar butterflies well up inside her belly making her feel dizzy, like only Jaxson can do to her. It never seems to fail how he can always make her feel so giddy and nervous and elated at the same time.

"Okay, okay! We can stay and go to their festivities," Calley secedes with a sigh and she smiles up at Jaxson. She nervously pulls her hand from his and shifts her weight in the bed.

Luc, who has been lying silently on a second bed in the room, gets up and heads for the door.

"Where are you going?" Calley asks nervously.

"I just want to go for a walk," Luc says and leaves the room, shutting the door quietly.

Chapter Thirty

THE NEXT MORNING, THE DINING hall was abuzz with talk about the day's carnival and all of the booths that would be displayed.

"I heard there's a booth with something called Coo-coo clocks from a place called Germany from the mortal's realm! They are clocks with little birds they call 'Coo coos' that pop in and out of the clock each hour and go 'Coo-coo, Coo-coo, Coo-coo' to call the number of hour of the day!" one person shouts excitedly at a table as Calley, Luc and Jaxson walk by.

"They haven't ever heard of a Coo-coo Clock before?" Calley asks a little sarcastically.

"Well, had you ever heard of the *pinunda* or the *Bonamaru* before coming here? Had you ever even heard of the Lipus or the *Majori* before coming here?" Luc asks, looking sideways at Calley.

"No, I guess not," Calley answers back, sticking her tongue out at Luc playfully.

After a breakfast of ham steaks, eggs and toasted bread, the group heads out into Amobem to explore the carnival. Booths line both sides of the main street. People fill the streets already, lining up at booths and exchanging gold for merchandise.

Music plays from somewhere Calley cannot determine. She cannot see a place set up for enough instruments to be making the sounds she hears as it spins an entrancing tune. Jaxson swoops to Calley's side and scoops up her hand in his. She looks down at his hand in hers, feeling the sparks of electricity that always excite her and create those giddy feelings in her belly. She smiles drunkenly up at Jaxson.

Oh my goodness, he is so cute! Calley thinks as she feels herself fall suddenly, totally and completely, and then she feels herself being lifted off the ground, weight-lessly floating just above it, being propelled only by the strong, electric grip of Jaxson's hand over hers. *Is this what it's like to fall in love?* Calley wonders as they pass different booths in this manner.

It's a few minutes before Calley realizes she's been staring at her hand in Jaxson's while walking down the street, where anyone can plainly see her affection for him; anyone and everyone including Luc.

Luc! Calley thinks and she drops Jaxson's hand and whirls around to find him. He is nowhere in sight. "Where did Luc go?" she asks Jaxson.

"I honestly don't know. I was kind of distracted," he says, picking her hand up again, cradling it in both of his and looking into her eyes. His eyes seem filled with warmth, comfort, and a love that Calley hadn't noticed in them before. The green of his eyes seems more vibrant, brighter, and bolder here. Against the black of his eye-brows, the black locks of hair that sweep his forehead, Jaxson's features are strikingly handsome. Again, Calley feels herself swooning and catches herself this time.

"Well then, shall we see what they have?" Calley asks and pulls Jaxson to the closest booth to them.

One booth is selling stuffed animals which are made with real animal fur. Calley doesn't really like that one much, but when Jaxson buys her one, she politely takes it and thanks him with a kiss on the cheek. Once again electricity shoots, this time emanating from her lips, down and throughout her body. She shivers involuntarily at the sudden invasion which leaves her feeling weightless again.

Simultaneously, Jaxson turns his face to hers and for a second they look at each other, only inches apart. Time seems to freeze, nothing in the world exists but for the two of them. Calley's heart leaps in her chest, doing cartwheels.

"Come see the amazing 'Coo-coo Clock'! Brought all the way from the Realm of the Mortals, from a land they call Germany!" a man shouts from a booth nearby, yanking Calley out of her trance.

"Oh! Have you seen them before? I have! My mom and step-dad have one in their kitchen!" Calley says enthusiastically and drags Jaxson, who sighs and chuckles slightly, by the hand over to the booth.

By lunch Calley and Jaxson return to the *Basculae Illumbar* Inn, hoping to find Luc. When he is not in their room, they ask Philomena if she has seen him.

"No, I'm afraid I have not seen your companion since this morning at breakfast. I'm sorry. I do hope he isn't lost," she states genuinely.

"I'm sure he's fine," Jaxson says as they walk back onto the street. "There are still so many booths we haven't visited yet. Shall we go and see what they are?" Jaxson suggests, then offers, "Or, would you rather see if we can't find Luc?"

"No, you're right. I'm sure he's fine. He's a grown man practically, right? He can take care of himself," Calley says, mostly attempting to alleviate the guilt she feels welling inside her.

Why should I feel guilty anyway? It's not like we're dating or anything! It's not like we're a couple....

"Let's go see what else is out there! And, I want to try to figure out where that gorgeous music is coming from!" Calley proposes happily.

"Oh, I forgot to tell you! That's the *Basculae Illumbar*! Come on, I'll show you!" Jaxson leads Calley across the street, through a couple of booths, through a couple of shops and up a hill behind them. At the top of the hill just overshadowing the rest of the town is the largest, most elegant tree Calley has ever seen.

Couples sit or stand under its branches. Most of them just stare into each other's eyes dreamily. That same music that accompanies the carnival does seem to radiate from the *Basculae Illumbar* just like Jaxson said. Small, pink *peonies* alight every tiny branch of the tree. Thousands of them make their home in any open spot. The entire tree is made of these *Peony* flowers. There is not a green leaf on the tree anywhere. An aroma similar to roses but softer is overwhelming the closer they get to the *Basculae Illumbar*. When the wind blows through the branches and across the flowers, the music gains momentum and volume.

"It's the flowers?" Calley says shocked, eyes wide open and blinking in disbelief.

"Their magic translates the wind into musical tones which enhance the romantic atmosphere. I'm sure you've felt their influence while we've been walking around this morning," Jaxson explains.

It's true that Calley had been feeling unusually giddy, more like a twitter-pated fool than normally. *So, is that what is really going on here? But, I had these kinds of feelings for Jaxson before we even came here. No, it might be 'enhancing' as he said, but they are my true feelings,* Calley assures herself.

A commotion under the *Basculae Illumbar* brings Calley out of her thoughts and she follows the gazes of everyone around toward one couple under the *Basculae Illumbar* who are kissing. 'Ooohs' and 'Aaahs' emerge from the crowd which grows as word spreads throughout the streets of the event taking place at the tree.

Calley hears someone say, "Another couple is being blessed by the *Basculae Illumbar*!", while another person says, "Their union will last throughout all of time!" Curious, Calley watches as the *peonies* fall from their branches just above the couple. Emitting a soft glow, they break up into pieces as they fall so that hundreds of glowing, pink flower petals envelope the couple mid-kiss, covering them from head to feet, seemingly sticking to them as with glue.

An eruption of applause breaks the whispers and murmurs, interrupting the couple which is the spectacle to be seen. As they each lift their head apart from the other's and look out over the crowd, the petals are released from their hold on the couple's bodies and they fall to the ground. Cheers and well-wishes for the couple are shouted from all gathered at the site.

Once again walking along the streets, among the vendors and festival-goers, Calley falls right in sync with Jaxson's stride despite the discrepancy in their heights. They seem to fit together like two pieces of a puzzle as they walk side by side and hand in hand.

Although still aware of the world around her, Calley still feels like there is a bubble around Jaxson and herself, secluding them. A bubble in which only he and she knows how each other feels, in which only he and she exists and nothing else matters.

"Oh what beautiful dresses!" Calley says as they walk up to a booth selling dresses advertised as 'Home Grown'. Like everything else on display, they are bright and colorful. With full skirts that flare when twirled in, the dresses look like upside down flowers; the skirt takes the shape of the petals with sections of fabric layered in a way to represent some kind of a tulip hybrid. Calley lets go of Jaxson's hand and reaches her hand out to caress the fabric. The soft peach colored fabric of the skirt is as smooth as silk, as light as tulle and as soft as mink. It is unlike anything Calley has ever seen or felt before. Peach color begins at the waste and spreads out through each 'petal' of skirt leaving a tinge of a darker, pinker hue on the ends.

"We have developed a special spell which causes the tulips to grow to the height of a person; so we can use their petals for the skirts. It is a family secret," a girl about Calley's age says as she approaches Calley. The girl is larger around than Calley, but doesn't appear overweight. She is plump, with red curly locks of hair that drape over her shoulders and down her chest. She wears a dress like the one Calley admires, except that it is a baby blue hue and doesn't seem quite as full in the skirt.

"You mean, these are the actual flower petals used as the skirt?" Calley says amazed, still holding the skirt of the dress as she talks to the girl. "How do you keep it from tearing? How do you make it so thin and light?"

"Those are family secrets too I'm afraid," the girl says and winks at Calley. "But, I can tell you that we have spent many years developing our techniques which allow us to grow the tulips just this way. Would you like to try one on?" the girl asks gesturing toward the one Calley had been admiring.

"I would love to! Do you have a dressing room or somewhere for that?" Calley asks as she scans the booth.

"We do in indeed," the girl answers. "Follow me." The girl leads Calley under a canopy which reaches somewhat into the street away from the booth itself. At the back, on the side of the booth, there is a room designated for trying on the dresses.

Inside the dressing room, Calley carefully puts on the dress. A knock at the door startles her.

"Miss? Do you have it on?" it is the girl who showed Calley to the dressing room. "May I come in?"

"Sure," Calley answers hesitantly. The girl enters the room careful not to open the door so far that anyone outside could see in.

"Oh good! It seems to like you!" the girl says as she touches Calley's waste.

"I'm not so sure," Calley starts and shows the girl how the dress is loose over her hips.

"Oh, that's no problem at all!" the girl starts whispering words in some language that Calley doesn't understand. Gradually, the dress becomes more fitting to Calley's waste, hips, and bust. In only a minute's time, the dress embraces every inch of Calley's body tightly but comfortably. She turns to look in a mirror positioned on the wall in the room.

The girl Calley sees in the mirror is gorgeous, graceful, and elegant! Certainly, this reflection could not be herself, Calley, that same tom-boy who'd grown up climbing trees in torn blue jeans and who'd sworn she'd never wear a dress as long as she lived!

"See! It loves you!" the girl says stepping back and admiring her work with the dress.

Calley smoothes her hands along the sides of the dress; unable to determine the exact word for how it feels to the touch. It feels weightless on her shoulders, almost as though she were wearing nothing at all.

"It's so beautiful," Calley says longingly. "But, I don't have much money. How much does it cost?" Calley asks shyly.

"Don't you worry about that! The young man you were with has taken care of it and this now belongs to you," the girl says and she turns to leave the room. With a hand on the door knob, the girl half turns back to Calley and says, "Oh, and if you are planning on attending the banquet this evening, I know the best place to get your hair done! A few booths down from us, there's a salon shop where my cousin works. She's just magical with hair! You should stop by there and see what she can do for you!" With that, the girl slips out of the room the way she came in, making sure that no one outside can see in.

Calley takes a minute to just look at herself in the mirror when a familiar voice outside speaks to her. "Well? Do I get to see it on you, or do I have to just use my imagination?" Jaxson asks from outside the dressing room.

"Um, I don't know," Calley says, suddenly nervous and self-conscious. A sick feeling floods her stomach as she thinks about what Jaxson might think of her when he sees her in this dress. *Will he think I'm beautiful? What will he do when he sees me like this?* Calley wonders nervously.

"Tell you what, if you don't come out and show me, then I'll just have to come in there and see for myself!" Jaxson threatens teasingly.

He wouldn't really, would he? Calley wonders.

When Calley hears a hand on the door knob she says, "Okay, okay! Just wait a second." She looks herself in the eyes, takes a deep breath and opens the door, striding out as confidently as she can manage.

Watching him circumspectly, Calley stands just outside the dressing room feeling awkward. A sly smirk creeps across Jaxson's face, turning into a full blown drunkard's grin.

"Okay, you're making me nervous," Calley says, biting her bottom lip and looking aside then back at Jaxson. "Say something! How do I look?" she pushes.

"There aren't words that would do justice to describe your beauty! You look magnificent! Beautiful! Stunning! Breathtaking! I'm left without words for there are none to adequately describe you!" Jaxson exclaims as he covers the distance between them in a flash and pulls Calley into his arms. He looks down into her eyes and Calley feels her knees weaken all at once and she actually loses her balance. Had Jaxson not been holding her so completely, she would have fallen to the ground.

Breathlessly Calley says, "I better get changed," and she eases herself out of Jaxson's grasp and escapes back into the dressing room. Once the door is shut, Calley leans with her back against the door and breathes heavily, her chest raising and lowering quickly as she looks up at the ceiling. Unused to attention from the opposite gender in such a manner, Calley doesn't know what to think or how to feel. So overcome with flattery, Calley must consciously slow her breathing and calm herself.

Is it possible? Calley looks back into the mirror at her reflection again. *Am I really breathtakingly beautiful? Is it maybe just the dress though? It can't really be ME that's so beautiful, can it?* Calley shakes the thought from her head.

Cautiously, Calley undresses and puts on the night gown she has worn since escaping Hazel and Saunder. Looking at herself in the mirror, now again in the dirty, now worn, night gown that had looked and felt so beautiful when Calley first saw it while lying in bed in Hazel's house, she now notes the transformation and concludes that her beauty must in fact be due to the dress.

How could anyone possibly think this was breathtakingly beautiful? Calley thinks to herself as lifts her arms, raises her shoulders and drops her arms back at her sides allowing them to slap when they hit her sides in an "I give up" gesture. She shakes her head slightly, now feeling more inconsequential and much less extravagant than only minutes before. *Oh well, back to being me again,* Calley thinks as she scoops up the dress in her arms and leaves the dressing room.

"It's getting late, we should head back to the inn," Calley says when she walks up to Jaxson again. He stares at her blankly for a moment, as if not quite registering who she is. "Jaxson?" Calley says again, raising an eyebrow at the boy who stands frozen in a different kind of stance than before when she'd stepped out of the dressing room.

"Right, of course we should get back and see if Luc has returned yet," he says and takes her hand in his, leading her back onto the street.

Back at the inn again, they spot Luc sitting at a table in the corner of the dining hall, sipping something from a thick, heavy clay mug. He looks up and sees them just as Calley approaches the table, trailed by Jaxson behind her.

"Luc! Where have you been all day? We've been worried about you," Calley says as she takes a seat next to him at the table.

"I just wanted to be alone is all. I spent much of the day up by the *Basculae Illumbar*, watching the couples that came there," Luc says looking at the table.

"Oh, we went up there today too, right after lunch," Calley says glancing over at Jaxson and then returning her gaze to Luc. "But, we didn't see you there."

"There were a lot of people there. And, I was sitting a ways from the tree, in the trees away from the town. So you wouldn't have seen me anyway," Luc says somewhat dolefully.

"Luc, are you all right? What's the matter?" Calley asks, lowering her head under his and turning her face up so that he has to look her in the face.

He stifles a chuckle and lifts his head from his hands, finally looking at her. "I'm fine, Calley. I'm glad that you have been enjoying yourself here," Luc says and smiles at her while shaking his head.

Just then, Philomena appears at the table side. "Are you folks going to be having your dinner here tonight? Or, are you planning on attending the banquet at town hall?" she asks, looking at each one of them as they discuss it.

"We hadn't really decided that just yet," Jaxson begins to answer and he looks over at Calley.

"Oh, if this is your first time here, you really should go! The food is wonderful! And, they bring in performers from all over Calueria for entertainment while you eat. It is a formal banquet, so you will need to have something nice to wear," Philomena says as she eyes the three in their worn, dirty clothes. "At any rate, there are plenty vendors here that are selling that sort of apparel that you can go explore. There's still time before the banquet begins," she suggests.

"Well? What do you think, Calley? Would you like to go to this banquet?" Jaxson asks, looking at Calley.

"I forgot to mention that there'll be a dance afterwards! All of the couples here for the celebration are encouraged to join in. And, my dear, you seem to have two partners of your own to choose from! You have your hands full with these two!" Turning to leave, Philomena adds, "Just let me know if you decide to stay here so I can have a meal for you ready!" and she walks away.

"I think it sounds amazing!" Calley says looking at Luc and then at Jaxson. "Should we all go?" she asks still switching her look from one boy to the other and back again.

"I'm in! I think it sounds like a blast!" Jaxson says sitting straight in his chair and leaning into the table.

With his hand over his mouth, holding his head up while leaning against the table, Luc looks at Jaxson almost menacingly. He takes a deep breath and closes his eyes before speaking.

"I'm not sure. She did say 'couples' and we three are hardly a 'couple'." He says blankly, staring into the wooden crevices of the table.

"But, I could dance with both of you! I guess not at the same time, you could take turns..." Calley tries to suggest. "I just think it sounds like such an amazing time!

It wouldn't be the same with either one of you missing," Calley says as she extends her hands, her right holding Jaxson's hand and her left gripping Luc's hand.

She looks from one boy to the other and back again while she waits for a response. Jaxson squeezes her hand in his gently and smiles at her, while Luc's hand sits still and cold under Calley's.

"Luc?" Calley asks pleadingly, looking at Luc.

"Sure, I'll be there," Luc says, glancing at Calley and then at Jaxson. He gets up from the table and goes up the stairs.

"I wish I knew what was bothering him so much," Calley says as she watches him leave.

"I'm sure he'll be fine. Well, I need to go find me something to wear to the banquet tonight. Do you need to get ready too?" Jaxson says nonchalantly as he gets up from the table.

"I think I know just where to go," Calley says, thinking of the salon the girl had told her about. "I'll see you at the banquet later!" Calley says and she rushes out into the street.

Chapter Thirty-One

CALLEY LOOKS HERSELF OVER IN THE mirror, not entirely sure she is seeing her own reflection. It's like before, when she first tried the dress on, except that now her hair and face don't even look like her own anymore either! She looks at this majestic, elegant lady in the mirror who seems to mimic every movement she makes simultaneously. On top of her head, the hair is gathered into tiny braids which form a sort of crown. From there the hair falls almost perfectly. The hair is curled into perfect golden ringlets that fall over her shoulders and down her chest. Even her face is decorated with colors to accentuate the blue of her eyes, the reddish-pink of her mouth and the light pink in her cheeks.

Well, I guess I'm ready. I wonder what Luc will think of me dressed up like this. I don't even look like me. I wonder if he'll even recognize me, Calley thinks as she turns to view herself sideways in the mirror. Calley sighs heavily and thinks, *I guess I should get going.*

***

At the banquet, everyone who enters is first introduced at the door to the rest of the guests present. Using some kind of volume spell, the attendant at the door speaks the name of the person currently entering the room. A line of people stems from the entrance into town hall and out along the side of the street when Calley reaches it. There she waits until she is at the entrance. Her heart beats hard in her chest, beating against her rib cage like a rabid animal trying to break free. Her palms are hot and moist; her stomach is twisted into knots. Even when she does finally sit down at the table, she doesn't think she'll be able to eat anything.

"Your name please?" Calley is asked by the attendant at the door.

"Calley-" she begins, "Catherine Alleynia," she finishes. Although unsure what has made her give her full name, Calley feels appropriately introduced when she hears it echo throughout the hall. It seems fitting to her that she should be introduced to all these strangers in such a prominent manner given her attire and overall appearance. It's not like any of them are going to recognize her once she's back in her ratty, worn clothing with her face washed and her hair back up in its pony tail again.

Upon entering the Town Hall, Calley realizes that the majority of it is lowered into the ground. She arrives at the top of a staircase which grants access to the main floor. The building that is Town Hall is one long rectangular room. All around the room, at her current level, there are walkways like balconies that reach the entire length of the room and oversee the main floor.

People are gathered sparingly on the balconies and in large quantities on the ground floor. Tables are set up in rows in the middle of the room where many people are already dining. All along the longer walls of the main floor, there are tables that are lined with foods of various kinds; some vibrant in color and extravagant in nature, and others more simple and plain.

At the end of the room there is a large stage set up where a performance is taking place. When Calley reaches the bottom of the stairs, she hears whispers spread from the people around her and she thinks she hears her name, 'Catherine Alleynia' being spoken several times. Every time she turns to see where it was spoken from, the people divert their eyes to the floor or away from her and they stop talking all together.

"Calley!" Jaxson says, pushing his way through a crowd. "There you are! I was beginning to worry that maybe you'd gotten lost or changed your mind. I heard them announce a 'Catherine Alleynia', but I wasn't sure it was you until I saw you coming down the stairs," he says coming up beside her and taking her arm in his.

Jaxson appears transformed almost as much as Calley does. He wears a formal green tunic with a leather black vest laced up around his chest. His black trousers are seamless and wrinkle and dirt free.

He's even shaved! Calley thinks. *I didn't even realize just how much facial hair he had before!*

"You look absolutely magnificent! Shall we?" Jaxson asks and leads her to the banquet tables which are lined with all sorts of foods that Calley has never seen before.

"We serve ourselves apparently," he says, handing her an ivory plate. He picks up a slice of ham, some chicken legs (at least, Calley thinks it must be chicken), and then reaches for some kind of black meat with a red center. It looks like a beef steak, but it's not black due to the cooking. Calley simply chooses a small slice of the ham and follows Jaxson as he continues to load his plate with items that smell fishy, are green and gooey and something red that is dry and hard like a cracker, but turns to liquid where broken. It reminds Calley too much of blood so she doesn't take one for herself. Finally, they find a pair of seats together at a table.

"Have you seen Luc yet?" Calley asks Jaxson as he begins digging into his food.

"Not yet, but don't worry. He'll be here, I'm sure," Jaxson says, not even looking up from his plate.

He must really be hungry, Calley thinks as she watches Jaxson inhale his food. Although there is some food on her plate, she doesn't touch it. Instead, Calley looks around the room searching for Luc.

While her head is turned to look at the staircase which leads down into the main floor, Calley doesn't notice when someone takes the seat next to her on her other side from Jaxson.

"There you are, my friend!" Jaxson says, looking up from his plate and over at the person.

Calley turns to look and there is Luc with a plate full of food sitting next to her. Luc, like Jaxson, is dressed in fine, formal attire. His tunic is a light tan color with a dark brown leather vest and dark brown slacks.

"I said I'd come," he reminds her, winking and giving her a half smile. "You look amazing, Calley! Beautiful like always," he says, turning the half smile into a full one.

"You do too! I'm glad you decided to come!" she says, hugging his arm.

"Ladies and Gentlemen, allow me to introduce to you the *Omnibe in Unom Tractu Cernuus,* the All in One Stretching Acrobats!" an attendant announces throughout the hall from somewhere near the stage.

Up on the stage a group of people have assembled. Every one of them is about the same build and height, male and female. All are similarly dressed in some kind of skin tight spandex. They begin climbing on top of each other, building a pyramid. Where their hands meet to grip each other, they seem to meld together. Where hands grasp bare feet, the hand and foot meld together. Finally, the last person reaches the top of the pyramid by climbing up her fellow performers like a ladder.

Once at the top, she lifts her hands in triumph and the audience bursts into applause and cheers. Then, the pyramid begins to disassemble by the people on the top sliding down on both sides of the pyramid, like one can do with cups after building them into a pyramid; they just slide down smoothly on top of each other.

Starting at the bottom again, the group begins to assemble themselves into another pattern. This time they build themselves into an arch. It amazes Calley that they can stay up there at the top without falling to the ground.

I guess they can do that because of the way their hands and feet can be joined like they are. It's like they're all just one person the way they flow from one to the next. There are no breaking points where they can lose balance or shift weight, Calley thinks as she watches the group build themselves into yet another amazing structure that seems impossible to create: the shape of a heart.

The audience goes crazy with cheers and whoops and applause. When all performers again have their feet firmly on the stage, they take hands and raise them up, and then they swing them down into a unison bow. Calley claps until her hands go numb amazed at the abilities of the performers. Jaxson whoops and cheers while Luc just claps and smiles.

Next, a couple takes the stage; a man and a woman. Music begins to play and the couple being to dance across the stage. The woman makes leaps that reach almost to the balcony above and lands in the man's arms. Their movements are so fluid, so complete and unified that it becomes difficult to determine where the man begins and the woman ends.

It's beautiful! It's symbolic of the matching that the Basculae Illumbar does and the reason for the whole celebration, Calley thinks as she watches, entranced by the couple on stage.

A few more acts are performed on the stage, each one unique and amazing. Each one shows Calley a part of this world that she never would have dreamed possible. At last, the final act takes their bows and leaves the stage.

"Now, Ladies and Gentlemen, if you will please rise from your seats, we will prepare the room for the ball," the attendant announces. Everyone in the room stands at their tables. The attendant says something in that strange language Calley doesn't recognize and the tables and chairs all disappear. Musicians take the stage, setting up instruments; some of which Calley knows and others that Calley can only guess at what their purpose is.

It has grown darker outside as the sun sets. Before Jaxson can say or do anything, Luc takes Calley's hand and asks, "May I have the first dance?"

"Of course!" Calley says, noticing how Jaxson lowers his head slightly to Luc as if to say, 'Well played'. Jaxson falls back to stand beside the wall and to wait for his turn with Calley.

As the music begins, a woman sings. Her voice is mesmerizing as she weaves an enchantment over the crowd of dancers. Luc leads Calley around the room, spinning her out here and there and dipping her on occasion for fun, leaving the two laughing. Calley had worried about the dancing part because she'd always been somewhat of a clutzoid and was always tripping, spraining ankles, and bumping into things.

Calley is reminded of how fluid Luc's own movements always are; how completely in control of his body he is. She seems to fit perfectly in sync with him as they spin and twirl around the room. Although Luc never misses a step, Calley often steps on his feet or trips over her own. Luc never fails to keep her on her feet though. He lifts her with ease and never seems to notice when she has stepped on his feet. She giggles nervously every time she does, but he just brushes it off and keeps on going.

The song comes to an end all too soon and Jaxson is there at Calley's side asking for his turn around the dance floor. Before letting Calley's hands go, Luc holds one up to his mouth and kisses it gently, sending warmth from her hand up her arm and throughout her body.

"Thank you for the dance," he says and releases her into Jaxson's care.

Calley feels confused as she watches him walk over to sit on the wall at the side of the room. *Does he love me?* She wonders to herself. Before she can consider the answer, Jaxson is leading her around the room in his own fashion.

He spins and twirls himself and her in an elaborate dance. It reminds Calley of swing dancing, but it's not quite the same. He lifts her into the air, holding her waist and twirls around in a circle. Every touch feels electric and makes Calley tingle with excitement.

After being held above him, Calley is slowly lowered so that she slides along Jaxson's chest. He holds her there so they are face to face for a moment. Calley's heart races like a wild horse in the open. As Jaxson starts to lean his face into hers, she lowers her head onto his shoulder.

I'm not sure I'm ready for anything serious, I'm not sure I want him to kiss me... she thinks as she breathes in his intoxicating essence. *Oh my goodness, he smells good!* She can't help thinking this as his scent floods her senses.

A moment later, Jaxson places Calley on her feet. Feeling light-headed and giddy, she almost loses her balance. She holds onto Jaxson's arm for support as they again take the dance floor. This time, he takes things slower and easier for her.

When the song ends, Calley looks back to the wall where Luc had gone to sit. He is not there.

"Did you see where Luc went?" she asks Jaxson.

"I'm sorry, I didn't," he answers. "Well, are you up for another round?" he asks, holding out his hand to her.

"Sure! Just, go a little slower please? I'm not quite as good a dancer as you are!" Calley says apologetically and she places her hand once more into his. It's like a snap when her hand meets his, sending electric shockwaves throughout her being. She welcomes the feeling with anticipation and nervous excitement.

A few songs later, Luc is still nowhere to be found and Calley is growing tired.

"Mind if we take a break?" she asks Jaxson as another song comes to an end.

"Of course not! Would you like to go outside for some fresh air?" he offers.

"That sounds great," she says and lets him guide her up the stairs and out into the night.

They find a log bench just outside the town hall and Calley thankfully takes a seat in it. Jaxson carefully sits down next to her, just so that they are still touching. He reaches for her hand and she allows him to take it in his.

"Do you feel up for a walk?" Jaxson asks.

"Sure, I guess," Calley answers, dreamily.

With one hand in his, Calley wraps her free hand around Jaxson's arm, leaning her head into it as they walk. The path becomes steep as they head up a hill beside the town hall. Once at the top of the hill, they see the *Basculae Illumbar* which glows and hums with the breeze that activates the magic of the tree as it brushes across the *peonies*. New *peonies* have filled in any gaps that may have been created when falling to cover couples throughout the day. Calley hardly suspects a thing when Jaxson leads her up to and under the tree. She glances around them and sees couples spread out sparsely around the tree. Most of the people are inside the town hall dancing or eating.

Jaxson turns Calley so that she faces him. "Calley, I have been holding something back from you for some time now," he begins and then, looking at the ground, he hesitates. "Calley, I think…" he starts and then stops. Then, looking at her with fierce eyes that seem to burn straight through her, Jaxson says, "Calley, I love you!"

He bends down without hesitation and before she knows it, his lips meet hers. His arms encircle her, cradling her back, holding her up. He kisses her fiercely, passionately. That electric charge that usually just tickles Calley races through her systems now, bringing them all to life with sharp, electric awareness. Calley kisses him back, her heart bound to beat right out of her chest. Her body feels bound to explode with the electrical current that charges through her veins, bones, muscles and along the surface of her skin.

Suddenly, glowing lights begin to float all around them, twirling and encircling them. Lost in his kiss, Calley is ignorant to anything outside of herself and him and their embrace. The flowers that fall don't break apart and grip to Calley and Jaxson as they had done to the couple earlier that day. Instead, they spin around them, blinking brightly as the go. In a moment, the two are surrounded completely by the whirlwind of swirling flowers from the *Basculae Illumbar*. Calley unlocks her lips from Jaxson's when she hears the torrent of wind around them.

Couples that were lazily lounging underneath the tree before now stand in amazement. They have never seen this kind of response from the tree. It usually just does as it did earlier; the petals of the *peonies* break apart and stick to the couple, supposedly blessing them with their magical touch. A crowd begins to gather at the *Basculae Illumbar* to see what is going on.

Jaxson holds Calley closely while the flowers swirl wildly around them. When she turns her eyes back up to him questioningly, he plunges his lips onto hers once more. The torrent of whirling pink flowers that fly around them begin to spin faster and glow brighter. Their soft tune from before is now a hurricane of harmony and melody, intensely playing out their song in the ever growing torrent around Jaxson and Calley. It is exciting, invigorating and frightening all at once.

"Calley…" is spoken from somewhere in the darkness outside of the rim of light given off by the tree, so softly that no one can hear it amidst the torrent of flowers and the song of their magic. No one hears it, except for Calley.

Breaking away from Jaxson's embrace abruptly, Calley looks in the direction where her name had been spoken from. The flowers that had spun so ferociously around Jaxson and her now fall to the ground, lifeless. All of their color has gone from them and they rest on the ground in little, white shreds. A flash of Luc's face just inside the tree line is all Calley needs to see before she takes off at a sprint in his direction.

The crowd breaks out into murmurs, confused at what has just taken place. Jaxson stands alone under the *Basculae Illumbar*, inside of a circle of shredded white *Peonies*. He watches as Calley runs away from him. When she disappears into the tree line, he stares down at the ground at the drained, dead flowers. Shortly, the crowd becomes silent as they turn their attention to the lone man standing in the circle of dead flowers.

Calley searches frantically through the trees for Luc, sure that he was there and that she had seen him. He'd seen her and Jaxson… in that way… kissing! He'd seen them under that tree! He'd seen the way the *Basculae Illumbar* was 'blessing' them!

What must he be thinking? I have to find him and… apologize,… or something! Calley thinks over and over in her mind.

For over an hour, she searches the trees. Then, she searches the streets of the town, hoping to find Luc hovering in some dark corner. Returning to the town hall, Calley searches the faces in the crowds still gathered around the room. Murmurs flare up as she enters the hall. She doesn't notice; she is on a mission.

When she doesn't find Luc in the town hall, Calley goes back to the inn.

Maybe he went back to the room... Calley hopes as she enters the inn.

Upon entering the inn, Calley seeks out Philomena, grabs her arm and asks her, "Have you seen Luc? Has he come in here or gone up to our room maybe?"

"No, dear, I haven't seen your companion tonight. Is he missing? Has something happened?" Philomena asks, suddenly alarmed.

"You could say that," Calley says and she let's go of the woman to turn around and sprint up the stairs to their rented room.

Bursting inside, Calley searches every corner of the room. She even looks under the beds, behind the dressers and in the wash tub. Luc isn't there.

Calley falls back onto a bed and rolls onto her side, bringing her knees up to her chest. She submits to the fears and emotions that overwhelm and confuse her. Tears break through the flood gates on her eyes and overrun her barricades. A deluge of tears fill the pillow that Calley buries her face into.

After a few minutes of continuous sobbing, Calley hears a knock at the door.

She lifts her head off the pillow and asks, "Who is it?"

"It's me, Jaxson. Calley, are you okay? Can I come in?" Although this was his room too, Jaxson shows Calley respect and space by waiting outside the room while she decides whether or not she would like to have company.

"Yes," Calley says wearily and she lays her head back onto the pillow. Black smears from her eyes sideways across her face and down onto the pillow.

As Jaxson approaches, he stops to take a tissue which he brings over to the bed Calley lays on. Gently, he dabs the tissue on Calley's cheeks, wiping up the black smears.

"You couldn't find him?" Jaxson asks mournfully, aching inside from his own rejection.

Calley shakes her head without lifting it from the pillow. She doesn't trust her voice to speak steadily.

"I know you have feelings for him. But I had dared to hope that your feelings for me were greater. I had hoped that you loved me, too," Jaxson says casting his eyes onto the ground and lowering his hand from Calley's face.

"I do love you, Jaxson! And, I love Luc. I love you both, don't you see that?" Calley says, lifting her head and sitting up in the bed. "I don't want to hurt either of you. But, I can't choose one of you without hurting the other one." She looks into Jaxson's eyes. Those same fierce green eyes that had burned just earlier that evening are now but lightly flickering as he gazes back at her, evidence of the pain he's feeling.

"If you would like me to spend the night somewhere else, in case Luc comes back, I can," Jaxson offers sitting up straighter in the bed, ready to stand at a moment.

"No, he's not coming back here tonight. I'm positive of that. He'll want to be alone. He'll want to run free tonight," Calley says, gazing out of the window and imagining the Mutatie Lipus running through the trees under the light of the moon.

"I see, well, good night then," Jaxson says as he begins to stand.

"Wait," Calley says as she grabs his hand. "Luc may want to be alone right now, but I don't. Please lay with me? Just hold me?" Calley pleads with Jaxson. "As my friend? I… I just don't want to be alone is all."

Helpless to argue or refuse her, Jaxson lies down behind Calley and reaches his arm around her. She snuggles into him, relaxing and feeling the electric tingles start to vibrate through her. Together, they fall asleep.

Chapter Thirty-Two

JUST BEFORE DAWN, CALLEY WAKES up. Jaxson
has turned his back to her and lies there peacefully sleeping. Not wanting to disturb him, she carefully gets up
from the bed, changes her clothes behind the screen for
the wash tub, and slips out of the room. Without knowing
where she will go, she walks aimlessly.

Thoughts fly through Calley's mind about the
night before. *I love Jaxson. I love Luc. I LOVE them! I
love them BOTH! What did the Basculae Illumbar do last
night when Jaxson and I kissed underneath it? What does
it mean?* Calley walks with her eyes on the ground,
watching her every step. *They say they've never seen it do
that before. They say the legend of Amos Shatworth was
the only known example of a reaction from the tree that
powerful. Does that mean that I am meant to be with
Jaxson?* Calley looks up briefly and sees that she has
walked all the way to the town hall. Looking down again,
Calley thinks, *But, what about how I feel about Luc? I
love him. I know I do. Does that mean we can't possibly
be together?*

Calley looks up again to see that she has climbed
the hill leading to the *Basculae Illumbar*. She looks over
the tree, through its branches and at all of its innumerable
flowers. Her eyes follow the branches down to the trunk
of the tree where she sees a figure sitting against it. There
is no one else around but for this lone figure.

As she draws closer to the tree, the figure sees her
approaching and stands. The glare from the glowing *peonies* combined with the rising morning sun makes it nearly impossible to see this person's face. She realizes the

figure is very tall, lean and fit. She recognizes the frame and stature, but can't be certain until she gets a little bit closer.

Finally under the tree, Calley can clearly see Luc standing there, seemingly waiting for her.

"Luc! I was so worried about you! I don't know what to think about all that is going on! I never wanted to hurt you! I would never want to hurt you! You're my best friend and I..." Calley tries to explain as she closes the gap between them but as soon as she reaches Luc, she is cut short.

Luc takes her into his strong arms, leans over and kisses her hard and heavy. Warmth immediately radiates throughout Calley's body, making her relax completely.

Flowers come to life on every branch of the tree, not just the ones over their heads. Each blossom takes flight and begins swirling around Luc and Calley as they stand in their embrace under the *Basculae Illumbar*. Every blossom lights up the area with a golden radiance. Pink and gold flashes of bright beams strike out and away from the couple as they remain in their embrace, unaffected by the goings on. Spinning pink and gold *peonies* begin to change, to transform into flapping wings holding up beautiful tiny women: fairies.

As each new fairy emerges from its blossom, a beam of brilliant gold or pink light shoots out from within the swirling circle around Calley and Luc. The roaring, buzzing song that the fairies sing brings people out of their homes and inn rooms. Gradually, people gather around the tree which is now barren. The branches are without a single bloom.

They gawk at the couple, amazed and bewildered at the *Basculae Illumbar*'s transformation and the unexpected appearance of these tiny little fairies. The song they sing is not unlike the one created when the breeze blows across the *Peonies*, but it is more elaborate, more complicated and immeasurably more beautiful. Calley and Luc become aware of their surroundings as the fairies each begin laying kisses on their cheeks. After gifting their kiss to Calley and Luc, the fairies each depart into the sky disappearing as they rise up.

The crowd's murmurs grow into a tumultuous roar that brings Calley and Luc back down to reality, and they look all around them at the throng of an audience they have. All at once, Luc is torn away from Calley's embrace and she falls back against the tree.

Jaxson tackles Luc to the ground with his arms around Luc's waist, throwing himself on top of him in a fit of jealousy.

"She's mine! The *Basculae Illumbar* blessed us just last night! We spent the entire night together! She told me that she loves me!" Jaxson yells getting back onto his feet and breathing heavily.

"It wasn't like that! Come on, Jaxson, stop it!" Calley shouts, placing herself between the two boys.

Luc gets up off the ground and brushes himself off. "It's Calley's choice. Why don't we ask her whom she'd rather be with? Me, a stable, caring, generous and kind young man; or you, a selfish, self-centered, conceited snob who thinks that women should worship the ground you walk on?" Luc's voice raises gradually as he says this and he positions himself defensively.

"Why you!" Jaxson yells and starts throwing punches at Luc.

Luc dodges and catches the punches, without returning them. Yet, he taunts Jaxson even more by saying, "That's right, I know what you really are after! You want her power! You want her pendant! You don't truly love her! If you did, then the tree would have done just like it did for her and me just now! Instead, your flowers turned to little shredded white bits!" Luc spits out in a rage.

Jaxson, now furious, lands a punch square on Luc's jaw. Luc stumbles backwards a little, still smiling. Calley jumps between the two boys, yelling, "Stop this! Stop it all! I love you both!"

"See, Jaxson, she loves us both! That means she loves me as well!" Luc says, smiling and rubbing his jaw with his hand. "Why would she choose someone like you when she has someone like me as an option?" Luc says, his eyes changing color and shape, changing into his wolf eyes.

With Calley still between them, Jaxson lurches forward swinging his fist hard and fast. Calley turns to Jaxson just in time to block his fist with her face. She is knocked to the ground, a tiny drop of blood trickles from her upper lip.

"Calley!" Luc says and lowers himself to her side.

"I'm fine," Calley says, shoving him away from her. "Just leave me alone. You're just as bad as he is. You're not any better." Wiping the blood from her lip, Calley looks at it and shakes her head. She gets up and looking from one boy to the other, Calley says, "I love both of you, and you have both broken my heart." She turns and runs away from them as fast as she can manage into the trees away from the village.

"Wait! Calley!" Luc shouts and chases after her.

Jaxson just stands there, still breathing heavily, tired and sore all of a sudden. "I don't understand. How could the tree have blessed us, if it could also bless them like that?" he mutters, turning around and slowly walking back through the crowd.

"Sonny, I may have the answer you seek," an old woman at the back of the now dispersing crowd says to Jaxson.

"You, old woman? What do you know of what has taken place here?" Jaxson asks skeptically.

"I know much of how the *Basculae Illumbar* operates. I've been around and have seen it work for many years," she says, following just at Jaxson's heels.

"Okay then, tell me why the tree blessed two men with just one woman?" Jaxson asks, turning and stopping abruptly.

"The girl must have pure love in her heart, and the boy must also have pure love in his heart for the *Basculae Illumbar* to bless their union. Pure love is selflessness, generosity, caring, kindness to all beings, forgiveness and tolerance. That girl has true power; she has the purest love one can possess! That alone is the strongest magic in existence!" the woman exclaims.

"Then, it is true. I don't deserve her..." Jaxson says, looking at the ground. "But, the *Basculae Illumbar* blessed us last ni-" looking up, Jaxson realizes that the old woman has disappeared. He looks around the crowd, searching for the woman, but she is gone.

Jaxson returns to the inn where he runs into Luc as he enters their rented room. "Hey, I'm really sorry about the way I handled that situation. It was wrong of me to have acted that way." he asks, holding out a hand to shake with Luc.

"I also over-reacted." Luc says as he gathers his things into a pack, stopping briefly to shake Jaxson's hand.

"You didn't find her?" Jaxson asks, watching Luc pack frantically.

"No, it was as if she just vanished. I couldn't even smell her anymore, which worries me far greater than not being able to see or hear her. She could have hidden, but I still would have picked up her scent. I'm worried that something bad has happened or is going to happen to her if we don't hurry and go after her. Come on, I'm going to need your help," Luc says and hands Jaxson a pack.

Chapter Thirty-Three

LIFTING HER HEAD, CALLEY realizes that she can hear waves crashing against a shore not far away. As soon as her eyes grow accustomed to the glimmer of sunshine off of the water, she sees that she has made it to the sea at last. How she got here is a mystery as she has no memory. The last thing Calley remembers is Jaxson and Luc fighting over her and her running into the woods away from them.

Is this another nightmare? Am I dreaming again? Calley wonders as she looks around.

Seeing a campfire near her that is smoldering and some gathered wood next to it, Calley brings the fire back to life as the cool morning sea breeze sends shivers up her back. Calley sits and stares into the dancing flames as she warms herself near it. She tries to remember how she got to the beach at last.

I remember running and crying. I remember I tripped on something. Calley wraps her arms around her knees which are brought up to her chest. She rocks slightly using her feet. *Then, I remember nothing. Just waking up here...*

An old, feeble woman walks along the beach. Calley sees her and waves. Suddenly, she remembers something: the *Duz de Prundencum*. The woman seems to know Calley and quickens her pace to join Calley at the campfire.

"Ah, I see you have woken up. Good, good, very good. I trust you feel better now?" the woman asks in a deep, raspy voice.

"Do I know you?" Calley asks, confused. "Are you the *Duz de Prundencum*?" she asks as she eyes the old woman suspiciously.

"Oh, no, no, you don't know me. And, no, I'm nothing like that old fart!" the woman says, chuckling to herself. "I found you at the mouth of the *Aurura Crena*, almost here to the beach. You had collapsed from exhaustion. I assumed you had about run yourself to death," the woman's raspy, deep voice does seem familiar to Calley, but she can't seem to place it with anyone that she's met recently.

Calley looks back at the *Aurura Crena*, at the mouth which opens to the beach and the *Libania Fretum*. Calley can even see a small cave through which, she assumes, the *Flu Lumens* flows through. She can see it lead all the way to the ocean not far from where she is. "How did you manage to bring me all the way over here in your condition and at your age?" Calley asks suspiciously.

"Oh, now don't be like that! I saved your life, you know!" the old woman sputters out defensively and she takes a step back uneasily.

"Calley...Calley..." Calley's father's voice rings in her ears.

"Daddy?" Calley thinks, sure that she can hear her father's voice in her head.

"Calley, you cannot trust this woman. She is the witch who has pursued you in your dreams ever since entering this world. Do not let her deceive you!" The words echo inside of Calley's mind.

"Well, my dear, are you going to just sit there all day or are you going to come with me now?" the old woman inquires, holding out a hand for Calley to take.

"What do you mean 'come with you'?" Calley answers a question with a question and completely ignores the hand held out to her.

"Oh, don't tell me you've forgotten! You promised me when I found you that you would come with me as soon as you'd gotten some rest," the old woman asserts.

"Why should I go anywhere with you? You still haven't answered my question: how did you, an old, frail and feeble woman, carry me all the way over here nearly to the ocean's edge from the *Aurura Crena*?" Calley persists, growing uneasy and exposing that fact by shifting her weight where she sits in the sand.

The old woman's eyes take in the shift in weight and obvious discomfort in Calley's posture. "I see. Well, shoot, he has warned you," the woman says, still keeping her eyes glued on Calley's every movement. "And, I thought I might have a little fun before the final reveal took place. Oh well," the woman says, dropping the façade.

A moment later, black misty smoke begins trickling out of the woman's ears, nose and mouth. As it pours out, the skin of the old woman begins to shrivel, dry and crack. It is as if the old woman is a balloon and now all of the air is being let out of it. It continues to shrivel and shrink while the black misty smoke billows just above the old woman's would-be body.

Cackling breaks the silence. "Recognize me now, *Dea Regia*?" High-pitched, nasal laughter penetrates the air, turning into the cackling of the Striga from Calley's nightmares. A swirling, whirring mass of black misty smoke hovers above what is left of the old woman's body.

Calley looks down where the body had laid to find only sand being blown around with the wind. Standing, Calley starts to back away from the black misty smoke slowly.

"Just where do you think you're going? I told you I would have you! And I will have you today!" The disembodied voice then begins chanting some incantation or spell in that same, strange language of magic.

Suddenly, Calley's feet begin sinking in the sand. The sand seems to be pulling her into it and no matter how she pulls her legs up, it is to no avail. Downward she continues to be dragged. She begins to panic and scream, crying for help.

"Oh, my dear, I'm not going to kill you! You're much too valuable alive! If you would stop fighting and just come with me, you would see that!" the Striga says. Taking the form of a woman with her dark mass of energy, the Striga advances on Calley and reaches a dark, whirring energy hand up to Calley's shirt collar. She picks up the chain on which Calley's pendant has remained hidden until now.

"Calley... Calley..." again, Jethro's voice echoes in Calley's mind.

"Dad!" Calley tries to answer back in her mind. *"Dad, where are you? Why does she want me so badly? What is with this stupid pendant?"*

"Calley, you must listen to me now. There isn't time to answer your questions and for that I'm sorry. You must repeat these words aloud, 'Magic hidden within, Love expressed without, Pendant portal open, Power now the devout'!" Jethro instructs Calley while the Striga keeps on talking.

"You know, this has all been just too easy. To begin with, your own father gives you up by attempting to contact you in a dream," the *Striga* scoffs and goes on almost to herself, "Though I don't know what made him think I wouldn't have noticed such an exchange taking place under my own roof," she scoffs again and shakes her head.

"Anyway, I'd expected at least some fight out of those drooling, love-sick boys who keep following you around. I never could get you alone," the Striga twists the pendant around in her fingers as if weighing it. "At least, not until that *Basculae Illumbar* that is, which made it all too easy," a wispy sigh escapes the Striga's throat. "I forgot to thank you for using your full name when being introduced at the *Basculae Illumbar* Banquet! I never would have found you so easily! And now, just imagine how the rumors will spread! '*Dea Regia* Alleynia is real!' More than that, '*Dea Regia* Alleynia is alive!'" Sharp, nasal laughter erupts into the air again and the woman shaped mass of black energy shakes as it does.

"Magic hidden within, Love expressed without, Pendant portal open, Power now the devout!" Calley spits out, shutting her eyes as if expecting some great explosion. Nothing happens.

"Oh, no! Whatever will I do?" the Striga chortles in her throat, dropping the pendant back onto Calley's chest. "What now? Is Daddy trying to help you use your magic?" she says condescendingly.

"Now, the elements are at your control. Whatever you can imagine, they will obey your command. As long as it is within reason, the elements cannot deny you your desire," Jethro says. *"Now, defeat that witch!"*

Whatever I imagine, within reason, will be done... Calley thinks. Remembering her nightmares, Calley gets an idea. She concentrates her thoughts on the ocean. Calley's peridot pendant begins to glow brightly and lifts off of her chest, floating just at eye level.

"Oh, no you don't!" the Striga shouts and begins murmuring in that same language as before.

The sand around Calley begins to thicken and again it starts pulling her downward. She concentrates on the ocean, feeling the rhythm of the waves, tasting the salty essence of the sea, knowing every inch of its vast entity. Calley imagines the sea rising up, gathering into a massive wall of water that just waits her command.

Sand reaches Calley's throat and begins to creep up onto her face, still dragging her down. *Bury her in your depths! Take her to a watery grave! Let the sea be her eternal prison!* Calley thinks to the ocean.

As soon as she thinks it, the ocean surrounds the Striga and all of her black misty smoke in a watery bubble. Her incantation ceases and the sand stops pulling Calley into it. Calley watches as the bubble encasing the Striga is dragged out into the sea, pulled deep into the depths of it. Inside the bubble, a storm rages, lightning strikes, whirring black clouds spin and churn.

Calley reaches her arms up and out of the sand which falls away dry and arid once more. She climbs out of the hole which is quickly filled in with new sand. Lying on the beach, Calley closes her eyes and listens to the gentle cull of the waves as they prepare to bombard the shore anew.

"Calley, well done," Jethro says from beside her.

Calley sits up hurriedly and turns to see her father, standing on the beach a stone's throw away from her. She stands and begins to run toward him.

"No, Calley, I'm afraid I am not with you in physical form right now," he says, shaking his head. "How I wish that I were so that I might hold you and comfort you!"

Silent tears drop from Calley's eyes as she drops her arms by her sides and holds herself away from her father's apparition. "What do you mean you aren't in physical form? I can see you clear as day," Calley argues disbelievingly.

"What you see before you is my spirit. I have caused that it should leave my body so that I may be here to guide you. I can only appear to you now because you have subdued her. I do not have long before my spirit must return to my body, so I will attempt to answer your questions," Jethro says calmly, lovingly.

"The night you disappeared..." Calley suggests eagerly.

"That night they came for us. She came for me," he says, emphasizing the 'she' and 'me'. "I don't know how they found us, but I'd always known she inevitably would. Her name is Anngora, and she will come for you again. She is not dead. Although the sea will keep her imprisoned for some time, it will not be able to keep her forever," Jethro says, regretfully.

"But, where are you now, Dad?" Calley asks, perplexed at the notion that he is only a spirit and not really there with her.

"I am imprisoned in her fortress, where I must regrettably remain captive until she is freed from her own watery prison. Only she knows where this fortress is and how to release my cage." Seeing fresh tears well up in Calley's eyes, Jethro continues saying, "It will be okay, Calley. You are strong! Go back to your mother. Be a teenager and enjoy your freedom. When you are of age, a mentor whom I have arranged with long ago will find you and teach you to harness the power that resides within you."

Calley reaches up and touches the pendant.

"It is the portal through which your power can safely be used. It's your *Qui* stone, your birth stone and the stone of your family's power. Your ability to love without bounds, without limits, your unconditional love is your greatest attribute and your strongest power. Share it and it will grow!" Jethro tells Calley. "You must prepare yourself and become stronger. Anngora will come for you again," he says forebodingly.

"Dad, I want you to come home," Calley says as a tear drop rolls down her cheek.

"Pumpkin face, I love you so much!" He clears his throat and says, "When you are ready to return to your mother, repeat these words, 'Through time and space,

Separate matter from mass, Split the elements apart, Pull me through the looking glass'. A portal will open through which you may pass into that world once more. You must choose carefully where you reenter that world. Modern mortals do not have the ability to comprehend all that exists in this universe. Your mother knows nothing of this world or of your true heritage. It is a secret you must continue to carry if you wish to keep her safe. Good-bye, Calley. I love you!" With those last words, Jethro's apparition vanishes.

Calley drops to the ground on her knees and forearms, her fists clenched and her head resting on the sand between them. She weeps softly. Behind her, she hears pounding in the sand; someone is running up behind her. Apprehensively, she whips around, getting onto her knees with her arms up, ready to defend herself if necessary.

Jaxson and Luc stop in their tracks about ten yards away from Calley, surprised by her quick reaction. Once she sees them, she relaxes and stands up. They walk the rest of the distance to her.

"We were worried about you. Luc thought something bad had happened to you," Jaxson says, out of breath, as they reach her.

"I couldn't pick up your scent anywhere. Just after you ran into the woods, it was as if you just disappeared without a trace," Luc says protectively.

"I sort of did. The Striga, the one from my nightmares, she found me. She's probably the one who made you two say all those things and fight the way you did. My dad said that her name is Anngora. It was probably all a part of her plan to capture me. She said that she had been trying to get me away from you two," Calley says, finally feeling true exhaustion as if she really had been running all night and all day, she falls back to the ground again. "I didn't even find the *Duz de Prundencum*..." Calley mumbles as she looks into the ocean.

"Was that your father just now? That apparition?" Luc asks curiously.

"Yeah, why?" Calley asks, looking up at him for a moment.

"Because, that was the Majorus, Jethro. He is the *Duz de Prundencum*, the *Majuscule Intellego*," Jaxson answers, completing Luc's thought.

"It's in the rest of the rhyme you never let me complete. At the end it says,

'Jethro, he is called, the *Duz de Prundencum*'," Luc finishes.

My dad... a Majori? The ... Majuscule Intellego? ... And... the Duz de Prundencum? It is too much for Calley to take in at the moment. *Okay, well then there's a lot I don't know about my dad, isn't there?* she asks herself, trying to make light of the new knowledge.

Sitting on the sand, leaning on one arm and looking down, Calley says, "I need to go home. My dad told me how to... open a portal... I guess." She looks up at the two boys standing over her.

Luc lowers himself, crouching, bending at the knees. He reaches out a hand to Calley's face and wipes some sand from her forehead. He looks over her dirty, tear-stained face and says, "You are the most beautiful creature I have ever met! I will wait here for you as long I must; until you are ready."

Calley reaches out her hand to hold his. She smiles at him thankfully. Then, she looks up at Jaxson. As if on cue, he too drops down and he kneels on the sand next to Calley.

"I have been foolish to think that I had any sort of claim on you. I will be worthy of your love! I will earn it gladly!" Jaxson says, looking Calley in the face. He reaches his hand to her face and caresses it along her cheek and down to her chin. He rubs his thumb over her bottom lip longingly. Then, he withdraws his hand suddenly and says, "Well then, is this 'good-bye', or 'until we meet again'?"

"I don't know," Calley answers honestly. "I hope we do meet again, someday," she says, glancing at one boy and then at the other.

She sits up straight and leans forward, and re-membering the words Jethro told her to speak to open the portal Calley says, closing her eyes, "Through time and space, Separate matter from mass, Split the elements apart, Pull me through the looking glass," and the sand before her begins to swirl and melt into a shining pool of glass.

In it she can see her mother and Arthur sitting on her bed. Mom is crying, holding a picture of Calley when she was a small girl. They are talking about her, what she was like as child, how she has grown, and how proud they are of her.

Not there, I can't go back there. It would scare Mom and Arthur to death! I'd give them a heart attack. I wonder how long I've really been gone... Calley thinks. She imagines the woods where she rode Ginger that night she left that world to come to Calueria. The image in the pool of liquid glass changes. There are trees; there is the field where Ginger loves to graze. Scanning over all of this, Calley spots the place where she had fallen from Ginger that night so long ago now.

"There it is. That is where I must go back," she says and looks up at the boys. "I do love both of you, very much! I will see you again! I promise!"

Calley leans forward, dipping her head onto the liquid glass. As soon as she does so, she is sucked into it and the entire pool seems to shrink into nothing. In the end, there is no sign that anything significant has taken place there. Jaxson and Luc exchange glances; they each let out a sigh, stand and silently head back toward the *Aurura Crena*.

Chapter Thirty-Four

"CALLEY! OH, ARTHUR! COME quickly! She's here!" Mom yells and rushes to Calley's side where she lies on the ground.

"Mom?" Calley says, stirring and sitting up. She looks around and sees the same circle of mangled trees and bushes that she and Ginger had gotten into just before she fell and hit her head on the rock.

Was it all just a dream then? Maybe I dreamt it all... Calley begins to wonder as she sees Mom come jogging up to her.

"Calley! We were so worried about you!" Mom says, taking Calley into her arms and squeezing her tightly. "When Ginger came home last night and you weren't with her, I started to panic! I was going to call the police, but Arthur was the one with the stable head who calmed me down and suggested that we follow Ginger to you. He said that since you've raised her from a colt, your connection should be strong enough that she could lead us back to you if we took her out again. And, he was right because here you are and she led us straight to you!" Mom cries openly while embracing Calley.

Last night? So, I haven't been gone for months? I know I was in Calueria for months... Calley thinks as she rests her head on Mom's shoulder while in her embrace.

***

Weeks pass and summer vacation begins to draw to its close. School begins again and before Calley knows it, her birthday is fast approaching. She agreed to be part of the town's 'Coming out Ball' to her mother's pleasant surprise.

A day before the ball, Calley and Mom are in her room, practicing doing Calley's hair for the ball the next day. Calley chose a light pink dress with a full layered skirt that reminded her of the dress she'd worn in Calueria. Of course, she couldn't share that information with Mom. Although, she did think of one way she could tell her...

"Mom, I had a dream last night. It was about the Coming out Ball," she says, looking up at Mom who raises her eyebrows and smiles, nodding her head for Calley to continue. "I was dressed in this gorgeous gown that was made from tulip hybrids that were grown using magic to reach the length of a person. It was a peach color where the petals of the skirt met the waist line and it spread down the petal to the tips. At the tips, there was a pink color that just barely lit them up. It was so soft to the touch too, Mom! It was as smooth as silk, as light as tulle, and as soft as mink! Wearing it was almost like wearing nothing at all!" Calley says happily, watching Mom in the mirror in front of them.

"Oh, my! That sounds amazing, Calley! Wouldn't it be wonderful if it really were possible to use flowers for the skirts of our dresses! What I would give for a dress made from rose petals!" Mom giggles as she tries to imagine this.

The next evening plays out just as it should. Calley is beautiful and radiant. She wears her light pink dress with off the shoulder cap sleeves. Her hair is in an up-do with twists and little strands of hair curls as it hangs down, bouncing with every movement she makes. Every girl who is 'coming out' tonight must first be introduced before she can enter the room. When Calley enters the building, she is led up some stairs to a balcony where she is instructed to wait until she hears her name called.

Other girls are waiting there as well. As each name is called, one girl at a time steps onto the balcony, into the light and begins descending another staircase that leads from the balcony into the ball room below. It reminds Calley of the town hall where she attended the *Basculae Illumbar* banquet. A small pang grips her heart as she thinks about the friends she left there.

This is where I belong. They are where they belong. I didn't belong there anyway. I am where I need to be, Calley tries to reassure herself and it works a little. Calley puts on a smile as she hears her name being called.

"Catherine Alleynia!" the announcer speaks into the microphone. Calley steps onto the balcony, suddenly blinded by bright stage lights that are all pointed onto her. She remembers to smile and tilt her head like Mom had instructed her to do.

Don't trip. Don't trip. Don't trip. Calley thinks over and over in her mind as she lowers herself carefully onto each step. *This would not be a great time for acting like myself!*

Finally at the bottom of the stairs, Calley releases a sigh of relief. Mom is waiting there at the bottom for her, beaming with pride, a tear rolling down her cheek. Arthur stands beside her, also beaming proudly as he smiles at Calley.

"Calley, you were just perfect! You are so beautiful!" she says as she opens her arms for a hug, which Calley grants gratefully.

"I didn't trip on the stairs, Mom! I was so worried that I would and I didn't trip on the stairs!" Calley says, resting her head on Mom's shoulder.

Mom pulls back and looks at Calley in the face, "You are becoming a grown woman, Calley. With that, you are learning grace, poise and balance. I knew you could do it! I am so proud of you! I love you, baby!" Mom says, leaning in with Calley's hands in hers and kissing Calley on the cheek. Then, Mom lets go of Calley's hands and says, "Come, I want you to meet some of my friends. I want to show you off!" Arthur follows closely behind.

After being dragged to several tables and introduced to so many people that she could never hope to remember any of their names, Calley breaks away from Mom and slips into the gardens outside of the ball room. Calley walks up to a stone wall that rises only to her waist and is covered completely in green vines. She leans over the wall and rests her head in her hands supported by her elbows on the wall.

I wonder what Luc and Jaxson are doing right now… I wonder what they would think of this place. That thought brings a giggle to Calley's mouth. *Luc would probably hate it. He'd probably rather be out here in the garden where I am now. But, Jaxson would be right at home in there, dancing around all those finely dressed ladies and gentlemen,* Calley imagines the boys as if they are there. *Oh, what am I thinking? They were probably just a dream anyway. I mean, come on… I'm the daughter of a Majori from some very different and strange realm that you can only get to through portals… yeah, right!* Calley sighs and lays her arms across the wall, resting her head on top of them. *It was nice though…*

"Beautiful gardens aren't they?" someone says as he comes up beside Calley and leans on the wall in the same manner that she is.

Startled, Calley lifts her head and looks at the newcomer.

"Luc!" she yells and lunges towards him with her arms wide open. She hugs him tightly and breathes in his scent. He likewise breathes her in.

A clearing throat behind her startles Calley once more, and she turns to find Jaxson standing there behind her. She whips around and rushes at him with her arms open.

"Jaxson!" she says as she closes the gap between them. Calley wraps her arms around him, just as she had done with Luc a moment before, hugging him tightly. Jaxson lifts her feet off the ground and spins them around in a circle.

Releasing her hug, Jaxson sets her down. Calley steps back and addresses both of the boys, "I missed you guys! I'm so glad that you're here for this!" she says, glowing with joy.

"We'll always come when you call, Calley," Jaxson says.

Confused, Calley asks, "I called?"

Luc reaches over to Calley's neck and lifts the pendant by its chain and says, "Calling doesn't always require words." He smiles at her and she holds the pendant in her hand. She stares at it, blinking blankly, trying to comprehend what they were telling her.

Did I call them with my thoughts? I was just thinking about them. I was thinking about how they would like this party. Was I missing them too? Calley asks herself. *Yes, of course I was. I am always missing them,* she answers herself.

"But how?" Calley asks, looking up at the boys in complete bewilderment.

"Don't you know? You opened the portal. Daughter of the Majori..." Jaxson says, opening his eyes widely in puzzlement.

"Daughter of the Majori... But, what does being a Majori have anything to do with it?" Calley asks confused.

"Only the Majori have the power to open a portal between the realms," Luc answers patiently.

"If I opened the portal here, then how did you guys get here from there?" Calley asks slowly, trying not to confuse herself.

"I thought I heard you calling my name, and then I looked up and there you were, dressed as you are now, here in this garden, inside of a liquid pool of glass like the portal you opened at the beach," Jaxson answers.

"And I saw your face. You held out your hand towards me, and the portal appeared around you. As soon as I touched it, I found Jaxson and we knew where we were," Luc adds.

"Well, I'm glad you're both here. Now I can relax and have some fun!" Calley says as she takes the boys, one on each arm, back into the ball room, smiling and almost skipping as she goes. "Come on, I want you to meet my mom!"

~*~*~*~

Meet our Author:

Jessica Munn

I am the proud mother of 4 and am happily married to my best friend. After spending 7 years as a stay-at-home mom, while my husband served in the army, I earned my teaching degree. My favorite job will always have been being a stay-at-home mom!

My childhood was spent taking care of my 4 younger siblings. It wasn't the easiest of childhoods. I would escape reality into every book I read! Reading became a passion. I would read constantly. That's when I began having my crazy dreams from which all my inspiration comes. So at a very young age, I started putting my dreams to paper.

My mother was an integral part of my love for reading and writing as it was her continuous encouragement of my imagination that drove my desire to write. She would help me put my ideas to paper and create my own little story books. Throughout the years, my love of writing grew. I joined my high school newspaper and became an editor. My dreams of someday becoming a published author never subsided! My crazy dreams that fuel my imagination combine with my love for the art of literature to create Calueria and Calley.

****

www.ingramcontent.com/pod-product-compliance
Lightning Source LLC
Chambersburg PA
CBHW070105030726
47506CB00002B/606